Now That I'm Gone

A Faison Quay Murder Mystery

By

Michael James Stewart

Dedicated to
JULIAN H. HUFFER
my husband, my love, my life,
who has continuously believed in me
and
encouraged me to constantly reach.
Thank you for forty-six fabulous
years and counting.

CHAPTER 1

"Excuse me, Mr. Quay," interrupted David Granpré, his Majordomo and personal assistant.

"Dr. Redfearne telephoned several moments ago and enquired as to your state of readiness. He suggested, since he was running several minutes behind schedule, he would just have Ernie drive up to the front door and you could join him there, instead of him coming up to get you."

"That will be fine, David. Thank you."

Faison took a long gaze at David as he withdrew from the library and enjoyed, as always, everything he saw. David, with his six-foot frame, clad in a muscular and trim shell, carried himself with an air that could only be termed polished and professional. The fact that he had a thirty-inch waist, gorgeous green eyes, a beautiful wide smile that displayed perfect white teeth, long-fingered yet masculine hands and blonde hair, didn't hurt either. The five years he had been working for Faison seemed to have passed in a blink; his total devotion appreciated and never taken for granted.

Having heard Faison address his economics class at university, David had sought the job with, as he put it, "the famous Faison Quay". After graduating with honours in Art and Languages, he wanted to travel, continue to learn and have some fun. He had reasoned there was no better way to accomplish all of those goals, while earning an excellent wage, than to, directly and intimately, work with the sole owner of Key Holdings International. Each day that passed reconfirmed the correctness of that decision.

Over the intervening years, a deep bond of respect had developed between both parties to the point that David was an integral component of Faison's life, both personally and professionally - a curious blend of Personal Assistant, son and business confidante summarized how Faison saw David. David, in turn, responded with respect, deference, humour and an unwavering loyalty. The invisible line between them was never crossed; it would ruin everything as far as each was concerned.

Easing out of his leather-bound armchair, Faison stood and stretched his six-foot, two-inch, body then headed out of the library, through the grand salon, along the gallery into the hall where he decided to tackle the stairs, instead of the elevator, to access his suite. One of his many habits was to always use the loo before going out; his governess had insisted that he 'never knew when he would get another chance so he should take advantage of every opportunity'.

Once finished and having meticulously washed his hands, he retraced his steps back downstairs to the entrance foyer, where Basil, his butler, was waiting with Faison's coat. Next, David handed him a package, approximately four inches by twelve inches by one-half inch, impeccably wrapped in Faison's custom 'Key'-embossed gold paper, plus a standard, business-size, envelope.

"I hope you both have a wonderful evening, sir. Please remember to check with the maitre d' before you sit down for dinner, just so that he knows where to have your specially ordered meal placed."

"Thank you, David. I appreciate you taking care of that, as always."

As Faison spoke, Basil opened the door, stepping aside to allow David to reach inside the elevator on the right, press 'Ground', and then step back to allow Faison entry.

With the door quietly closing, David offered a gentle, "Have a good evening, sir."

Faison Quay VI, as the sixth descendant to carry the now-famous appellation of Faison Quay, had built the privately held family business from an inherited value of three hundred million dollars to nearly one hundred and thirty five billion dollars and had dramatically diversified the company in the process. Originally founded by the Quay family progenitor, Faison Quay, as a Quebec City-based shipping firm, Compagnie de maritimes du Quay, the Quay family moved to Toronto around the beginning of the twentieth century and anglicized the company name to Key Shipping, assuring the proper pronunciation of the company name by the English, while retaining the family name of Quay. Faison's father, Faison V, branched into mining and oil exploration; but, it was the present Faison who changed the company to Key Holdings International and diversified into international commercial and residential construction and management, diamond mining and retailing, six-star hotel construction and management, aircraft leasing, cruise line, security protection, pharmaceuticals, telecommunications, international breweries, fruit and carbonated beverages, food processing and dozens of various other businesses. Through his dynamic tutelage, the numerous Key companies attracted the top executives and personnel, in their specific fields, due to Faison's 'hands-off' approach and well-above industry compensation levels. He expected nothing but the best from each person and always received even more.

The private mirrored and walnut-clad elevator, with Carrara marble flooring and Swarovski crystal light fixtures, swished past the eighteen floors and deposited Faison into the marbled lobby of Quay Mansions, the elegant and beyond-exclusive condominium, erected twenty-two years before by Key Construction, in order to provide the location, calibre and ambience desired by Faison Quay,VI, Dr. Stark Redfearne and their son, Faison VII. It took only a moment more for the doorman to clear the way for him to reach the curb, where Ernie was waiting to help him into the back seat.

"Sorry I was a little late, Fai." was the greeting offered from Dr. Stark Redfearne, Faison's partner of twenty-three years.

"You look rested." as he kissed Faison.

"No problem, luv. Actually, I was enjoying the extra time listening to Chopin and daydreaming."

"That's typical of us. I have been daydreaming all the way home. It must be the fact that neither of us really wants to go out tonight." said Stark.

"As always, once we get there we'll enjoy ourselves. It's just the thought of having to make small talk with people we haven't seen in ages and who really don't, for the most part, give a damn about anyone but themselves."

"Faison, you know better than that. Most of the people who will be there tonight are decent, caring, socially-conscious, individuals whom we have known for years...and in the case of a few, you've known your whole life."

"Touché, Stark. Just keep an eye on me, as I will you, so that we can let each other know when it's time to leave."

"Right! And when I do give you the signal, you'll blurt out that you are 'in the middle of a conversation and will be through in a moment'. Once again, I will look like a party-pooper and you as the poor soul being dragged from the festivities by your boring partner.'

Feigning shock and surprise, Faison retorted, "Moi? Not me. I'd never do anything like that, would I?"

"Yes, dear....all the time; but, that's all right. It is part of your charm," Stark jokingly responded.

"By the way," Stark continued, "before we arrive, and it is too late to find out what's going on in that mind of yours, have you given anymore thought to us joining Andrew and Fort on the cruise we are giving Andrew for his birthday gift, tonight?

"Yes I have; and, yes we are. You were absolutely right when you reminded me that they have been after us for several years to take some time and go on another cruise with them. They're both a pleasure to travel with and now couldn't be a better time for us to get out of this grey autumn weather. Sooo.... ," reaching into his breast pocket, Faison retrieved the business envelope David had given him and handed it to Stark.

"You never cease to amaze me. I only suggested it when we were talking, around lunchtime. I never expected you to make up your mind so fast, never mind do something about it." Stark said with a smile.

"I merely placed a quick telephone call to Olav Pederson, at Key Cruise Lines, in Copenhagen. He assured me that the owner's suite would be available during the cruise we had already booked for Andrew and Fort. Presto! He faxed that confirmation to me mid-afternoon."

While still holding the envelope in his left hand, Stark reached over with his other hand and took hold of Faison's warm and tender hand. Without having to say another word, they both knew how happy the other was. Classical music, from CFMX, softly played in the background, the armoured Jaguar Vanden Plas purred through the traffic and all was wonderful.

Moments later, Ernie manoeuvred the car to the curb, jumped out, opened the passenger's door on his side, allowing Dr. Redfearne to alight, and then Ernie scurried around the rear of the car to open Mr. Quay's door. The ritual had long ago been established, during the first day Ernie was on the job. Faison had proceeded to open his own door and Ernie had responded by suggesting 'quite possibly he was not the correct individual for the position of chauffeur, since he was of the old school that felt it was quite proper to carry out all aspects of the job without being assisted by others, including his employer'. From that day forward, Ernie proudly conducted 'his job' and did so with a level of professionalism rare in this day and age.

At almost the same moment the Jaguar came to a halt, and before Ernie could begin his routine, an unobtrusive black Crown Victoria pulled in behind and stopped. As the driver slammed the gear selector into 'Park', two tuxedo-clad men emerged, Mario Badali, from the front passenger side and, Barry Wolfenden, from the back, right door. They stealthfully swooped in behind Faison and Stark, after they had united on the sidewalk, and remained ten feet back in order not to draw attention.

Neither Faison, Stark, nor, their son, Veetwo, ever left the protection of their home without the crème de la crème of armed, plain clothes, security officers, from Key Protection International, following either in a car or on foot. In addition, with rare exceptions, the automobiles, including a Rolls-Royce and the Jaguar, used to chauffeur the three, were always armoured to the highest standards. One could never be too careful, given the position and wealth Faison's family enjoyed.

Inhaling deeply, Faison and Stark took each other's hand and casually headed for the imposing entrance of the Royal Ontario Museum, the building that housed JK's, where the actual reception and dinner was to be held. Usually open only for lunch, JK's did a solid evening business hosting private dinner parties for discerning people who wanted an out-of-the-way, yet central and easily reached location to impress their friends. Faison and Stark loved JK's, so it was not an unpleasant venue choice.

Having grown-up prowling the galleries of the ROM, Faison was concerned the current familiar-feel to the ambience was going to be lost with the pending massive addition and renovation of the original building. Stark and he had generously donated five million dollars toward the construction of the highly anticipated two-hundred million dollar project and, in so doing, had just hoped the visually stunning cluster of crystals, designed by architect Daniel Libeskind, to be insinuated amongst the existing complex, would enhance and not detract from the original 1912 and 1932 buildings. The only problem they were going to have to deal with was the closure of JK's, once the construction started. Hopefully, Jamie Kennedy, the owner and brilliant chef, would open a new location nearby.

After a brief ride, the exclusive elevator's door to JK's opened, instantly exchanging the exquisite quiet for the confusing, and irritating, din of chatter, glasses and a jazz trio. Faison and Stark were immediately embraced and kissed by the guest of honour, Andrew Poyntz and, his partner of twelve years, Fortunato di Palma. Although at least a decade separated the two couples, they had developed a strong and caring relationship filled with humour and the mutual love of travel, great food and wonderful wines, especially Canadian. Stark had met Andrew when Andrew, as a hired consultant, was overseeing a Time and Motion Study of the

Emergency Department of St. Michael's Hospital in downtown Toronto and Dr. Stark Redfearne was Deputy Chief of Staff. Stark and Andrew immediately established a friendship. Within a very brief period of time, Stark and Faison, through socializing with him, recognized the inherent analytical and deductive talent Andrew possessed and determined it was innate, since Andrew's father was the world-famous physician and thinker, Dr. J. Merreck Poyntz.

Andrew, at five-eleven, had a slender build, fine-boned facial features with big blue eyes, a perfectly proportioned nose, kissable lips, boyishly rosy cheeks and a smile that would break the hearts of the most jaded.

At six-one, and a trim bodybuilder's physique adorned with an olive complexion, jet-black curly hair, full deep-red lips that framed a broad smile featuring enough ivory to outfit a baby grand, and a personality that would melt granite, Fortunato was Andrew's ideal match.

"Happy birthday, you old fart", Stark offered as he inconspicuously place the card and gold-embossed package, David had so meticulously prepared earlier in the day, into Andrew's hands.

"We're so glad that you came. We honestly thought that you might want to avoid the gaggle of guests."

"You know us only too well. If it were anyone else, we'd probably have pulled some 'emergency' out-of-town trip to attend to something terribly important," Faison responded.

Not wanting to be left out, Fort chimed added, "Darling, haven't you attended enough overseas face-lift parties, to last you a lifetime?"

With that, the four of them roared with laughter and both Faison and Stark inwardly felt glad that they had indeed decided to attend. It was always the same when they got together….kibitzing, laughter, wit and just generally great company.

"We'll let you get back to your guests; but, please don't abandon us completely. You know how much we hate to 'work a room'."

"Don't worry about that, Fai, you're sitting with us at our table; and, before you ask, yes, the Maitre'd is obviously aware of that, so you will eat," Andrew assured.

Only a rarefied cluster of very close friends and family ever dared to call Faison by the sobriquet Fai. It wasn't that he detested the appellation; to the contrary, he just long ago decided that it might be abused by acquaintances attempting to elevate themselves, prematurely, to friendship or people attempting to ridicule him.

Therefore, it was not until Faison granted permission, that anyone was allowed to use Fai, when addressing Faison. Stark, Fort and Andrew were the only ones who did, on a regular basis. Faison's parents, from his birth to their deaths, had almost exclusively used Fai and that, more than anything else, contributed to Faison's limiting its' use.

Before either Faison or Stark could thank Fort and Andrew, they felt someone come slightly between them, take hold of their respective elbows and utter, "Hello, Fai and Stark, how are you doing?"

Turning with just their upper torsos, they immediately recognized the grasper to be none other than the odious Gino Esposito, erstwhile gossip columnist for 'HERE' and one-time manager to a bevy of no-name starlets and harlots, who was generally referred to, out of earshot, as 'one of the world's great slimes'. His pasty-skinned, deeply-creased, face was accentuated by an oversized hooked nose, beady eyes and a mouth spread beyond its natural dimensions by too many, unsuccessful, face lifts. It sat on top of a five-foot-five bag of potatoes draped in mismatched clothing and adorned with enough gold-plated jewellery to embarrass a pawnshop owner. From as long ago as Faison could recall, Esposito had fancied himself as a friend and invaluable guest, when in fact absolutely no one could stand him being in the same room, never mind nearby. Ever the party crasher, all he needed to know was that there was to be a party attended by famous names, the wealthy, or people of position. He would arrive and be so bold that he would just sit at someone else's place. This absurd behaviour was tacitly allowed because of the fear most had for his vicious tongue and them not wanting to be on the receiving end. Of course, security being what it was at Key Mansions, Gino had never been successful at invading any function held by Stark and Faison, even though he had tried on numerous occasions.

Without skipping a beat, Faison flashed a disingenuous smile and in low, but firm, voice, curtly proffered, "Remove your hands from our persons or I will have you charged with battery. Should you think I jest, then don't." Esposito, momentarily stunned, began to say something but was interrupted by Faison continuing, "You disgust me and everyone else in the room, yet common courtesy and breeding, and the fear most have of being attacked by your crude mouth, and poison pen, usually protects you. This evening is a celebration of a dear friend's birthday and should not be marred by your insulting antics, typically aided by your oft too frequent trips to the open bar. Therefore, before you say or do something you'll regret, I suggest you merely retrieve your coat and fade gracefully from the scene."

Blanched and momentarily chastened, Gino Esposito sputtered, turned and charged toward Andrew and Fort. "Did you hear what that arrogant son of a bitch said to me? Are you going to allow that, knowing that I can make or break everyone in this room?"

All it had taken was a nod of Faison's head and, by the time Esposito had blurted out his two threatening sentences, Faison's tuxedoed protectors had quietly come from behind Gino and scooped him up by his elbows. With his feet swinging in the breeze, and his eyes bulging from his face, the gentlemen efficiently removed him from the dining room while he frantically screamed, "You'll regret this, Andrew Poyntz, for letting Quay get away with this. Nobody does this to Gino Esposito. You'll pay dearly, mark my words!"

Before the stunned silence could be broken, Faison turned to Andrew and, smilingly, said, "Once again, Happy Birthday." With that, the entire room started cheering and clapping. Obviously, the assessment of their general disgust and dislike of Mr. Gino Esposito had not been overestimated by Faison. "Andrew, I can assure you, he can't hurt you and won't. He's all mouth and no substance. The last thing he'd want is for anyone outside this room to learn of his embarrassment. He's like the little boy who lurks in the bushes and shoots peas through his peashooter at unsuspecting people passing."

"I sincerely hope you are right. All I need is a pissing match with a skunk."

For the next forty-five minutes, Stark and Faison meandered through the room receiving kudos from everyone, including the occasional stranger, and making small talk with their many friends present.

With a trumpet fanfare and an announcement from Fort di Palma for everyone to find their assigned table and chair, the room, for the next several minutes, reminded Faison of a mouse maze filled with drugged rodents. The fact that everyone took the process so seriously, to the point of insisting that each chair had to be occupied by the specified diner, made it even more absurd. As if it really mattered who sat where? Unless, of course, Faison mused, with a slight smirk appearing at the corner of his mouth, the occupant of a predetermined chair was going to be poisoned. Since Gino Esposito had not even been invited, he immediately ruled that possibility out.

Now That I'm Gone

The head-table was the only round, specially set up for the occasion, since the restaurant's regular seating consisted only of square and rectangular tables. To Faison's immediate left Andrew, the guest of honour, had placed himself, Fort and then Carlton Parkhurst and, his, closeted, new partner, Robert Earlton, Tory Member of the Ontario Provincial Parliament. On Stark's right, newly-out Liberal Member of the Federal Parliament and Minister of State for Eastern Europe, The Honourable Marleena Anastasia Czahnivsky, or Mac as her close friends called her, and her partner of nearly twelve years, Ziam Ngout, an early Miss Black Canada, originally from Ethiopia. The table was the perfect balance of intellect, age and background to make for interesting dinner conversation.

Stark and Faison knew all of their tablemates socially, but other than their hosts, none too well. Having been completely out for most of their lives, they had always had difficulty with men and women who insisted on living a double life by playing both sides of the net at once. Hiding in the straight world, lest a professional promotion be lost, or family peace be shattered, while cruising for sexual companionship, whenever they could circumspectly manoeuvre, was not the way to ultimately garner respect or acceptance in either world or, for that matter, within themselves. Faison and Stark usually kept anyone who switch-hit at a distance, without ever being demeaning or rude.

For those reasons, plus the innate loathing they shared for ultra-conservatives, it was, with diffidence, that they attempted to conduct any conversation during the next forty or fifty minutes with Robert Earlton, seated opposite. He, unfortunately, embodied the worst of both, closeted and an ultra-conservative. Coming from a long line of provincial power brokers and politicians, Earlton, and his family's tentacles, past and present, oiled their way through life, using and abusing anyone who could advance their position or wealth. Rumour had always had it, that nothing was beyond the Earlton dynasty. Of course, many had tried to maim them, or at least their reputation, but no one had succeeded.

Each course had been presented and consumed leaving only the cheese and fruit, accompanied by thirty-year-old Madeira to be savoured. As Faison sipped the port, Marleena Czahnivsky said, "Andrew, how have you been coping since we last saw you?"

"Not too bad, but still having the odd moment, especially since the files were delivered."

"What files? What's all this about?" inserted Robert, never one to miss an opportunity to demand to know every detail of everyone's woes and misfortune.

"Oh, nothing really. Marleena was just referring to the last time she and Ziam were over for dinner, several weeks ago, and I was a bit down. Although my Father and I weren't especially close, I'm still experiencing the odd pang of remorse that we were never really close in the way most fathers and sons are."

"For God's sake, Andrew, it's been four months since he passed away. Move on," Robert insensitively retorted.

Stinging from the tone and tenor of the rebuke, Andrew maintained his outward demeanour and calmly responded, "I am moving on, Robert, but it's something that takes time. It would be a lot easier if my Father had not left such a cryptic will, with me being the one charged with deciphering it. On top of that, he left me his professional and personal files and I'm at a loss to know why."

"What do you mean he left you his files? Aren't they the property of his patients?" Robert Earlton continued.

"Actually, that is a misconception. Patients' files belong to their doctor; and, in the case of my Father, he kept very detailed files on all of his patients. In addition, he was a voluminous diarist, recording the minutest details of each day's occurrences. In reading the randomly selected bits, thus far, I am staggered by the contents. It's amazing what personal dirt individuals confide to their doctor. I'm just getting into one file that appears to be detailing blackmail and suicide and seems to involve some prominent people."

"That sounds fascinating but could also be quite a burden for you," Ziam offered. "I don't really know if I'd be able to keep the information secret, especially if I knew any of the people involved."

"I'm afraid it may very well become an enormous onus, given that so many of the people Father treated, and refers to, are, or were, residents of the Beach and I, having been born and raised there, know, directly or indirectly, most of them.

"In the case of the blackmail I mentioned, I've only just started reading the copious entries. Thus far it appears to involve some old-time politician or prominent citizen, but in only the most cryptic fashion. Unfortunately, I don't have the time required to really wade through everything in order to tie all the pieces together to obtain a clear picture of the apparent intrigue."

"Well, I guess it doesn't really matter how quickly you get to it since you've got the rest of your life to do it. You can make it a hobby and spend the odd snowy evening playing snoop," offered Carlton Parkhurst.

"Yes and no," Andrew responded.

"My Father's will included a very curious passage involving the records, me, and a specific period of time. Once the files and diaries were delivered, several weeks ago, I only have one year and then I am mandated to report to his executor what I've done with the contents. It's bizarre and quite confusing; since, I haven't a clue what Father wanted me to do with them. It's as if he's testing me, except I don't know what's the test."

Fortunato interrupted Andrew by gently placing his hand on his thigh. "Excuse me, birthday boy, but it's time for the speeches. That means you have to sit there and let us say nice things about you."

"You mean we have to lie and pretend that we really like him," Stark jibed?

Everyone encircling the table roared with laughter and then Fort stood and asked for the ear of the room. For the next twenty minutes, praises flowed, starting with a loving tribute from Fort, followed by Faison, Stark, Marleena and Estella Karsway, Andrew's sister.

Responding, Andrew thanked everyone for their gifts, which would be opened later at home, and for all the kind words and wishes. It wasn't until he thanked Fort for being his partner, and the complete joy that he had given him from the very first moment they met, that he was brought to tears.

Finally, with everyone possessing a full stomach and a warmed heart, the dance music started and the room arose in ragged unison. Andrew and Fort led off the dancing and were the sole occupants of the dance floor for the first number. At the end, the surrounding audience clapped and cheered the Terpsichorean couple, then joined them in dancing, for the rest of the evening. Even Faison and Stark broke with tradition and partook of the opportunity. Both were very good ballroom dancers, having been raised to be skilled in all the social niceties, but rarely found the desire to dance with each other. They usually used the excuse that it was too difficult to decide who was going to lead. When they did dance, Faison usually led.

Normally, Faison and Stark would leave an event such as this around eleven or eleven-thirty but given the guest of honour and the fact that they had promised to provide Andrew and Fort a lift home, they stayed to the bitter end. After the last guest had left, Fort opened a bottle of Dom Perignon, poured four flutes and toasted Andrew once again, and, then, the friendship the four assembled so enjoyed.

Andrew finally announced that he was going to open the gift that Stark had slipped into his hands so many hours before. Quickly, the gold key-embossed paper was on the floor, the box within pried open and Andrew and Fort sat there agape and in stunned silence. Inside the thin box was a photograph of the four of them standing on the private sun deck of the owner's suite of the Key Mariner and across the face of it was scrolled, 'Let's do it again, ten days from now, Love Stark & Faison'.

Fort spoke first. "You guys can't keep doing this. It's too much."

"Who says?" Stark queried. "It's a great excuse for all of us to get away right after Thanksgiving for two weeks and cruise down South America's east coast."

"Absolutely", chimed in Faison. "We'll fly to Barbados next Tuesday afternoon, then board the ship Thursday evening, have three days at sea, visit Fortaleza, Brazil, three more days at sea then two days in Rio, two more days at sea and then end up in Buenos Aires. If you can get the extra time, we can even stay on board for another two weeks and end up in Valparaiso, Chile, after circumnavigating Cape Horn."

"Buenos Aires will be more than generous. Plus, the fact is, I don't think we can get away for anymore time. As it is, if we take off too much more time, we're going to get fired and then you'll have to put us on Key Holding's payroll", Fort contributed.

"Well, I've told you both many times that could be arranged. The main thing is, we are going to have a great time, get some sun and rest. Now, let's get you two home. Faison and I need to get to bed so that we can get some much needed beauty sleep."

Once all the guests had departed, the bodyguards had quietly gathered the gifts; neatly packed them in cartons obtained from the restaurant; loaded them in the car; and, were motionlessly guarding the room from nearby the elevator lobby.

Ernie headed down Queen's Park Circle, around Queen's Park, in which the Ontario Provincial Legislature building was located, proceeded down University Avenue to Gerrard Street, where he turned left and continued along to Parliament Street. Navigating a turn to the left and then a quick turn to the right, the Jaguar found itself on Spruce Street and a minute later, at Lilac Lane, and Fort and Andrew's corner-lot Cabbagetown home. Cabbagetown, located in the east-central part of downtown, contains the largest collection of

Now That I'm Gone

Victorian houses in North America and features abundantly treed streets that are lined with lush gardens emitting pungent fragrances. The trip had taken less than ten minutes with the quiet only being broken when Stark and Faison bade goodnight, then hugged and kissed Andrew and Fort. After the car doors were closed, Ernie waited until the gifts were unloaded from the Crown Victoria by the guards and delivered to their foyer. As the two couples waved to each other, Ernie stepped on the accelerator and headed home to Key Mansions.

It had been a wonderful evening.

CHAPTER 2

Time collapsed between the evening of the birthday party and Thanksgiving dinner. Andrew and Fort had confirmed that they would only be able to go as far as Buenos Aires, while Faison and Stark had decided to take advantage of the opportunity to stay on board and cruise to Valparaiso, knowing that Andrew and Fort would not mind flying back to Toronto by themselves. Who wouldn't enjoy flying in the ultra comfort of Key Holdings International private Bombardier Global Express Jet? One hundred feet long and a wingspan of ninety-four feet, with a compartment at forty-eight feet by eight feet, the personal jet transport of the owner and Chair of Key Holdings International was outfitted with every conceivable creature comfort. Fire-resistant silk moiré, leather and deep-pile carpet complemented a disappearing queen-size bed, disappearing dining table, two luxurious chesterfields, six reclining chairs, a gourmet galley, shower equipped bathroom, and a staff, consisting of Captain Vinita Rialto, First Officer Ali Vanshee and valet, Marcel Trembley. Capable of flying eleven thousand kilometres non-stop, at a speed of up to 950 kilometres per hour, Faison and Stark rarely travelled distances using any other aircraft. On occasion, when there were to be more than twelve passengers, rather than reconfigure the Global Express, Faison would grudgingly use one of the larger planes operated by Key Aviation.

The flight to Barbados was twenty hours away. It was Monday evening, Thanksgiving Day, and the last big holiday get-together before Christmas. David Granpré, Majordomo extraordinaire, had been planning the banquet for weeks and had not overlooked a thing. Fresh-cut flowers were everywhere and arranged in appropriate-sized antique vases of porcelain, crystal, silver and gilt. The formal dining room was set with fourteen place settings of Wedgwood's Caernarvon bone china, Puiforcat's Royal sterling silver flatware and St Louis' Gold Thistle crystal stemware, upon crisp, white, damask table linen. Chef Michel Bocier had created a festive fall-themed Thanksgiving Feast, consisting of puree of yam soup with maple syrup crème fraîche, French-roasted turkey, two dressings featuring, celery from Stark's family, and, sage with onions from Faison's, garlic riced-potatoes, parsnips, almond spinach soufflé, Italian plum tomato and fiddleheads salad, pumpkin pie with brandied whipped cream and cranberry apple pie with homemade cinnamon ice cream, ending with fresh fruit and assorted cheeses served with Faison's private reserve forty year old, oak cask-aged Madeira.

Due to the travel plans for the following day, Faison had set the invitation for arrival earlier than he would normally have preferred; cocktails for six o'clock with dinner at seven. That would provide the appropriate one and one-half hours for dinner and another one and one half for visiting, before everyone would depart at ten.

First to arrive were Marsha Redfearne, at thirty-two, Stark's baby sister and, her on again, off again, live-in Brock Streeter. Basil had barely taken their coats when the other elevator door opened and Faison VII, known as Veetwo, stepped into the spectacular foyer with his fiancée, Felicia Pomeroy and, Veetwo's lifelong friend, Douglas Cheung and, his wife, Victoria Sartoni.

There was no more elegant and dramatic entrance to a penthouse in Toronto, or probably any other city in the world, than the one perched atop Key Mansions. The forty-foot square, inlaid marble-floored hall soared thirty feet into the air and was centred with an antique bronze statue spewing water down itself into a marble-ringed catch basin. Upon exiting either of the twin, private, elevators, guests could look directly across the hall to a wall of glass that shielded the forty-by-forty foot formal dining room and the incredible view of the Toronto skyline. Depending on the occasion, or for that matter even the moment, drapes could be drawn across the entire length to create a completely different mood and appearance, assisted by an extensive computer-controlled lighting system. Along the wall to the right was the cloakroom, an elevator accessing the guest suites, the entrance to the formal gallery walk and a ten-foot expanse of glass doors opening to the terrace. Along the left wall were doorways, both concealed and obvious, that lead to other areas of the main floor of the two-floored penthouse. At the north end was the concealed door that led to the personal suites of David Granpré, Majordomo and Basil Kellet, butler, next the entrance to the elevator that carried Faison, Stark and Veetwo upward to their private suites and, to the right of that, another door that led to Faison and Stark's office suites. Known as the family gallery walk, because its north wall was lined with ancestral portraits and photographs, the most southerly opening led to the family dining room, garden room, kitchen, wine cellar, offices for David Granpré and Basil Kellet, plus laundry, storage and day-staff quarters. Flanking the centred elevators along the north wall were the twin staircases that swept from the foyer to the wide balcony and the wall of north-facing glass and French doors that opened to a lushly planted formal terrace. The guest suites of the west wing were accessed from one end of the balcony and the east wing, which consisted of Veetwo's six-room suite to the north and Faison and Stark's lavish suite and terrace to the south, from the opposite end. On many formal occasions, the hall had acted as a ballroom, accommodating the fancy footwork of the revelling guests, while the orchestra would be positioned on the wide balcony, overlooking the foyer.

"Hi, Aunt Marsha. Where's my hug and kiss?" Veetwo said as he thrust his arms toward Marsha.

"Come here you little brat and I'll give you a spanking, never mind a hug and kiss", Marsha responded.

"OOOh, promises, promises! All talk and no action", countered Veetwo.

"Hey, you two, haven't you heard of incest?" Felicia jocularly offered.

"Didn't you know that's how we plan to keep all the money in the family?" Veetwo added as everyone roared with laughter.

"Come on," Veetwo said, "let's go find Father and Dad."

"You'll find them in the salon, sir."

"Thank you, Basil." Veetwo acknowledged as he escorted the others down the long, art-lined, gallery toward the grand salon.

Rarely did anyone rush along the forty-foot long, fifteen-foot high, ten-foot wide, arched passageway. The entire south side featured ten-feet-high solid glass doors, framed by the soaring arches, which opened onto a spectacular forty-by-forty foot terrace, which, in turn, overlooked the downtown of Toronto. Opposite, on the north side, the arch-framed walls were lined with part of Faison and Stark's extraordinary collection of Canadian art. One could revel in a dramatically lighted, brilliant display consisting of two Tom Thomson, two Lawren S. Harris, six A.Y. Jackson and four each of A.J. Casson, Frederick H. Varley, Arthur Lismer, J.E. MacDonald, Frank Johnston and Franklin Carmichael in addition to a dozen other artists including Edwin Holgate, Paul-Émile Borduas, Alfred Pellan, L.L. FitzGerald, Jean-Paul Riopelle, Ronald Bloore, Harold Town and, of course, Alex Colville.

Fortunato di Palma and Andrew Poyntz arrived several minutes later, closely followed by Marleena Czahnivsky and Ziam Ngout.

Finally, around twenty after six, Arthur Baum and his partner of forty-five years, Chaim Mitzner, entered the grand salon, offering abject apologies for being late.

Graciously, Faison countered, "My darlings, the only thing that matters is that you are here, along with all our other dear ones. What would you like Basil to bring you?"

"A gorgeous, twenty-five year old, hung, six-foot, blonde Adonis and a bottle of Viagra will be fine. If that's not available, we'll both have Dubonnet on the rocks with a twist."

"You best be careful, Arthur, you know how dynamic our staff is and how they usually are able to successfully fulfill any request," Stark mockingly chided.

As the room erupted into gales of laughter, Veetwo raised his voice and said, as he blew exaggerated kisses, "It's alright, Uncle Arthur, I still love you. Dad is just jealous that you can still crave twenty-five year old blondes."

"One for Veetwo, zero for Stark", Chaim added as the rest of the guests laughed even harder.

The banter and cocktails continued until Basil appeared in the doorway and silently clasped his white-gloved hands in front of him. Faison didn't need to check his wristwatch to know that it was precisely seven o'clock and time to serve dinner. An unobtrusive nod between Stark and Faison was all that was needed for them to rise in unison, extend their right arms toward the doorway and say, "Ladies, gentlemen and Arthur, dinner is about to be served. Please follow Basil."

With a very slight bow toward the guests, Basil turned and slowly made his way to the formal dining room. Flanked by forty-foot-wide walls on both the north side, which looked into the reception hall, and the south side, that afforded a spectacular vista of downtown Toronto, the room was elegant and yet inviting. Rich walnut panelling along the forty-foot wide east wall featured intricately carved wainscoting and several magnificent large works of eighteenth-century English art, while the glass west wall looked onto the illuminated garden terrace. During formal dinner parties, either David or Basil would guide the guests to their place cards to be seated. Many aspects of protocol would be employed in determining the correct placement, the guests of honour always seated to the right and left of Stark, at the west end of the table, and to the right and left of Faison, at the east end of the, normally configured, twenty foot long, table. Given the evening was restricted to family and very close friends, formal protocol had been suspended, allowing the participants to be greeted by David and invited to randomly place themselves around the exquisitely presented table. Once settled, they removed their crisp linen serviettes from the Q and S monogrammed gold rings and placed them on their laps, anxiously anticipating the feast that awaited them. The grand crystal chandelier suspended from the thirty-foot high ceiling had been dimmed allowing the candlelight to dominate and cause the entire room to appear in a somewhat muted, ethereal, state.

"As you know, we don't say grace, since she can take care of herself, so please don't wait on us to start, once you are served," Faison jested.

With that pronouncement, the door to the kitchen opened and two servers appeared each carrying a soup tureen with a silver ladle. The efficient placement of the soup plates segued to the seamless and impeccable serving of the first course. Immediately after the two servers departed, David and Basil followed with a crisp and perfectly chilled Chateau des Charmes Late Harvest Riesling and poured the prescribe amount into the first wine glass to the right of each guest.

After the soup had been consumed and the spoons placed at 'four o'clock' in each of the soup plates, the two servers appeared and innocuously retrieved the plates and their silverware and placed them on large silver salvers, strategically resting upon the marble-topped cabinet along the wall. Next the used wine goblets were removed and the servers, with their loaded trays, retreated.

In what seemed only a moment, the door to the kitchen once again opened, this time revealing Chef Michel Bocier triumphantly pushing a giant, silver-domed, walnut trolley followed by the two servers each bearing a large silver tray loaded with covered silver serving dishes. With a dashing swoop of his arm, Bocier retracted the dome to reveal a stunning, perfectly browned, turkey. After the traditional quiet applause subsided, he whisked out the carving knife from between a folded white linen serviette and, with lavish strokes, applied the whetstone.

Mesmerized, the diners sat enraptured by the performance, whetting their taste buds for what was about to be placed before them. As each plate was mounded with sliced turkey, one of the servers spooned out each of the accompanying vegetables while the other server took the finished plate to the next guest lining the table. After the fourteen plates were served, Chef Michel closed the dome and then watched as the two servers worked their way around the table offering gravy to each guest. Once they finished their anointing and had returned to flank the trolley, Faison thanked Chef Bocier for a superb presentation and then watched as the staff, except for David, disappeared to the kitchen and everyone began to devour the main course.

All it took was several forks of food for Veetwo to exclaim, "I don't know how Michel does it; but, he outdoes himself every year. This is fabulous."

"Hear, hear," added Chaim. "May I propose a toast to our wonderful hosts," raising his wine glass and saluting it toward Faison and Stark.

"To Faison and Stark," was the unanimous response, as all the other glasses were raised.

The remaining courses paraded past the assembled guests at an elegant pace that allowed for the preceding course to settle slightly before the next. Finally, when there was nothing more to be offered in the dining room, Faison asked David if he would please ask the staff to come into the dining room for the traditional thanks.

David disappeared and a moment later reappeared, followed by Chef Bocier, his sous chef, three kitchen assistants and the two servers.

Faison waited until David and the other seven had fully entered and then said, "On behalf of Dr. Redfearne, Veetwo, and our guests, I would like to thank each of you for providing us with such a delicious feast and a seamless presentation. Happy Thanksgiving."

Once again, "Hear, hear", echoed through the room.

The smiles on the faces of the staff indicated just how much they appreciated the recognition. As they filed back to the kitchen, David and Basil broke away from them and headed for the dining room doorway. Faison and Stark stood, followed by the guests, and they randomly sauntered back to the salon, where Basil had already placed the liqueur cart and was awaiting requests.

Although an enormous and elegantly formal room by any standard, the forty-by-eighty foot Grand Salon retained a feeling of intimacy. Apricot, pastel lime and muted gold formed the basic colour scheme, with intricate crown moulding, inlaid hardwood floors, and Persian accented carpets complimented the groupings of custom-made Barrymore white damasked-covered chesterfields, armchairs and patterned occasional chairs. Both the south and west walls featured full-width floor-to-ceiling windows softly draped in silk. The forty feet on the east side, south of the gallery entrance, opened onto the terrace. A full-size, antique, Heinzman concert grand piano graced the northeast corner, just by the entrance to the entertainment and billiard rooms.

"My god, guys," complained Marsha Karsway. "I don't know where I put it all."

"If you look very carefully, you'll notice that your right leg is appreciably larger than your left, my darling", Stark offered with tongue in cheek.

"You always were a bitch," she countered, "and, much to my frustration, a skinny bitch."

"Well, none of you have a thing to worry about. How do you think Chaim and I feel when we look in the mirror on the ceiling of our bedroom while were making love and all we see is the Michelin tire boy astride the Hindenburg," laughed Arthur.

"TMI, TMI, too much information, Arthur, way too much. My god, Arthur, please, not on a full stomach", Marleena shrieked, accompanied by a mock gesture of pretending to get sick.

"One thing's for certain", Fortunato interjected, "with the four of us on the plane tomorrow, it's going to really have to flap its' wings to get off the ground."

"Oh, you lucky buggers, I wish that we were going. How come were not going", Marsha jokingly asked.

"Because you're straight and would ruin all the fun. Anyhow, Brock asked us not to offer to take the two of you because he said you'd be so busy ogling all the gorgeous men you wouldn't have time for him. On top of that, quite frankly, we don't want you competing with us for the attention of all those poor married men accompanying their wives. They need rescuing from their ennui and the four of us are the ones to do it."

"Stark, how can you be so cruel to your poor little baby sister?", Marsha purred as she curled her lower lip. "I'm always willing to throw you my rejects."

"By the way", Faison chimed in, "have you two finished packing?"

"All but our toiletries and medicines", Andrew said.

"Yeah, and I've had to do all of it since Andrew has been spending every single spare minute on those damn records he got from his dad", Fort added.

"I just can't put them down", Andrew stated. "The files and diaries are really getting interesting. The more you delve, the more dirt appears. I can't believe the stuff my father was privy to. Not only that, the bits and pieces he garnered from general conversations and observations that he realized were part of things he had previously been told. He made notes about all of it. The problem is, when you come across something, you might not be able to fit it to something else that you already read until you come across something else that makes it possible to fit the pieces together to finish that particular puzzle. I have learnt about all sorts of things, from illegal abortions to prominent drug addicts, thefts, partner swapping, counterfeiting, bank fraud, loan sharking and the beginnings of a blackmail scheme that involves some big movers and shakers. I just haven't being able to put all the pieces in place on that puzzle."

"The two week break will do him good", Fort interjected. "I think he's become almost obsessive about trying to figure out why his father left them to him."

"You're probably right on both counts", Andrew ruefully responded. "It's just such a conundrum. Father never did anything without a good reason. Unfortunately, he never really afforded me the opportunity to get to know him so I can't contemplate what was in his mind when he entrusted the files and diaries to me. He was always working and seemed to prefer his patients to his family – at least that's what Mother used to say. Whatever it was that he expected me to do with that copious anthology of files and diaries, I just hope I can discover it before the one year time limit arrives."

"Honey, I'm sure you will, but, no matter what happens, I'll still love, and respect you, and that's the most important thing, n'est pas?"

"Mais oui", Andrew responded with a smile, "Absolument".

"Listen, you two, enough with the treacle. I'm going to go into insulin shock", joked Faison. "Who's for a movie in the cinema and who's for a game of billiards?"

By this time, Basil had unobtrusively filled all the liqueur requests and, with drinks in hand, the group dispersed. Douglas and Victoria, along with Felicia and Veetwo, opted to see who could best whom at billiards; while the remaining guests headed for the luxurious media room to melt into individual leather-wrapped recliners and fight to stay awake while attempting to select and watch a movie from the DVD library inventory of well over one thousand. True to form, everyone eventually fell asleep well before the ending, causing David to stop the show and gently waken Mr. Quay and Dr. Redfearne, who in turn roused the others. Filing back into the salon, they were reunited with the others who had long-since finished their billiard game and had made their way back to the comfort of the eiderdown-filled chesterfields for quiet conversation.

Gesturing to the assemblage, Faison said, "Is everyone alright to find their own way home or would you like to have Ernie drive you home?"

"We should really walk home in order to burn off some of the calories we put on tonight; but, given the hour and the fact that none of us would ever walk anywhere we didn't have to, we'll be quite able to get ourselves home. Thanks, however, for the thoughtful offer", Arthur said, sensing everyone's wishes.

"Since no one else will be requiring Ernie, I'll ride along with him while he drives these three sleepy characters home, Father", Veetwo announced, indicating Felicia, Douglas and Victoria.

Moving to the foyer, the guests were each helped into their coats by Basil. Once the donning had been completed, he deftly rolled a small trolley from the cloakroom and positioned it by the door to the elevator. As Faison and Stark hugged and kissed each couple goodnight, David, unobtrusively handed Stark a gold, 'Key'-embossed, gift bag that Stark then handed to one of each couple. This was a tradition always carried out at the end of a festive occasion such as Thanksgiving, Christmas and Easter. In the gift bag was an assortment of meat, vegetables and condiments from that evening's repast and included an appropriate bottle of wine. Faison and Stark felt that leftovers were the best part of a festive dinner and were missing at one's home if they had dined away from their place. Even Felicia had been given a full-sized goody bag since Veetwo had already told David he would be dining at Felicia's the next evening.

When it came to Andrew and Fortunato, Faison said, "You won't need a bag, this time, since we'll be together and having a scrumptious meal on the plane, as we fly to Barbados. We'll pick you up at three. Hope you have a good sleep."

"Believe me we will and I can assure you Andrew is not going to be doing anything on his pile of paper. He desperately needs his sleep", Fort assured.

The elevator door closed, Faison and Stark once again thanked David, bade him goodnight and headed toward their personal quarters.

CHAPTER 3

The morning schedule rarely varied, not because Faison and Stark had become inflexible but because they enjoyed the ritual that had evolved over the years. Awaking naturally between eight and nine, and having usually slept through the night, both would head to their double bathroom, empty their bladders and then proceed to the adjacent state-of-the-art gym, where their personal trainer would already be working out. For the next forty-five minutes, each of them would be put through their personally choreographed routine. Following that, they would shave and shower and proceed to the breakfast room in their suite. While reading the Toronto Star, they would consume freshly-squeezed orange juice with lots of pulp, Red River porridge, or oatmeal porridge, with honey and milk, eggs, either lightly scrambled, soft boiled, poached or lightly basted, homemade multigrain bread and with butter and homemade marmalade or jam , fresh fruit, occasionally a piece of cheese for Stark, and a pot of one of Twinings' Teas, possibly Prince of Wales, Princess of Wales, Ceylon, English or Irish Breakfast, Earl Grey or Lady Grey. Fridays varied only in that instead of working out they were pampered in the spa part of the gym, each receiving a massage, pedicure and manicure. On weekends, eschewing the gym, and allowing staff time off, they usually scheduled brunch with friends at one of the many restaurants in Toronto that provide fabulous arrays. When nothing was planned, David would make certain the normal services were provided, staffing appropriately.

After breakfast on weekdays, at ten fifteen, Stark and Faison would emerge from the suite, to be greeted by David, who would escort them to their respective, adjoining offices. Once Faison was settled at his desk, David would present the leather-bound, gold key-embossed, folder, from under his left arm, which contained the daily reports from the companies that made up Key Holdings International. Faison, as Chair and Chief Executive Officer, received daily reports from the Chief Operating Officer of each company owned by Key Holdings International. Each company's report included a synopsis of the preceding day's operations, the current status of any legal proceedings or situations, all current financial information and any personal correspondence between the COO and

Faison Quay VI. As Faison reviewed each, David would await any instructions Faison would issue.

Stark, as Senior Vice President, oversaw special projects undertaken by the KHI companies and received the appropriate daily communications in order for him to monitor and guide the progress of each mission.

At one-thirty, each weekday, they always adjourned and Faison would join Stark for a light lunch, served in the garden room.

Once the repast had been consumed, and several glasses of wine had been enjoyed, it was time for them to go to their respective offices, and continue their respective work.

From two forty-five on the afternoon of Tuesday, October fifteen, Andrew, Fort, Stark and Faison enjoyed the raptures of being pampered with a private jet, limousines, ocean-going suites, butlers, Fortaleza, Brazil and the sweet, warm air off the coast of South America. At ten twelve, eight days later, on Wednesday evening, October twenty-three, their world started to unravel.

Tenuously, Morden Holmgren, Captain of Key Cruise Line's 'Key Mariner' approached, looking ashen and more serious than usual, bowed very slightly and said, "Excuse me, Mr. Quay, but may I speak with you, privately, for one moment."

Sensing the urgency in Captain Holmgren's voice, Faison excused himself from the rest of the party, stood and then followed the captain over to a quiet moment of the dining room.

As Captain Holmgren extended his right hand containing a folded piece of paper, he quietly said, "I'm so very sorry for having to intrude on your dinner, sir, but I felt this message, which just came in for you, was so important you would not want it to be delayed being given to you."

Hurriedly, Faison opened the note and read,

Dear Mr. Quay:

It is with sadness that I communicate to you the news that I received just moments ago.

At approximately 8:15PM, Toronto time, an automobile careened out of control, mounted the curb and crashed into the side of Messrs. Poyntz' and di Palma's home. Unfortunately, the gas meter was ruptured on impact; the car burst into flames and, subsequently, their home exploded and has been totally destroyed.

Anticipating your desire to return to Toronto immediately, as a group, I have dispatched the plane to meet you in Rio de Janeiro, when you arrive there tomorrow. Additionally, I will have the

Tom Thompson Suite ready to receive Messrs. Poyntz and di Palma upon your return.

Please be assured that Key Security personnel are already on site and liasing with the police and will be posted there, until you state otherwise, in order to secure the property.

If supplementary information develops over night, I will have your briefing notes waiting for you aboard the plane.

Loyally,

David Granpré

Feeling as if he had just been kicked in the stomach, Faison grasped the back of a nearby chair, quietly thanked Captain Holmgren, breathed deeply and then headed back to the blissfully naïve trio sitting at the table gazing inquisitively across the dining room as he approached.

Not saying anything until he reached the table, he crouched between Andrew and Fortunato and softly said, "I'm so very sorry to have to give you this note that Captain Holmgren just received".

Fort took the extended paper, slightly turned so that Andrew could also read its' contents and seconds later started to tremble. Simultaneously, they both muttered, "Oh my god".

"How can this be? How could our home have been destroyed?" Andrew continued.

"What about Sadie and Max, our beloved tabbies?" Fort interjected, his voice breaking into tears.

"Come on, we'll go back to our suite and I'll call David to find out any more details that have come in since he sent the note. In the meantime, rest assured that we'll be back in Toronto before dinner and by that time the police and Key Security will have a lot more details." Faison consoled.

After Faison called David and was unable to gain any more information, the ship's doctor administered a sedative to Andrew and Fortunato to insure they got some sleep. In the morning, after a light breakfast, during which very little was said, the four of them disembarked ahead of the rest of the passengers and headed by awaiting limousine to the Rio de Janeiro airport and the solace of the Global Express.

Except for the occasional mumble and incoherent statement, neither Andrew nor Fort made any effort to communicate, instead just alternating weeping with silence. The five-and-a-bit hours were torture for everyone but fortunately passed quickly.

David Granpré had requested special expediting courtesy treatment from Canada Customs and Immigration that, of course, given who was involved and the special nature of the situation, they were more than happy to provide.

Ernie was waiting for them as they emerged from the Private Aviation Terminal. The instant all were settled in the Rolls-Royce, Ernie sped toward downtown Toronto. No time to worry about baggage, an extra bodyguard detail would take care of that matter. Time was of the essence, especially for Andrew and Fortunato.

The flashing lights from the gas utilities' trucks and police cars could be seen by the passengers three blocks away, as Ernie manoeuvred the limousine onto Spruce Street from Parliament Street. As they drew closer, the multiple strands of yellow police tape seemed to be strung everywhere and people streamed throughout the floodlighted mound of rubble, while gawkers clustered across the street.

Stunned by the realization that this was not a dream but an horrible reality, at first Andrew and Fortunato were unable to do anything after exiting the car but hold on to each other. Finally, the enormity of the situation brought them both to sobbing that quickly turned to keening heard by all. Faison and Stark just quietly put their arms around them to cosset them but said nothing.

Noticing the arrival of Mr. Quay's limousine, Key Security's site supervisor, Moriyama Ito, moved quickly through the crowd and gingerly positioned his burly body close to Faison. Almost two minutes passed before Faison turned and noticed his presence. As soon as he did, Ito leaned over to Faison's ear and whispered, "If you can get them over to my car, I have something that will make them feel somewhat better."

Faison furrowed his brow as if to question the request but Moriyama Ito merely jerked his head toward the direction of his car and started to walk in the same direction. That prompted Faison to do the same to Stark, who caught on immediately.

"Would you two come with me for a moment?"

Robotically, they turned and walked with Faison and Stark to the Key Security vehicle. Agent Ito introduced himself, extended his sadness over the loss of their home and then opened the rear door on the passenger side of his car. Pointing to the back seat, he said, "I think these two little fellows are going to be very happy to see you two."

Simultaneously, Fort and Andrew shrieked, "Good lord, Sadie and Max. How did they survive? Where did you find them? Thank you, thank you, thank you." as they hurriedly picked up and cuddled their much loved cats.

Responding to the barrage of questions, Ito offered that the two cats had been found barely an hour before, when the Fire Marshal's crew were lifting some of the debris from the basement. The cats appeared to have been shielded from the main force of the explosion by a small, sturdy, antique table in the lower level under which they must have been lying.

Realizing this was a perfect opportunity to get their dear friends away from the horrible scene and back to the peaceful setting of Key Mansions, Faison suggested that they take the cats, and let Ernie take everyone back to their place. With numbed nods, they moved toward the Rolls. Just as he bent to enter the back seat, Andrew reared, gasped and shouted, "Oh my god, what about Father's records. I can't have lost those. Fort, they were in the wine cellar, for safekeeping. We have to go see if they survived. Fort, we have to. Please, please, now."

"Calm down, Andrew, we can't get to the wine cellar yet, it's buried under the entire structure. We've got to hope for the best and let the Fire Marshal finish his investigation before the rubble can be moved in order for us to access the wine cellar."

Turning to Faison, Andrew pleaded, "Please make certain that your people watch everything that is happening, especially when they get into the lower level and the wine cellar. I must know if the records are all right. They're really the only thing I have left from my father and I have to complete what he's asked me to do....whatever that is."

"I promise you, my staff will safeguard everything and not just the wine cellar. I'll instruct Moriyama Ito to have anything that is revealed that is repairable or not damaged to be removed from the debris and placed in a storage truck that he'll have brought to the site immediately." With that, Faison disappeared for a minute and then returned, got into the front seat. Ernie closed the door and then drove them home.

Sensing they would want to have a very quiet evening and an early bedtime, David Granpré, Majordomo supreme, had arranged for the lights in the Tom Thompson suite to be dimmed slightly and the gas fireplace to be flickering when they entered. Two sweat suits lay folded on the long Carrara marble counter in the bathroom and two white terry cloth robes hung from the stylish clothes tree

Michael James Stewart

adjacent to the shower stall. The muted hum of the candle-ringed whirlpool completed the comforting welcome.

By the time Fortunato and Andrew had showered and soaked, slipped on the cuddly sweats and re-entered the main part of the suite, a kitty litter pan had been inconspicuously placed against the wall behind one of two large down-stuffed chaises. Across the room, close to the fireplace, a candlelit table had been set with two place settings of china and crystal and Basil, the butler, was standing unobtrusively by one of the two chairs waiting to assist the first of them into their chair. After serving the soup, he reminded them of the wireless call-button placed on the table within reach of both, bowed and noiselessly departed. Barely had Basil disappeared when Sadie and Max peaked from under the dust skirt surrounding the bed, perked up their ears, and then raced to the laps of their masters. Once they had nestled, Fort raised his glass of wine toward Andrew and offered, "My darling, no matter what possessions we've lost, thank goodness we have each other, Sadie and Max, and tonight especially, Fai and Stark."

CHAPTER 4

Coming out of a deep sleep and sitting bolt upright, with eyes appearing to pop from their sockets, Andrew blurted, "Shit! I forgot to call Dardi McIntyre. She must be beside herself thinking that Sadie and Max are dead."

"What are you babbling on about? I was having a wonderful dream one minute and the next I hear you raving on about daddy and a tire being dead. What's going on?"

"Fort, I suddenly woke up realizing that we didn't call Dardi when we got here and let her know that Sadie and Max were found alive. She must be so upset worrying about us and how we are coping with their deaths. Please dial her and hand me the phone, I've got to tell her the good news."

The phone rang five times before the answering machine kicked in with the recording of Dardi's voice stating she was not available and please leave a message. At the beep, Andrew excitedly told her they were back in town, Sadie and Max were alive, the four of them were staying with Faison and Stark until further notice and she should call them as soon as she got the message.

Over the next two days, Andrew refused to go anywhere; instead he just sat in their suite, stroked one or both of the cats and sunk deeper into depression. Fortunato had called both their employers and told them what had happened and said they would just continue as if they were still out of town. After breakfast each day, he visited the site of their former home for a few minutes but deftly avoided anyone he knew who might be milling around. He just couldn't bring himself to discuss it. As it was, he could barely bring himself to look at the slowly reducing pile of debris. Particularly painful was the view of each dump-truck load of shattered furniture and building components disappearing down the street. How could their beautiful home be there all safe and sound one minute and completely destroyed the next by a simple car accident? Nothing seemed to make sense. He couldn't bring himself to even think about what would come next. He knew he should but how could he? Where would they start? Everything was gone. There was so much to do, such as talking to their insurer, the police, their lawyer, an architect and contractor, etcetera but absolutely no will to do it. Faison had assured him that he could take care of everything but how could they ask that of him? How could they not? It just seemed too much to handle by themselves. Of course they would let Fai help and would appreciate everything he did to make this all go away as quickly as possible.

After dinner, the third evening after their return, while the four of them sat in the salon having liqueurs, Faison, looking dour, leant slightly toward Fort and Andrew, lowered his voice and said, "I have some very sad news to tell you. Shortly after noon today, the Coroner's Office, with the aid of the Fire Marshal, confirmed that a body that had been discovered, a short time before, buried under a mass of debris, in the basement of your house, was that of Dardi McIntyre. I don't recall you saying that she was actually planning to move into your place."

Instantly, both Andrew and Fort burst into tears, with Andrew wailing with sadness, "It can't be. She can't be dead. She was only to go in twice a day and spend some time with Sadie and Max so they got fed, a clean litter box and didn't feel totally abandoned. She had planned to go in on her way to university each day and again before bedtime each evening. This has to be a mistake. Oh, god, it just has to be a mistake."

"I'm so sorry, but it has been definitely confirmed that it is Dardi." Faison continued, "Do you know who her next of kin is and where they can be reached?"

Fort, sobbing, weakly offered, "She was from Cape Breton. Sydney, Nova Scotia. Shit, her poor parents. She was their only child and they were so proud of her getting into the University of Toronto's architectural school. I'm quite sure that we don't have their telephone number but I'm sure we could get it through information."

"I'll have David get their number and then one of you should give them a call. I presume they'll want her shipped back to Cape Breton, once she is released from the coroner's. We can take care of that without any problem."

"What do you mean? Why would the coroner be involved?" asked Andrew.

"It's just routine," Stark offered. "All deaths that occur without a doctor present require an autopsy. They'll have probably conducted it this afternoon and will release the body tonight or tomorrow morning. I'll check with them to find out their schedule. Once you find out the family's wishes, I'll take care of the rest."

Hoping to get their mind off the tragedy of Dardi's death, Faison added, "I do have some good news for you, Andrew. About half an hour ago, the workers finally reached the wine cellar. They found that everything inside the cement room was saved. I've asked for your wine to be put into storage and all your father's records to be brought over here. They should be here before you go to bed."

Still lightly sobbing, Andrew smiled broadly and sighed, "Thank you so very much. What a relief. At least I can concentrate on them to get my mind off the rest. I don't know how Fort and I will ever be able to thank the two of you. It's amazing how seemingly strong individuals can become blithering idiots when their whole world comes crashing down."

Realizing this was the perfect opportunity to interject some much needed humour into the moment, Stark snapped, "Sweetie, you're always a blithering idiot. What's with this bullshit that it only happens after a catastrophe?"

For the first time in almost four days, the four of them roared with laughter.

Next morning, after the four had eaten breakfast together in the Garden room, Stark, having been told by Fort, after speaking with Dardi's stunned parents, that they would deeply appreciate her body being returned to Sydney, went to his office to make arrangements. Andrew could hardly wait to get to the records that had, by this time, been placed in a small office next to their suite. Faison and Fortunato had decided it was about time they both visit the site. The time had come for some hard decisions to be made and it would be easier if just the two of them did so once they personally reviewed the situation.

It was the first time Faison had seen the location since the evening they had returned. It seemed so desolate and surreal. The hedge still edged the corner on the front and street side of the lot. Cinder block outlined what had been the foundation and the last of the debris was being scraped out by the backhoe. The door to the wine cellar was agape revealing a totally emptied interior. Strewn about the yard were the last pieces of furniture and décor salvaged from the basement, waiting initial cleaning before being placed in the truck for removal to storage.

As Fort and Faison negotiated their way across the lawn, a shrill woman's voice penetrated the revving drone of the machinery, "Yoo hoo, Mr. Fort. It's me, 'ermione, 'ermione Tilsbury. 'ow are you and Mr. Andy 'olding up?"

Turning, the two of them saw peaking around the big maple tree at the corner of the lot a diminutive lady, barely five feet tall, clad in a threadbare, washed-out, powder blue patterned cotton housedress, with rollers and a scarf adorning her head, a cigarette hanging from the left corner of her mouth and well-worn pink cotton slippers on her red, knee-high socks clad feet. The over-all look was depression-era bag lady.

"I've been trying to catch y'ur eye ever since I saw y'u arrive back the night after it 'appened but y'u never looked over towards my 'ouse and y'u knows 'ow I don't like to come outdoors, 'specially with all them strangers and noisy machines."

Hermione Tilsbury, at eighty-three, was a fixture in this part of Cabbagetown, having moved there from England, in 1938, as a newly arrived immigrant, with her new husband, Harold. Over the intervening years, neither of them had ever lost their cockney accent. Widowed for two years, she had become somewhat of a hermit and had become more and more reliant on Fort and Andrew to do her shopping and errands. They didn't mind and she appreciated their kindnesses.

"It was kind of you to come over and enquire about our health, Hermione. We're doing fairly well, all things considered, although we are having a great deal of difficulty with the fact two people died in this accident."

"What d'y'a mean two people? There was only one in the car, weren't there? I mean, I saw the whole thing, y'a know. When I heard the bang, I was right by the window and looked out. Mind y'a, I don't see too well in the dark but I couldn't help but see the man tryin' to stop the car from 'ittin y'ur 'ouse. He lingered after the car hit the house until the flash and the fire ignited. Can't blame him for running away just before the explosion. 'e might got himself 'urt if he hadn't run."

"Actually, madam, in addition to the driver of the car, unfortunately, a friend of theirs who was looking in on their cats also died in the explosion," Faison corrected.

"Eee, aren't y'u the one with the fancy car? Ooo, I do luv a Rolls. They're so posh, they are."

"Excuse me for being so rude, Hermione. Please meet Mr. Faison Quay. Faison this is Hermione Tilsbury."

"It's a pleasure to meet you, Mrs. Tilsbury," Faison said after taking note of her wedding ring. "Could you please clarify something you just said? In recounting the accident, you indicated that you first heard a bang that was followed by you seeing a man trying to stop the car from hitting the house and that he lingered by the car until there was a flash that was then followed by an explosion. Is that actually the order in which you saw the events?"

"Ya, it sure is. Exactly the way I saws it and the way I told them rude coppers who asked me if I'd seen anything. The fact is, I don't think they believed me cuz I 'eard one of them say as they walked down my front steps that I was so old that I probably couldn't see very well and got things mixed up into the bargain. But I didn't. I know whats I saw and I saw that man trying to save that poor driver."

"Mrs. Tilsbury," Faison continued, "did you happen to notice anything earlier in the evening in or around the house that you didn't tell the police?"

"As I said, them wanker cops were so dismissive of me, I answered them only what they asked. Anyways, there wasn't anything else, except the usual timer light coming on. By the way, Mr. Fort, how's y'u able to set that to go off at different times every night? Sure is a clever system, I guess."

Before Fortunato could respond, Faison continued, "You mentioned that the man who tried to help the man in the car ran just after the flash and before the fire. What fire? Where was the fire?"

"The fire that started after the flash. It burned for a minute before the explosion. That's why the man who'd been 'elpin' the other guy was able to get back to the protection of his truck before the place blow up. Y'a know, that damn explosion broke me windows on this side of the 'ouse and damn near scared the shit out of me. I'm too old for surprises like that. By the way, how'd I get my windows fixed?"

"Hermione, I'll notify my insurance adjuster about your damage and have him arrange for them to be replaced immediately. I'm so sorry that they were damaged and you were upset. Andrew and I are very grateful that most of the damage was contained within our property."

"Fort, I think we should let Mrs. Tilsbury get back inside before she catches a cold. But, before you go, I do have one more question for you, Mrs. Tilsbury. Do you happen to remember what kind of truck the man was driving, its' colour and, lastly had you ever seen it before?"

"Of course I remember what kind of truck it was. It was a big dark green tow truck. As for ever seeing it before, I saws it earlier that night, around six o'clock, just when the local news was starting on the telly. I heard a truck idling, so's I looked to sees who was polluting the neighbourhood. It was the same tow truck. He was just sitting there, for about ten minutes he was. Then I saws h'm later, again, when he drove by after the fire had been doused."

Bowing slightly, smiling and shaking her hand, Faison said, "Thank you so very much for being so informative and gracious. You've been an enormous assistance. Would you like assistance getting across the street and up to your front door?"

"Ooo, you are a gentleman, but I'm fine, ducks. You're right though, I'm gunna catch me death if I don't get inside. Next time you come by, Mr. Fort, bring Mr. Andrew and this Mr. Quay over to me 'ome and I'll serve tea and scones. I make them from Granny's recipe and there bloody good. Toodley do."

As she crossed the road and Fort watch, Faison gazed off into space assessing what he had just heard.

"What was that all about, Fai?"

"Her account of the events of that evening does not conform to what the police, and for that matter the rest of us, assumed happened. The series of actions she claims happened are completely different than if the car had merely mounted the curb, crashed into the gas meter and snapping it off, followed by an explosion and fire."

"That's exactly what the police said happened. In fact they have said the preliminary report indicates the driver lost control of his car as he turned the corner, stepped on the accelerator instead of the break, careened across the lawn and upon hitting the gas meter and side of the house smashed his forehead on the steering wheel and passed out. That's why he didn't escape from the car before it exploded and burned along with the house."

"Although, I have not seen the report, from what you had said, I presumed that's what it contained. The only problem with that is, it doesn't jibe with Mrs. Tilsbury's recollection of the events."

Protesting, Fort cut in, "Fai, she' eighty-three, for god sake. It all happened so quickly, I'm sure she got confused and remembered what happened out of sequence. Anyway, which ever the order of events, the end results were the same. Two people accidentally died and our home is destroyed."

"Fort, I hate to disagree with you but my gut feeling is that her account is correct and, if that is the case, then two people didn't accidentally die, they were murdered."

"Good god, Fai, do realize what you are saying? You mean someone was trying to kill the driver and their action inadvertently led to also killing Dardi?"

"I wish it were that simple, Fort, but I don't think it is."

With the anxiousness increasing in his tone, Fort pressed, "What then? I'm confused. If it wasn't the driver they were trying to kill....oh my god....no Fai....it couldn't be us they were trying to harm."

Placing his hand on Fort's arm in an attempt to console him, Faison said, "Fort, at this point I'm not quite certain if that is the case but it would appear that is what was being attempted. Fortunately, if that was the case, the two of you weren't harmed but, unfortunately, Dardi and the driver were."

Before Fort could say anything, Faison continued, "I want you not to say anything more until you come back to the car with me and we each write down our exact recollection of Mrs. Tilsbury's recount of the evening's events. Once we have correlated the two, we will have a better grasp of what actually happened. Then I would like to carefully compare it with the actual police report."

For the next twenty minutes, Fortunato and Faison quietly sat in the back of the Rolls-Royce, with the tables pulled toward them, writing out their respective recollections of Mrs. Hermione Tilsbury's conversation. Once completed, Faison opened the burled walnut cabinet door, withdrew a crystal decanter and two crystal glasses and poured them each a sherry. Once the bottle was replaced, Ernie pulled away from the curb and headed back to Key Mansions.

As the limousine approached the doorman awaiting the vehicle, Faison suggested, "Fort, until we have carefully compared our two accounts and then our synopsis with the police report, I think it behoves us not to discuss this possible turn of events with Andrew. He is already in a fairly fragile state and there is no reason to add to it at this point. However, I am going to discuss with him his father's reports, but please don't read anything into my curiosity."

Later in the evening, well after dinner and Andrew's return to pore over his legacy, in the office he had been provided, Faison knocked on the door and asked if he could enter. After making small talk for a few minutes, Faison inquired, "Have you been able to figure out what is so special about these files that your father wanted you to have them?"

"Honestly, the more I study the contents, the more I wonder. They are very detailed, with a shit load of personal observations in some, but not all. His diaries are also very detailed and sometimes even mention the same observations that were entered into patients' files. Knowing many of the patients and most of the people mentioned in the diaries still doesn't help me figure out what's so special about them that they should be left to me. I just wish Father had left some instructions as to what he wanted me to do with them."

"How would you feel about letting me review some of the material with an eye to figuring out if some pattern to them appears?"

"Faison, I would deeply appreciate your assistance, but I can't. Father was quite explicit. I was to have access to the material for one year during which time I was not to share it with anyone."

"Even though that is the case, there may be a legal way around it that would allow me to assist you. You'll recall, three years ago, you and Fort named me your Attorney by signing individual Power of Attorney forms. By doing that, you empowered me to act on your behalf, as if it was you rather than I taking the action. That being the case, I can act on your behalf in any situation including looking at the contents of your father's files. It's as if you are reviewing them when I am actually conducting the review."

"If that's the case, and I have no doubt your assessment is correct, I would welcome your assistance and advice."

"Do you have a copy of your father's will, Andrew?"

"Actually, Fai, he didn't leave a written will, per se. Instead, he left a video will. After it had been shown to us, Marsha and I requested a transcript be created, but the official will is in video format."

"Okay, the question then is, 'Do you have a copy of the video'?"

"It's somewhere in this mess. Just give me a minute."

Shortly, Andrew found the video and the two of them made their way to the media room where Faison quickly inserted the cartridge into the VCR, pressed a few buttons on the computer screen next to his recliner and then watched as the lights dimmed, the panels retracted and the screen flickered to life.

An upper torso and headshot of Andrew's father, Dr. J. Merreck Poyntz filled the screen and spoke,

"I am Dr. James Merreck Poyntz of Toronto, Ontario, Canada and am of sound mind. If you are watching this, I'm dead.

Now That I'm Gone

Although unusual, this is my last will and testament and revokes any and all other wills including any codicils I may have issued in the past. I name Roland 'Rolly' Witherspoon, my solicitor, my sole executor and authorize that he be paid the standard percentage, and no more, allowed by the Law Society of Upper Canada.

"Now that I'm gone, I want my only living heirs, my son Andrew and my daughter Marsha, both of Toronto, Ontario, Canada, to know that I had a wonderful life, filled with all the selfish pleasures I could cram into each and every day. Obviously my medicine came first, my political wheeling and dealing second, my research, writing and speech-making third and, unfortunately, my family fourth. In doing so, it was at the expense of my dear wife, who unfortunately predeceased me, and my two children. I cheated each of them in many ways, chiefly by leaving my wife to spend most of her life without an attentive partner and by not spending time with my children and experiencing them growing and becoming adults. Fortunately for me, their Mother was a wonderful, loving, person and provided them with the outward love that I withheld. For that I apologize; but, it just wasn't in my nature to be demonstrative. Instead I tried to replace my being there with possessions and a grand standard of living. In retrospect that was wrong.

"Had I been there for them, I honestly feel that Andrew would have followed me into medicine and eventually taken over my practice. Instead he chose to waste his life trying to solve the problems of large businesses, like so many other ordinary underachievers. Yes, Andrew, I know you obtained a Doctorate in International Finance and Economics, but you and I know that doesn't make you a real doctor, just an academic one.

"Marsha also underestimated her abilities and frittered away her opportunities to go on to university and amount to something in medicine. Ultimately, it's my fault that I failed to impress upon them the importance of them carrying on the legacy I had started.

"That said, I leave my son, Andrew, all my professional files and diaries, no matter where they are located, and instruct him that he is to report to Rolly Witherspoon, exactly one year after the receipt of the files and diaries, what he has done with them. He must tell the truth, no matter what that may be. In addition, I leave Andrew one hundred thousand dollars.

"To my daughter, Marsha, I leave one million dollars. The only reason I do so is because I think it is too late for her to change and become someone capable of earning enough money to maintain the lifestyle to which she has become accustomed. Use it wisely, Marsha, that's all there is.

"In addition to the above bequests, I leave the sum of four hundred thousand dollars to be divided equally amongst the three household staff, which has served our family so faithfully for the last many years, and my devoted nurse who was with me since 1971.

"If anyone named in this last will and testament challenges any part of this will, they will lose their bequest and all their rights to any further claims against my estate.

"This video was made by me, James Merreck Poyntz, this seventeenth day of May, nineteen hundred and ninety-eight, and witnessed by my solicitor, Roland 'Rolly' Witherspoon, who now will enter the picture and state, 'So witnessed this seventeenth day of May, nineteen hundred and ninety-eight.'"

The video ended, the sound of it rewinding could be heard as the panel closed across the screen. As the lights rose, Faison looked across to see Andrew sitting with his head slightly bowed and tears cascading down his cheeks. Faison did not know what to say first. Should he call Andrew's father an old bastard for treating him in this manner; should he keep silent and go and hug him; do both; or just do nothing. He opted for the hug. Andrew continued to sob and Faison continued to gently rub his back and rock him as his father should have done and didn't.

Finally Andrew whispered, "I never knew he felt so bitter toward me, especially about not following him into medicine. How could he not realize that if I had, everyone would have always gauged me by what my father had accomplished and not for my abilities and accomplishments? I would have always been Dr. J. Merreck Poyntz's son, Andrew, instead of Dr. Andrew Poyntz. At least by choosing my own path in life, I've been successful on my own. At least I thought I had, until I saw this. Since then, I've questioned my achievements and even my capabilities. Even in death he mocked me for having earned the wrong kind of doctorate, as if anything other than a medical doctorate is not worth anything. How could he have done this?"

"By his own admission, he never made the time to get to know either you or Marsha. I can honestly say that he is totally wrong when it comes to both of you. Completely and absolutely wrong."

Retrieving the videotape from the machine, Faison beckoned Andrew to follow him. Andrew wiped his eyes then joined Faison, who placed his arm around his waist and squeezed. Stark and Fortunato were seated in the salon and immediately noted the reddened eyes of Andrew when he and Faison entered. Fort signalled to Andrew to sit beside him and, once seated, placed his arm around him and drew him close.

"We've just reviewed Andrew's father's videotape of his will so that I could attempt to determine whether I could assist him in his review of the files and diaries he's been given. Contrary to what Andrew thought it contained, I didn't hear anything that would preclude me from reading them. Granted, I believe the confidentiality of the patients' records would transfer to any custodian; however, since I am already Andrew's Committee and hold his Power of Attorney, I can act on his behalf and, maintaining that confidence, access the files. Of course, so does Fort, which makes it even better. The more people sorting through that stack the quicker the job will be done."

Looking straight at Andrew, he continued, "Starting tomorrow, I want you to start sorting the files, placing them into groupings of Strictly Patients, Family Friends, Famous People and Community Leaders. Once you've done that, I want you to start reviewing their contents for anything, and I mean anything, that might indicate shocking, secretive or unusual events or behaviour. As you do that, remember that what is acceptable and normal today was not necessarily so many years ago."

"Honey," turning to Stark, "have you heard anything more about when Dardi will be released for transit back to Cape Breton?"

"As a matter of fact, I received a call from the coroner's office while you and Andrew were viewing the tape. She will be released tomorrow morning and, acting on her parents' wishes, she will be taken immediately to St. James' Crematorium. Her ashes will be ready for pick-up the day after tomorrow and the four of us will take her ashes and fly down Friday afternoon to Cape Breton and attend her funeral on Saturday morning. We'll return to Toronto late Saturday afternoon."

Before either Andrew or Fort could sink into another bout of sadness, Faison added, "I'm certain her parents will appreciate how you've handled this and will especially be pleased to have Andrew and Fort present for the interment."

Nonchalantly, Fort casually said, "We both deeply appreciate everything you both have, and are, doing for us, especially what you've done concerning Dardi." Quickly changing the subject, he continued, "By the way, Fai, I'd like to show you something on the Internet I came across. Can we use your big-screen office computer?"

Puzzled, but sensing some urgency in his voice, Faison responded in the affirmative, leaving Stark and Andrew to the open bottle of wine Basil had so thoughtfully placed, along with crystal goblets, on the coffee table, in front of the chesterfield where they sat.

Silent until they reached the far end of the long hall leading from the salon, Fort finally whispered, "Fai, I've been doing a lot of thinking since this afternoon and I think I've come up with something."

Putting his forefinger to his lips, he continued to briskly walk toward his office. Once the door was closed behind them and each had a glass of wine in hand, Faison said, "I presume it has to do with what we heard over at your house this afternoon and if it is, I'm very grateful you didn't say anything in the salon. As it is, Andrew, at this point, must not think anything is any further amiss than it already appears."

"I agree concerning Andrew and, yes, it is about this afternoon. If what Mrs. Tilsbury said actually happened and somebody was truly trying to kill one or both of us instead of all this being an accident, I think I know who might be behind it."

"Whoa. We haven't confirmed all of what she told us, other than correlating our notes. At this point it would appear that something nefarious took place but to make the leap from thinking something did, indeed, take place to trying to link the events to an individual, is too much, too rapidly."

"Normally, I would agree, Fai, but do you remember back to Andrew's birthday party and the scene that little shithead Esposito pulled? Remember, he threatened Andrew and said he would make him pay for allowing you to embarrass him in front of everyone?"

"How could I forget, but I can't believe he would go that far to get back at Andrew. Making threats and actually carrying through to the point of causing a death, never mind two, seems way too much even for that miserable bastard. Anyway, if these were murders, according to Mrs. Tilsbury they were carried out by a tow truck driver acting alone." Faison knew that, at this point, he was playing the devil's advocate but he wanted to draw Fort out as to how he thought Gino Esposito could be behind this pathetic act of mayhem.

Now That I'm Gone

"Fai, the di Palma family has been very well established in the Toronto community for almost sixty years. During that time, especially in the early days, a very few of the early immigrants relied heavily on old-world customs to carry out revenges and other reprehensible deeds. Now, please understand, I am not painting my ethnic community with a broad brush when I state that it would not be beneath Gino Esposito, nor beyond his capability, to have arranged for something to occur, even including murder. Even in this day and age, it is not that difficult to find a lowlife who is willing to do pretty much anything for free or next to nothing. Ethnicity has nothing to do with it, sociopathic behaviour does. In Gino's case, it would be very easy for him to find someone equally vile who would be willing to carry out his dirty work. In fact, if you were to check him out, I would bet he has an ironclad alibi for the night of the explosion. That way, he would think no one would be able to link him to it and he would get away with eliminating one or both of us."

"All of what you say may be true, Fort, but I think we have to move very judiciously and not jump to any conclusions prematurely. To do so, might cause us to overlook major clues that could lead us to the actual culprit or culprits. That is not to say that we shouldn't look at Gino Esposito very carefully, but we also have to look farther afield, since time is of the essence."

"I wholeheartedly agree, but what do you mean time is of the essence?"

"Fort, think about it. If someone is trying to kill one or both of you, I'm certain they have discovered that they did not succeed. If it was important to kill you before, they'll probably try again. Without being an alarmist, I think that is exactly what we have to realize and take adequate precautions so they are not successful. Additionally, for right now, I do not think you should discuss these concerns with Andrew. On the other hand, Stark must be brought up to snuff immediately so that he can assist us in getting to the bottom of this. Also, just in case you are wondering, I will be in touch with my contacts at police headquarters but I will not be providing them with anything we have uncovered up to now. To do so may impede, rather than assist, the investigation. We can move in broader circles, with less formality, than the police, especially utilizing all my capabilities, contact and person-power within Key Security. Does that approach sound acceptable to you?"

Somewhat flummoxed, Fort stammered, "Yes, yes, yes of course, whatever you say, of course. We so appreciate what you're doing."

"No thanks is necessary, Fort, this is about brothers helping brothers. It's that simple. Now let's get back to the guys and finish the evening with some upbeat conversation."

CHAPTER 5

Once the morning's ablutions and breakfast was behind him, Faison moved expeditiously to map out a plan of action. At the top of his list was contacting Règinè Ouellette, former Commissioner of the Royal Canadian Mounted Police and now Chief Operating Officer of Key Security. Her skills and contacts would help him immeasurably, or so he hoped. Ms Ouellette arrived within the hour after receiving his telephone call and sensed before she laid the telephone receiver back into the cradle the subject of the meeting. After all, she had had staff posted at the site within an hour of the explosion and had, intuitively felt the need to have her on-site people gather as much information as possible without alerting the police and fire marshal. She knew that would come, if and when Mr. Quay gave the go ahead.

Once Basil had placed a café latte in front of Ms. Ouellette and mug of Ceylon Breakfast Tea in front of Mr. Quay, he withdrew and Faison started, "What have your site staff discovered thus far?" His abruptness did not bother Règinè, to the contrary, since that was her modus operandi.

"Sweet bugger all, other than the obvious, that two people died in the subsequent explosion and fire. Moriyama Ito says he's smells a rat but has had to be very careful since the police and fire marshal are still pouring over the scene. I've got my contacts in the coroner's office, fire marshal's, and police all keeping their eyes and ears open. As soon as their reports are finalized, I'll have them. They've been promised within two hours but, if the past is any indication, it could be two days. Once that has occurred, I'll be able to provide you with a better assessment."

"I would expect nothing less; however, I'm extremely disappointed that Moriyama hasn't had his men surreptitiously canvas the neighbourhood, especially the immediate houses. As it stands, I have obtained more information concerning the night of the explosion and the events leading up to it than he has. It would seem obvious that the best source of information would be gathered from the eyes and ears behind the many windows overlooking the corner where the conflagration took place. That is where I obtained my information. As for waiting until the police leave the area, that's just not acceptable. For the most part, I doubt very seriously whether they have bothered to think outside the box and, therefore, probably still think the whole occurrence was just an accident. I want Ito and his people to pay a visit to every home within a one block radius, starting with the ones closest to the scene and then fanning out from there. The reason for them following that pattern is so that they can build on any information they receive closer to the centre of the event. The only house they are not to contact is that of Mrs. Hermione Tilsbury, directly across from the side of the property. She is the lady I have already spoken with and will be following up with very shortly. Additionally, I want all the information you can get on a green tow truck spotted in the vicinity on the night of the explosion. Who owns it, who was driving it and, if possible, what was it doing in the area? Make certain that information is gathered as discretely as possible. I have reason to believe the driver might not be a very nice person, if you catch my drift."

"I'll get going on this as I drive back to the office. By the way, I'm not making any excuses for the way we dropped the ball. It should be inherent in each one working for Key Security, including me, that there is always a possibility of foul play when something out of the ordinary occurs. Is there anything else?"

Smiling and attempting to convey appreciation for her professionalism in the way she apologized, Faison stood and asked, "How's your new granddaughter? I bet she's the apple of your eye. I'll also guess that I won't have to ask twice to see her latest picture."

Caught off guard, Règinè fumbled with her briefcase, found the photos and handed them to Faison. After he had made the appropriate comments, she placed them back into her case, stood, extended her hand and said, "Thanks for your understanding and direction. Without sounding obsequious, I truly do consider it an honour to work with you. I promise you we will not drop the ball again."

"Of that, I have no doubt. I'll look forward to your daily reports. Of course, call me at any time, should you feel it necessary."

Lunch was enjoyed by Andrew, Fortunato, Stark and Faison in the Garden room and then Faison headed out, not advising any of them where he was going. David, of course, had been told and had Ernie waiting at the front entrance when Faison emerged. Ernie loved intrigue and always sensed when he was a part of it without having to be told. It added to his adoration of his job. He especially loved it when there was just him and Mr. Quay. Ernie could fantasize about being Faison's right-hand man as they scoped out spies and other 'bad guys'. The destination or purpose wasn't important; his mind enjoyed creating adventure no matter what.

Instructing Ernie to stay put once the Jaguar stopped at the curb, Faison swung open the back seat passenger door, sprung from the car and headed directly through the wrought iron gate, which hung by one rusted hinge, mounted the moss-covered brick stoop, glanced in each direction to make certain no one was aware of his presence and then twirled the doorbell knob mounted in the middle of the flaking, weathered, red-painted door. Thirty seconds crawled by before he detected movement through the stained-glass panel that filled the upper portion of the door. Slowly the portal opened and an eye peered around the exposed edge.

"Oooo, it's me gentleman friend, Mr. Quay." Hermione Tilsbury continued, "I do so 'ope the nosey neighbours see this. They'll be thinkin' I've got me a suitor."

That was the last thing Faison wanted, as he quickly found protection after he stepped into the hall and hurriedly closed the door. It was better no one even knew that he was there, never mind why.

"Good afternoon, Mrs. Tilsbury, I do hope that I'm not intruding? May I have a few moments of your valuable time and ask a few more questions concerning the events of last week?"

"Of course, ducks. Come on in."

Leading the way into the front room, she made a sham effort to clean the path to the torn and stained, chintz slip-covered chesterfield, balling the strewn newspapers and chucking them behind an overstuffed armchair sitting next to where she instructed Faison to sit.

"Make yourself comfy, Mr. Quay, while I go and make us some tea. Sorry I don't have any fresh scones but I do have some Pantry Cookies and I bet y'u love them as much as I do."

Calling after her scurried footsteps, Faison protested, "There's no need to go to any trouble, Mrs. Tilsbury. Please don't put yourself out."

Two or three minutes passed, before Faison heard the shuffling of her slippers coming back down the long, narrow, hall from the kitchen to the living room. Thrusting the stamped metal tray before her, she announced with a flourish, "Ta, da. Tea's served. I've not had anyone to tea since me dear 'arold died. He did so luv 'aving people in and brag about me scones. But, it just doesn't seem like the thing to do now. Oh, don't get me wrong. This is an 'onour and a privilege and something that I won't forget in a long time. One lump or two? Milk?"

As she stopped to take a breath, Faison wedged in, "Just clear for me, thank you very much."

Before he could say another word, Mrs. Hermione Tilsbury continued, "Did you know the British Tea Council spent ten thousand pounds conducting a study whether you should pour the milk in before or after?" Not waiting for an answer, she proceeded, "They discovered that if the milk went in first it didn't change the taste of the tea because the milk warmed as the tea was added; but, if you pour it in after, the milk scalds and changes the taste. That's why I always put mine in first. I bet so does our dear Queen, don't y'u think?"

"That is quite fascinating and certainly makes a lot of sense. Regarding the Queen, the last time I attended an afternoon tea at which Her Majesty was present, I believe, if I'm not mistaken, she took her tea clear. Of course, a lot would depend on which tea was being served, don't you think."

Hearing that her guest had taken tea with the Queen was enough to leave Hermione's mouth agape and speechless, at least long enough for Faison to continue, "Since our last conversation, I was wondering if you have recalled anything that had slipped your mind back then?"

"Y'u know, it's queer that y'ud ask that, cuz I 'ave. Remember I told you about the man trying to help the driver? Well, the strange thing about that is, I recall that I saw 'im pull a piece of wood out of the driver's window just as the car careened across the lawn. I guess 'e was trying to pry the guy's foot off from the accelerator. The other thing was, y'u got me thinkin' after y'u asked me about the tow truck and I finally recalled while I was lying awake that night that the truck 'ad a big pitchfork on the door to the cab. Now I don't know whether that's any 'elp but I'm sure glad that y'u came along so I could tell y'u before I forgot again."

"Just one more item. When the man finally got back into the tow truck, after the fire and before the explosion, did he race away or wait until after the explosion?"

"Now that you mention it, it was sort of funny. 'e jumped in and y'u could tell that 'e was steppin' 'ard on the accelerator but 'e sure wasn't movin' too fast. But of course, what would he expect? Them trucks 'ave the pickup of an ugly whore."

Stifling a hearty laugh and suppressing even a smirk, Faison decided he had heard all that was new to report by Hermione, so he closed with, "Besides serving me a delicious cup of tea and my favourite Pantry Cookies, you have provided me with some very important and helpful information." Patting her hand, he continued, "If I could ask a favour, would you please keep all of what you told me to yourself and not share it with anyone. It is very important that this stays just between us. Okay?"

"Eeee, mum's the word. Me 'arold always said I could keep a secret better than a nun could hold back a fart. Y'u got my word, Mr. Quay, just our little secret. Care for some more tea, luv?"

"No thank you, Mrs. Tilsbury, but I'll take a rain cheque, how's that? Now, I really must be off, but I promise you, I will always be in your debt for the assistance you have provided. I'm also aware how grateful Andrew and Fortunato are to you."

"Mr. Quay, those two are wonderful boys who treat me with such respect. It's a bloody shame what's 'appened to their beautiful 'ome. When they bought it, it was in terrible disrepair. The previous owner was a real floozie that acted as a madam to any an' all whores who wanted a place to bring their customers. In the long run, it became nothin' short of a brothel with 'er as the main one. Eeee, she was a real loose chit. Rumour 'as it that her legs would spread quicker than warm peanut butter, if y'u know what I mean? The boys bought it from the bailiff and worked so 'ard to restore it back to 'ow it was when me and 'arold first moved 'ere. They 'ad me in a few times and I tell y'u it was a palace. I sure 'ope they can rebuild. Do y'u think they will? Oooo, I so 'ope. I don't want to lose them as neighbours; they're such good 'uns. Please send them me luv and tell them to come and visit me real soon."

Moving toward the door, Faison assured her he would pass along her wishes. After a slight bow and handshake, he opened the door, bid Hermione good afternoon and briskly moved down the brick path to the seclusion of the waiting car.

It was the hardest thing Ernie could do, just sit behind the wheel and let Mr. Faison Quay, VI, enter the car he was driving without offering assistance; but, if the 'plot' called for it, he would grudgingly cope.

As the Jaguar started to glide away from the curb, Faison autodialled Règinè Ouellette who answered after the first ring, having referred to the caller ID.

"Good afternoon, sir."

"Good afternoon, Règinè, I have obtained some additional information that I think will speed up the discovery of the tow truck in question. My source has just told me that the green tow truck had a pitchfork on the driver's door. Would you get on to that and let me know as soon as you know anything further concerning that truck."

"Thank you for the additional information. I'll be back to you as quickly as possible."

The line went dead from both ends simultaneously since neither required the niceties of a formal goodbye when it came to a call such as that. Brevity was not rudeness when time was the important factor, of that they tacitly agreed.

As the car purred its' way through the afternoon traffic and classical music wafted from the sound system, Faison ruminated on what he had learned thus far. The latest information brought everything together, making him certain, for the first time, that the events surrounding the destruction of Andrew's and Fortunato's home was deliberate and, thus, murder, at least when it came to Dardi and, more than likely, to the driver of the automobile. Once he had a few more pieces to the puzzle, he knew he would have to contact the police. The problem with that was he also knew that once he did, the police would interfere with his investigation and, more than likely scare the murderer, or murderers, deeper into hiding. The fact that nothing had been said, thus far, in the press about the explosion other than a driver had lost control of his car which, subsequently, had crashed into the Cabbagetown home Messrs. Poyntz and di Palma, causing the total loss of it and the accidental death of Dardi, was especially helpful. Whoever was behind it was thus far thinking they had gotten away with murder and would, therefore, be somewhat blasé. That would give Faison the time he required to track them down. Damn, he thought. Why did he have to bother with the police? Of course, he could hold back bits and pieces just long enough that he stayed one step ahead of them. They wouldn't need to know and he would appear as if he was cooperating with them.

Of course, there was another way he could go about his quest. He could call Detective Sergeant Gregor Ferguson, whom he had known for years, actually within days of his arrival from Scotland as a young, handsome, former Edinburgh police constable who was instantly popular throughout the gay community. Within a very short time he had been hired by the Toronto Police Department and, very quickly, worked his way up through the ranks to his present position.

Extremely astute, diligent, perceptive, fair and highly respected by his force, Gregor could keep a confidence as long as he felt that it was to the ultimate benefit of the case. Several times in the past, he and Faison had consulted on a professional basis when Règinè Ouellette required his input on several important cases. Even though they were solid acquaintances, they were always able to keep the professional separate from the friendship.

Faison's mental debate ceased with the ringing of his desk telephone, which displayed that it was Règinè Ouellette. "What's up?"

"Finally a break. The tow truck belongs to Trident Towing Service. According to their dispatcher, they have four trucks painted sea blue and only one painted green. Actually none of the trucks are owned by Trident. They are independently owned and work exclusively for Trident. When asked the name of the owner of the green truck, they got a little tight lipped. After some gentle prodding it turns out they haven't heard from him in a day or so and thought we were actually the police. Our cover was that we had been asked to locate the driver by a client who had had an accident and thought the driver of the green tow truck might have been a witness. That seemed to satisfy them to the extent they gave us his name. He's Marislav Anatole and he lives at 182 Pointer Crescent, apartment 304. In addition, he wasn't working the day of the explosion. What would you like me to do with the information?"

"Honestly, Règinè, I'd like us to sit tight for the time being so we can get a little bit more information about Marislav Anatole but, in reality, I think we've come to the point where we have to let the police in on some of the information we have thus far. To that end, I'll give Gregor Ferguson a call and provide him with just enough information for the police to locate him and to make certain that we won't get charged with obstruction down the road. It's important that I make it appear that it's no big thing; just something we thought the police should know about. For that reason I don't think you need to be in on the call. Your presence could, possibly, raise some questions in his mind that shouldn't be raised. Do you have anything to add?"

"Nothing, except that we are canvassing the neighbourhood and continuing to hound our contacts at the coroner's for a copy of the post mortem. I would appreciate it if you let me know if anything comes from your call. Otherwise, I'll be in touch as soon as I have any more info."

With a simultaneous goodbye, the lines went dead. Grudgingly, Faison dialled Gregor and was relieved when he got his answering machine. At least that would buy him a little more time.

The next morning, after Stark and Faison had finished with breakfast, David informed Faison that he had had a telephone call from Detective Sergeant Gregor Ferguson. Without hesitation, as soon as he reached his desk, he dialled Gregor. On the third ring, the Scottish brogue of Gregor whirred into Faison's ear. Over the next five minutes, after the perfunctory social banter, Faison filled the Detective Sergeant in on the basics of what he knew. Left out was Mrs. Hermione Tilsbury and most of the details she had related. All that was necessary was to let him know that the green Trident tow truck had been seen at the scene prior to the explosion and what the name and address of the tow truck driver was. Detective Sergeant Ferguson was in a much better position to follow up on Marislav Anatole and his present whereabouts than Key Security, plus, that was detail work that would divert valuable personnel and waste money and time. From past experience, Gregor would be so anxious to show Faison of what he was capable that as soon as he had something to report he would be on the telephone spilling everything he'd learnt. Before he cut off, Faison explained that he was leaving for a funeral being held in Cape Breton and would not be back in Toronto until late Thursday afternoon or early evening. Without saying any more, Gregor knew that meant that if he had anything urgent to report, he could reach Faison on his cell phone; otherwise, he should wait until Faison was back in Toronto.

Stark had personally gone to the crematorium to retrieve Dardi's ashes, saving Andrew and Fortunato the anguish. It also meant the four of them could go directly to the private passenger terminal without having to make any detours. While en route to Sydney, Nova Scotia, all agreed that as little as possible of the details surrounding Dardi's death would be conveyed to her family and friends. It was premature to even mention that it quite possibly was murder. Her parents and family had already had enough to deal with without having that added to the trauma.

The ensuing twenty-four hours compacted to a blur, being consumed with spending the evening amongst Dardi's family, enjoying their warm and unpretentious hospitality, a comfortable night's rest and the moving but simple memorial service the next morning. Following the reception in the church hall, catered by the women of the parish, Andrew, Fortunato, Stark and Faison thanked the McIntyre family for their hospitality and there kindness in allowing them to grieve with all of Dardi's family and friends and then departed for the airport and the return trip to Toronto.

Having been alerted, via his pager, by Ernie, that the limousine was one block from home, David and Basil were waiting when the elevator door opened and the four somewhat weary travellers stepped out. After thanking Faison and Stark for making it possible for them to attend Dardi's memorial service, Andrew and Fort headed for their suite and some quiet time alone. In turn, Stark and Faison headed for their suite with David following behind them at a discrete distance. A few minutes later Faison entered his office where David had patiently waited. David intuitively knew that Mr. Quay would want to spend a few moments alone with Mr. Redfearne but, then, would want to be updated on the latest information. Once both were seated, Faison behind the desk and David in one of two chairs placed in front, David opened his leather-bound notebook and started.

"Ms. Ouellette telephoned late last evening to inform that the coroner's report had been released on both Dardi McIntyre and the driver, one Monty Fitzpatrick, seventy-four years old, residing at 36 Sycamore Square. Mr. Fitzpatrick had been in frail health for the last seven years but was still considered well enough to drive. The report states that he struck his forehead on the steering wheel and was knocked unconscious. Unfortunately for him, his automobile was of pre-airbag vintage. The ultimate cause of death was the fire that consumed him and his car. Dardi McIntyre died from smoke inhalation. Both deaths have been ruled accidental. In your absence, I asked Ms. Ouellette to get as much background on Mr. Fitzpatrick as possible.

"Additionally, Detective Sergeant Ferguson telephoned shortly after lunch and reported they had located the green Trident tow truck abandoned on Cypress Street, which runs north-south between Eastern Avenue and Front Street, East, just west of the Bayview Roadway. The driver's door was ajar but there was no trace of Marislav Anatole."

"Thank you, David. You were quite correct instructing Ms. Ouellette to follow through on Mr. Fitzpatrick. I'll give Detective Sergeant Ferguson a call and let him know I'm back. Hopefully, by now they will have located Anatole and been able to interrogate him.

"By the way, will Veetwo be joining us for dinner this evening or is he out as usual?"

"Actually, he specifically mentioned this morning that he hadn't seen much of you lately and wanted to take advantage of the evening by dining with you and Mr. Redfearne. I believe he plans on having Miss Pomeroy here as well. At least I've planned on both of them being here for dinner, which is scheduled for seven, if that is acceptable."

"Thank you, David, that's perfect. By the way, would you please have Basil bring Mr. Redfearne and me a cup of tea and some Dad's Cookies? We'll both take it in our suite."

David smiled, knowing how much they loved Dad's Cookies, which were truly a Canadian passion, as well as afternoon tea.

As he left the office, Faison speed-dialled Detective Sergeant Gregor's cell phone and immediately heard, "It's about time you got back to the big city. I trust your trip was successful?"

"Sad, but very necessary. I understand that whilst we were gone you got lucky. Of course, I mean in the line of duty. Mind you, with your luck you probably got lucky personally as well."

"Actually....oh, I better not go there. I wouldn't want you to get jealous, being the old married man you are."

"Hey, a little less emphasis on the old bit."

Given the situation, Gregor would always wait for Faison to indicate at what level the conversation could go. Sometimes it would be strictly business and other times the more relaxed approach.

"I'm certain that David has filled you in on the discovery of the green tow truck?"

"Yes, he told me, but I do wish Anatole had been in it. I'd love to hear what he has to say about why he was in the area the afternoon and evening of the explosion."

"I wish he'd been in it also. Unfortunately, Faison, we'll never hear it from him. His body was discovered dumped behind an abandoned warehouse about a block from where we found his truck. The coroner visited the site and indicated that from the lividity he had been dead for at least twenty-four hours."

"Shit! It's never easy, is it? What was the cause of death?"

"We're not certain; but, he had severe head trauma so the coroner felt that, unless he discovers something else while conducting the post mortem, Anatole was killed by being hit on the head several times with a baseball bat that was found nearby."

"Any prints, or is it too soon to know?" Faison anxiously asked.

"Forensics conducted a preliminary dusting at the scene of its discovery and found none; but, hopefully, back in the lab they'll be able to bring some up."

"While I've got you on the phone, Gregor, I think you should know about something that we just remembered that may have a bearing on the explosion at Andrew's and Fort's home and the subsequent discovery of Marislav Anatole's body."

"Fai, the explosion was ruled accidental. Anatole's death is definitely murder. Are you going to tell me that his murder is directly tied to the explosion?"

"Gregor, I'm afraid so. It may go even deeper than that. Several weeks ago, Stark and I attended a birthday celebration for Andrew Poyntz held at JK's. Shortly after we arrived, Gino Esposito caused an unpleasant scene and I asked my bodyguards to remove him. As he was being taken to the elevator, he screamed threats at Andrew for having allowed him to be embarrassed. At the time, we just assumed that he was merely making vapid and empty threats. With the ensuing chain of events, I'm not as certain. It's rather coincidental that within weeks of that odious incident Andrew's home has been destroyed and three people, who can be linked in some way to it, are dead. Believe me when I say that I take no pleasure in reporting this nor do I accuse Mr. Esposito of being involved, either directly or indirectly. That said, it would behove us not to merely dismiss his threat, given the chain of events."

"I couldn't agree more, Fai. It's quite possible it's coincidental and can easily be explained once we speak with Mr. Esposito; but, it is too important to disregard. I'll speak with him and then get back to you as soon as I can."

"There's one other item, Gregor, and that is Marislav Anatole's apartment and its contents. Would you mind overly if I accompanied you when you choose to visit?"

"Not at all. Given the level of your assistance thus far, I don't think the department would have any objection to you being present when I conduct my search. In fact, it might be helpful if we went there prior to me meeting with Esposito. How about me picking you up in ten minutes? That's, of course, if you don't mind being seen in a police vehicle?"

"That will be perfect. Thanks, Gregor, I'll be down in front in ten minutes. Just make sure I sit in the front with you. We wouldn't want the tabloids to snag a picture of me riding in the back of a squad car."

Faison disconnected, buzzed David and quickly filled him in on his planned movements. With dinner at seven, he would have plenty of time to complete the search and make it back so he wouldn't miss dinner with Veetwo and Felicia Pomeroy.

CHAPTER 6

Larksbridge Avenue was starting to experience the subtle effects of gentrification. The farther one travelled northward from Queen Street, the more post World War I homes had been renovated. Decades of flaking paint had been scraped or water-blasted to reveal the deep-rust-shaded brick for which Toronto was famous. Made in the lower part of the Don River Valley, adjacent to the heart of downtown Toronto, southern Ontario, radiating outward from the city, benefited from the early craftsmen who utilized the local clay and waterpower to create the much-prized building material. Elaborate wood trim had been carefully restored and gardens, once again, reflected the early occupants who had emigrated, for the most part, from the United Kingdom. At the beginning of the second block, Pointer Crescent intersected. Situated on the northwest corner was a tawdry three-story walk up that had definitely seen better days. With the veranda having long ago been removed, the door appeared like a black eye on a bruised, weathered, face. Although the oft painted address numbers indicated '1 2', traces of the missing '8' confirmed that the decrepit edifice was, indeed, the home of the recently deceased Marislav Anatole.

Gregor had barely placed the car into 'Park' when the grimy Venetian blinds and tattered curtains on the windows ringing the intersection started to reveal beady eyes belonging to nosy neighbours fascinated with the latest interlopers. Faison and Gregor casually navigated the broken cement walkway, mounted the six steps and entered, what was, in reality, the building's second floor, due to the fact the first floor actually was partially below ground level. The wooden stairs creaked under their weight and the railing wobbled each time either touched it. Apartment 304 was the first on the right and took Detective Sergeant Ferguson only a few seconds to jimmy the ancient lock and enter the squalid bed-sit. It was immediately evident that Anatole's life had involved a modicum of creature comforts. To say the room measured ten by ten was to be generous. The linoleum floor, which pattern had long ago been worn away, was cracked and missing huge pieces, exposing the soiled planked floor. Directly to the right of the door was a cot, circa 1930, topped with a bare, urine-stained mattress. The only other furniture was a small dresser, with a small black and white television perched on top, and a shade-free floor lamp next to a tattered and stained winged-back chair that would probably be rejected by the garbage collectors. Draped over one wing of the chair, and reflecting just what a disgusting person Anatole had been, was a stack of tattered T-shirts splattered with the gustations of many meals consisting of fried eggs, chilli, coffee, ketchup, relish and chocolate ice cream. On the north wall there were two doors, one leading to a clothes closet and the other revealing a small three-piece bathroom that appeared to have been last cleaned in 1950. The medicine cabinet had long-since lost its' door, as had the toilet its lid. The bathtub appeared to have been where an enormous batch of tea had been brewed over three or four decades. The overall stench throughout the flat would permeate the nostrils of a porcelain statue.

"My god, I can't believe someone would live this way. I've seen kennels in better shape," gasped Gregor.

"To be honest, Gregor, I wasn't expecting much, but, apparently, even then I was overly generous in my estimate."

"Here's a pair of latex gloves, Fai. Better use them. Now, let's hurry up, before I vomit."

Expeditiously, the two combed what little there was. Under the bed, Gregor discovered a cardboard suitcase that appeared to have come from Eastern Europe. Unbuckling the two straps and flicking the latch, Gregor revealed the contents, consisting of a half-dozen black and white photos, most likely depicting Anatole's family; Canadian Landed Immigrant papers issued to Marislav Anatole, September 12, 1995 and his Russian passport which was bound by two stout elastic bands that restrained a wad of ten, faintly mauve, one-thousand dollar bills. Rarely seen anymore, because of the difficulty in cashing them, the bills featuring Elizabeth II, Queen of Canada, on the right front, with 1000 inscribed on the upper-right corner, had last been revised and issued in 1988. For the most part, the bills were rarely used except for criminal transactions and both Gregor and Faison knew that.

"Well, what do we have here? I think I'm in the wrong business, Fai. I didn't know driving a tow truck paid so well."

"They look almost un-circulated. Are the serial numbers consecutive?"

Fanning through the wad, Gregor, somewhat stunned answered, "The first six are, with the balance random numbers."

"Obviously, these were given to Anatole by someone who either maintains a stack of unreported cash or has access to large amounts of cash that isn't being withdrawn from a bank account," Faison concluded.

As Faison finished the sentence, Gregor lifted several issues of Playboy sitting on the floor beside the armchair and noticed a yellow piece of paper protruding like a bookmark. Gregor's quick scan of it resulted in him whistling and saying, "Look what we have here. It's a parking ticket dated almost four weeks ago, issued to licence plate number WTZ 7483."

Reaching into his breast pocket of his suit jacket, Gregor withdrew a small notebook, flipped through the pages, paused and then said, "Just as I thought, that is the licence plate number of the green tow truck that was owned by Anatole. Now that's confirmed, look at the address where it was issued."

Faison took the parking ticket, read the address and said, "That's less than two blocks from where Gino Esposito lives."

They both knew the next step had to be Detective Sergeant Gregor Ferguson going to pay a visit on the despicable Mr. Esposito and the sooner the better.

"I'll drop you off at your place, Fai, and then go by Esposito's. Given that it's approaching dinnertime, hopefully, I'll catch him in. Once I've spoken to him, I'll let you know what he had to say."

Dinner and the evening flew by, with just Veetwo, Felicia, Stark and Faison enjoying the rarity of a quiet family gathering. Being a warm evening, in spite of it being autumn, David had Basil serve coffee, tea and liqueurs on the south terrace, which overlooked the radiance of downtown Toronto. With gas heaters adding extra warmth, the setting was blissful.

Shortly after ten, David came onto the terrace, excused himself and told Faison that Detective Sergeant Ferguson was wishing to speak with him and asked if he would like to take the call in the Grand Salon or his office. Indicating the salon would be preferable; Faison followed David inside, sat down on one of two elegant, overstuffed, white damask-covered armchairs opposite the similarly upholstered chesterfield and picked up the wireless telephone that lay on the marble topped coffee table and greeted Gregor.

"Did you get lost or held for ransom?"

"Neither. The SOB wasn't at home. The concierge of his building indicated he had left about a half hour before I got there. Luckily for me, Esposito had tried to impress the concierge by telling him he was off to a big reception at the Granite Club for some famous person that the poor guy had never her of. By the time I got to the Club, the reception was well underway and I had the fun of interrupting Mr. Gino Esposito boring a large circle of wanna-be nobodies, by flashing my badge and asking him to come with me. I wish you'd been there. I don't know which was funnier, the stunned look on him or the rest of the people."

"What did he have to say for himself?"

"I took him to a small boardroom near the manager's office and asked him when was the last time he spoke with Marislav Anatole. He genuinely appeared totally confused at the question and told me he didn't even know anybody by that name. I then asked him whom he used when he required a tow truck and he responded that he merely called the CAA and took whomever they sent. After a few nondescript questions about his comings and goings over the last several weeks, I asked how he planned to punish Andrew Poyntz for the embarrassment he felt had been inflicted on him at Mr. Poyntz's birthday party."

"And?"

"He blew up and accused me of being in Poyntz's pocket and then ranted on about how he was a close personal friend of the Police Chief, most of the force, the Mayor, the Premier and every other mover and shaker there is and how I would pay for attacking him and adding to his perceived embarrassing situations. Cutting him off, I suggested that he better calm down and stop threatening me or I'd charge him with making threats against a police officer. At that point he sounded like an outboard motor that was running out of gas. He just sputtered to a stop and sat there looking like he had just been told his mother hated him."

"Eliminating the bluster, what is your take on the entire meeting?" Faison queried.

"Honestly, after another fifteen minutes of questions, I honestly don't think he was involved in any of the events at Andrew's and Fortunato's home or the subsequent deaths. He really is quite a simple individual who just likes to hear himself talk and appear important. To actually kill someone or even think of paying someone to do it is, I think, quite beyond him."

"You may be correct, and most likely are, but it might be prudent if you contacted the CAA to see if Trident Towing is used by them and, if so, if he has ever been assigned a tow truck from them. Also, it might possibly prove to be helpful if you had one of your officers canvas the area surrounding Anatole's apartment building, as well as all the tenants within the building, to find out if anyone ever saw him have visitors or do anything that appeared unusual. It's a long shot but at this point we really don't have too much to go on."

"I'll have both suggestions carried out first thing tomorrow and then get back to you."

"That will be very appreciated, Gregor. In the meantime, I have several things I would like to look into. Thanks for your openness. As always, I deeply appreciate it. Goodnight."

With Gregor's goodnight, the line went dead and Faison returned to the terrace.

The Friday morning ritual of massage and personal grooming always left Faison and Stark invigorated and feeling like the two luckiest people alive. Of course, their special lifestyle was never casually dismissed by them but always recognised as being blessedly unique. After breakfast in their suite, Stark and Faison headed for their offices and the daily routine of attending to the affairs of Key Holdings International. On top of the stack of daily, morning, reports, precisely placed in the centre of Faison's desk, sat one labelled, 'Règinè Ouellette, Key Security'. Flipping the file open, once he got seated, Faison rapidly digested the contents. It was a compilation of the canvas, carried out by Key Security personnel, on the neighbourhood surrounding both the explosion and Monty Fitzpatrick's home at 36 Sycamore Square.

Several neighbours of Hermione Tilsbury confirmed much of what she had already reported. They had also seen the tow truck driver close to the car when it was at the curb and then again after the car hit the house but before it exploded. None had mentioned the flash that she recounted, but that could be due to the angle at which they were viewing the chain of events. When asked if they had given similar information to the police, each individual stated, in varying ways, that they had been so upset or flustered when asked by the police they completely forgot about the additional information, it had come to them afterwards or the probing by the Key staff had jogged their memories.

Mr. Fitzpatrick's neighbours, for the most part, had only anecdotal information about him, except for his next-door neighbour, Mrs. Clova Horst-Schilling, who allowed that she and Mr. Fitzpatrick looked after one another after their spouses had died and that he was a very kind and gentle man who had suffered from deteriorating health for the last two years. She explained that even though he was only seventy-four, his heart had been in bad shape and he had had a quadruple bypass just last year. When asked about his automobile, Mrs. Horst-Schilling recalled that he had called for a tow truck to come and give him a boost several times in the last few months because he kept leaving his lights on which depleted the battery. When asked if she could recall anything about the driver or the tow truck she had remembered that it was green and the driver spoke with a Russian accent. As for the car, she had begged him to either get a new one or stop driving but he had told her that even though it was over twenty years old, he felt that it was good enough for him to use as a runabout and would probably outlast him. The last thing that she remembered was that he had called her to tell her that he was going out for a while and he said something about the car except she couldn't recall exactly what it was about.

Faison closed the file, immediately speed-dialled Gregor's cell phone and impatiently waited for him to answer.

"Gregor, I just received some information that I think links Marislav Anatole with Monty Fitzpatrick, the driver of the car that ploughed into Andrew and Fort's home. Do me a favour and get the telephone logs for both Anatole's home and cell phones and Mr. Fitzpatrick's home phone. Once you get them, please check to see if there was any contact between them on the day of the explosion. Give me a call as soon as you've got anything, okay?"

"I'll get onto it right away." Gregor smiled to himself and hung up.

Having convinced Andrew that he couldn't spend every waking minute poring over his father's files and records, Fort had suggested that the two of them go for a stroll through Yorkville and stop for lunch at Flo's Diner, their favourite casual haunt in Yorkville. Their one concession to Faison was to let Ernie drive them down and to wait in the area so they could telephone him when they were ready to return home.

By the time Fort could pry Andrew away it was almost eleven-thirty. Ernie met them at the front door with the Jaguar and in no time was heading south on Avenue Road. Once they had crossed Davenport Road, Ernie stayed in the left lane so that he could affect a left turn onto Cumberland Street. Just as he was turning, Fort decided that he would like for them to be let out right at the corner, next to The Four Seasons Hotel and walk from there. As Ernie quickly manoeuvred the car to the curb on the north side of the one-way street in order to accommodate the request a horn blared and a white Dodge Caravan swerved sharply in order to avoid hitting the right-rear corner of the Jaguar. With true aplomb, Ernie merely disregarded the noise and the accompanying middle-finger gesture, alighted from the front seat and opened the rear door.

"Thank you Ernie, I'm so sorry about the short notice," Fort offered.

"Not to worry, sir. I'll be waiting nearby. Just call me and let me know where you wish to be picked up and I'll be there in a jiffy."

"Oh, please don't wait, Ernie. I've decided that we'll slowly stroll over to Flo's and then go down to Harry Rosen's to order several new suits and do some other shopping. Later in the afternoon, I think we'll treat ourselves and go for afternoon tea at The Four Seasons. We'll just grab a taxi from there."

"Actually, sir, I don't think Mr. Quay would find that acceptable. Under the circumstances, I'll be waiting in the hotel's arrivals area for you, no matter when you are finished. Just take your time and enjoy yourselves."

Yorkville consists of eight to ten blocks of some of the chicest shopping in the world. Originally, just a village north of the settlement of Toronto, over the intervening two centuries it became a residential neighbourhood, which evolved, in the nineteen fifties and sixties, into a hippy haven of coffee shops, restaurants and rooming houses. By the seventies, chic boutiques started to open, followed by international "name" boutiques and shops. With its store-lined lanes, converted brownstone houses and sparkling new structures, the area had become a shopper and tourist's paradise.

Heading east, along the north side of Cumberland Street, Fort and Andrew spent the next forty-five minutes window shopping and making mental notes of several interesting shops that they would visit on their way back to afternoon tea. Finally reaching Bellair Street, they turned left and started north toward Yorkville Avenue. Just then, Andrew tripped on a slightly raised piece of pavement, resulting in him ungracefully plunging to the sidewalk. It happened so suddenly, Fort was unable to prevent the fall but he could assist in Andrew's recovery. As he bent, Fort noticed out of the corner of his eye an elderly woman slightly in front of them also trip and fall. Grabbing Andrew he pulled him to his feet and then rushed to the fallen lady.

Her brevet-clad feet faced him as he approached her lifeless body. Quickly crouching, he gently placed his hand on her shoulder only to realize she was not responding. Without a second's hesitation, he pulled his cell phone from his overcoat pocket and dialled 911. By the time the police operator had answered, Andrew was bent down on the other side of the inert body, gently calling to her.

The ambulance and the police arrived within seconds of one another and immediately told Andrew, Fort and the gathering crowd, to keep back. Rapidly, the two paramedics rolled her over and attempted to locate her vital signs. It only took a few seconds more to announce that all vital signs were absent and declare her dead.

The police immediately cordoned off the surrounding area with yellow plastic tape and a plain-clothes detective asked Andrew and Fort to accompany them into Sassafraz, the adjacent tony restaurant and bar where they would take statements. Identifying himself as Detective Constable Ng, he asked if each of them would produce some identification. As he was writing down all of the pertinent data, Fort realized that he should inform the Detective that they were not presently living at the address on file with their driver's licence. Once he heard that they were temporarily living at the home of Mr. Faison Quay, the Detective's demeanour quickly changed for the better. This time, smiling, he asked them to carefully recount everything they could about what they had just witnessed. Describing Andrew's fall, Fort added that they had not actually noticed the lady prior to her falling, since he and Andrew had been talking as they rounded the corner.

Just then a uniform constable approached and said, "Excuse me, Detective, but there are two men who have identified themselves as being employees of Key Security who may have information concerning the situation outside. Do you want to speak with them or should I just make notes and tell them we'll talk with them later?"

"Please have them come in right away." Turning back to Andrew and Fort he fired, "What's going on? Are they with you?"

Sputtering, Fort responded, "Absolutely not, at least not that I'm aware. I'm so confused at this point, all I know is one minute we were enjoying a quiet walk through Yorkville and the next moment my partner trips and falls, a woman in front does the same thing and then there are police everywhere."

No sooner had Fort finished his plaintiff recount than two dark-suited, burly men, both around six-feet in height appeared and presented their credentials to Detective Ng.

After thoroughly reading each of the offered credentials, Detective Ng said, "Okay, so you're Barry Wolfenden, nodding toward the younger of the two, and you're Mario Badali, acknowledging the older one, and you work for Key Security. So what?

"We've been assigned to follow, and look out for, Mr. Poyntz and Mr. di Palma by Mr. Faison Quay, the owner of Quay Security", Badali offered, while Andrew and Fort's jaws dropped in utter amazement.

"Keeping a safe distance so they would not realize our presence, we tailed them by slowly driving along Cumberland Street, not immediately noticing anything awry. It was only after the sudden chain of events that we focused on several items and connected them to dramatically change what we thought originally occurred", he continued.

"What do you mean by 'a chain of events'?" Detective Ng interjected.

"We were two cars behind the chauffeured car that brought Mr. Poyntz and Mr. di Palma to the corner of Cumberland Street and Avenue Road. Once their car had turned left from Avenue Road onto Cumberland Street, the white Dodge Caravan that was directly behind them, in the queue to turn left onto Cumberland, darted in front of on-coming traffic in such an erratic manner I thought the Caravan was going to hit the back of the Jaguar. When it didn't hit, we just dismissed the incident and concentrated on completing our left-hand turn so that we would not lose sight of the Jaguar. As we did turn, we suddenly realized they were being let out of the car near the entrance to the Four Seasons Hotel. With another car on our tail, we had no choice but to continue. Several car lengths ahead, we noticed a car pulling away from the curb so we signalled and then pulled in to the vacated parking spot. From that location we kept our surveillance of Mr. Poyntz and Mr. di Palma as they visited several shops and window-shopped the rest of the street. Incorrectly thinking they were heading for Sassafraz to have lunch, we felt that our parking place provided a perfect location from which to observe the entrance without being obtrusive. Only when they passed by the entrance to Sassafraz did we realize we might have to move. Several steps further and we realized they were turning up Bellair and we better get moving. We pulled away from the curb and, as we did, a white Caravan, which we now recognize as having probably been the same one that earlier almost hit the Jaguar, pulled out from the row of parked cars and raced through the stop sign at Bellair and Cumberland, continuing toward Bay Street in quite a hurry. Since we were more concerned about not losing our charges, we concentrated on getting up to the corner and turning onto Bellair so that we could see where they were going next. When we reached the corner, Mr. di Palma was helping Mr. Poyntz to his feet and we noticed the woman laying on the sidewalk several metres further up the block."

"This is all very interesting", Detective Ng interjected, in a terse and dismissive manner, "but what the hell has all of that got to do with the old lady falling and dying as a result?"

Looking at each other with confusion written all over their faces, the older of the two private detectives continued, "Because, I think you'll find that the lady didn't die from the fall. In fact, I think you'll find that she was probably shot."

"What?" Detective Ng, Andrew and Fortunato all blurted out simultaneously.

"What the hell are you talking about? She fell, probably on the same piece of broken sidewalk, as did Mr. Poyntz. There's been nothing to indicate any foul play", Ng countered.

"You may be right, but I don't think so. For well over a week, we have been aware that quite possibly someone was trying to harm Mr. Poyntz. That's why we've been assigned to protect him. Unfortunately, the events that have just occurred would indicate that protection is not only necessary but should, in fact, be increased and be more vigilant."

Andrew and Fort stared at Mario Badali in disbelief at what they had just heard; Detective Ng just stared out the window of the restaurant for a second, as if he was attempting to make sense out of Badali's thesis. Finally, he focused, leapt to his feet and ordered, "The four of you, stay here. I'll be right back."

Darting out the front door of Sassafraz, Ng rapidly made his way around the corner, ducked under the yellow tape and approached the body, recumbent on the pavement and being attended to by two people, a woman with salt and pepper hair, and a young man dressed in a trench coat and a knitted toque.

"Who the hell are you and who let you past the tape?" Ng irritatingly barked.

"I'm Hilda Passmore and this is Andy Quinn and we're with the coroner's office. Now, who the hell are you?"

Taken aback, Ng quickly regained his composure and stated, "Please forgive my rudeness; but, ever since I've arrived here I seem to be on the receiving end of one surprise after another."

"Well, never let it be said that I broke the chain", Passmore said with a wry smile. "I hate to tell you but she's been shot."

"Shit. Are you sure?" realizing he had just uttered a totally redundant question.

"Yes, but not in the usual way."

"What does that mean?" Ng said in an exasperated tone.

"It means that she was shot but not with a bullet", Hilda Passmore responded. "She was shot with a dart gun. Probably one like they use to tranquilize animals. You see, here deeply nestled in her hair at the back of her head, just above the nape. That little dark pin with a slight ring of packing around the shaft is a dart. I'll have to analyse the tip of it back at the lab before I can tell you what it had been dipped in, but, given the fact that it appears to have caused instantaneous death, it must have been more than an animal tranquilizer."

"Thank you, Dr. Passmore, for your very observant diagnosis. Better I know now than learn about it after the autopsy is completed. By the way, I do apologize for my manner a few minutes ago. It was unprofessional and not usually my style. It's just that since I arrived at this scene, nothing seems to be following the norm, whatever that is."

"Not to worry. I'll try to get the autopsy results back to you ASAP. If you need me before then, here's my card. Could I have yours?"

Once he provided his card to Dr. Passmore, Ng started to leave when Andy Quinn spoke up and said, "While you two were talking, I checked the victim's purse and discovered that her name is Margaret Palgrave and she is, I'm sorry, was, seventy-one years old."

"Thank you, Dr. Quinn, I was so busy I forgot to ask if anyone had found out that information."

Ng then bade them goodbye and headed back to the restaurant and the four men who were anxiously awaiting his return.

"Mr. Badali, you were, unfortunately, correct," Detective Ng offered in a sad but firm voice as he re-entered the restaurant. "Do you or Mr. Wolfenden have any other information that you may have recalled while I've been outside?"

Before the private security men could answer, Fortunato interrupted by asking, "Do you mean that the lady who fell in front of us was shot....murdered?"

"Yes, I'm afraid that's exactly what's happened", Ng answered.

"I didn't hear any gunshot. Did you, Andrew?"

"Absolutely not. Of course, I honestly can't even remember exactly how I fell, but I certainly don't think I heard any gunshot."

"You probably wouldn't have heard the shot, since she was, apparently, shot by a tranquillizer gun and they, usually, don't make a loud noise."

"It's got to have come from that white Caravan", Barry Wolfenden quickly inserted and, although I hate to say it, I'll bet it was meant for Mr. Poyntz."

"At this point in time, it certainly looks that way", Ng concluded.

"Oh, my god. Fort this just keeps getting worse and worse. What the hell is going on and what are we going to do?" Andrew desperately questioned.

"Andrew, Faison and I have kept a lot from you since the explosion because we didn't want to unnecessarily upset you. You already have enough emotional baggage to deal with since the death of your father", Fortunato explained.

Turning to Detective Ng, Fort continued, "While we were out of town about ten days ago, our house was destroyed as the result of an explosion. At first the police indicated it was just the result of an accident, but since then there has been a series of incidences that has led all of us, including Detective Sergeant Gregor Ferguson, to feel that the explosion was not an accident and that someone is attempting to kill my partner, or possibly, both of us. Today's occurrence just confirms it, at least in my mind."

"Mr. Badali, I tend to agree that Mr. Poyntz and Mr. di Palma are in imminent danger. Do you feel that you and other Key Security personnel are capable of protecting them or do you want additional police assistance?"

"Thanks, Detective Ng, for the offer but I can assure you that they will be very well protected. I'll call for their driver to come to the front door of the restaurant so that they won't have to walk too far in public view. Since the car is fully armoured, they'll be completely safe getting back to Mr. Quay's residence. Of course, once there, they are better protected than if they were residing in a fortress."

"That sounds perfect. Please make the call while I try to get in touch with Detective Sergeant Ferguson. He'll need to be brought up to snuff on the latest event and then he and I will decide where we go from here."

Less than a minute later an ashen-faced Ernie pulled in front of Sassafraz and a trembling Andrew Poyntz and Fortunato di Palma emerged from the restaurant's front door surrounded by Badali, Wolfenden and Detective Ng. Once the two were safely ensconced in the back seat of the Jaguar, Badali and Wolfenden raced to their car so they would be able to follow directly behind the Jaguar. Due to the multiple police and coroner vehicles blocking Bellair, the red-lights-flashing police squad car, assigned by Detective Ng to act as the lead escort, headed straight along Cumberland to Bay Street, followed by the Jaguar and the Key Security's Crown Victoria, with portable blue emergency lights having been placed on the roof, flashing. Once the three cars got a green light, the police escort turned on the siren, they turned left and sped north on their way to Key Mansions.

Faison and Stark were waiting when the still trembling Andrew emerged with Fortunato from the elevator. Once Basil had taken their coats, the four of them gathered and gave each other a loving group hug. With that, both Andrew and Fort broke into tears and uncontrollably sobbed. Waiting until they had regained their composure, Stark finally interrupted by saying, "Come on you two, David has several bottles of white wine chilling in the garden room and Chef Bocier has prepared a wonderful light lunch just for you."

Andrew started to decline but Faison and Stark wouldn't hear of it and lead them to the peace and quiet of the garden room. During the following hour, conversation was kept light, with Faison and Stark eventually able to inject the occasional bit of humour.

It was slightly after three o'clock when Faison felt that it was time for him to broach the chain of events, including earlier in the day, with Andrew and more directly and openly let him know the gravity of the situation. Over the next two hours, the four of them went over all of the occurrences from the initial explosion and the deaths of Dardi McIntyre and Monty Fitzpatrick to the murder of Marislav Anatole and the apparent attempt on Andrew's life that resulted in the murder of Margaret Palgrave. It was the first Andrew had heard of Marislav Anatole, his seeming involvement in the imbroglio and his subsequent murder. The totality of the cumulative actions eventually overwhelmed him resulting in convulsive sobbing. While

Faison and Stark quietly arose and walked across the garden room to the windows overlooking the city, Fort embraced Andrew and gently stroked the back of his head until he regained his composure.

With impeccable timing, Basil entered the room carrying a fresh bottle of perfectly chilled white wine and proceeded to fill the four crystal glasses sitting empty on the glass-topped table. Once he had retreated, Faison broke the silence by suggesting a toast to the quick solution to this nightmare and a wonderful future for the four of them. Andrew wiped his eyes and cheeks with a Kleenex Fort had provided, smiled weakly and said, "Please forgive me. I know I'm supposed to be much stronger than I've been, but I just had to let it all out. It seems that since Father died one shitty thing after another has happened. I can't fathom how somebody could hate me that much that they would be willing to sacrifice four people just to get at me. What the hell can be behind all this?"

"Without realizing it, I think you have put your finger on the crux of the crisis. Ever since your father died you have been upset, but it has only been in the last ten days that horrible things, directly or indirectly linked to you and Fort, have occurred. That said, I truly believe that somehow the explosion and subsequent four deaths are all linked to your father's files. If we thoroughly study them, I honestly believe we will uncover who is behind these terrible acts. The police can continue to hunt for the killer or killers of the four victims but only we can access the files and, hopefully, unravel the conundrum contained within. Given all you've been through today, let's just have dinner and a quiet evening here then get to bed early. In the morning, all four of us will meet in your suite, where all the files are, and concentrate on that task and nothing else. Agreed?"

Without hesitation, all four responded in the affirmative.

CHAPTER 7

Unbeknown to Andrew and Fortunato, Faison had called Règinè Ouellette before dinner and had discussed the day's events including the breakdown in the appropriate level of protection Badali and Wolfenden had afforded Andrew and Fort. Although they had handled the fallout professionally, Faison felt that they should have either been following them closely on foot or had called in a back-up team to be on foot while they observed from their car. Règinè agreed and assured Faison that would be the modus operandi henceforth. Once that had been dealt with, Faison queried Règinè as to whether she had received any additional information that would be of assistance, to which she had replied in the negative. She assured him she would follow up on both the coroner and police investigation of the Yorkville situation and report back as soon as she had any news whatsoever.

It was, therefore, not surprising to Faison when the telephone rang less than thirty seconds after he had seated himself behind his desk, which contained the Saturday morning reports.

Thanks to identi-call, Faison answered, "Good morning, Règinè, hopefully you have some good news for me."

"Good morning, sir. I do have some news that just reached me from my contact in the coroner's office. It appears that the dart that killed Margaret Palgrave, instead of Mr. Poyntz, yesterday in Yorkville, had been dipped in sarin."

"You do realize that means this is definitely not just someone with a grudge trying to wreak some havoc. This obviously involves professionals. When it comes to sarin, I can't imagine anyone even being able to get their hands on any. Once the police get hold of that report, they are going to go berserk and clamp the lid on that information so the press doesn't blast it across their headlines and scare the public. They're also going to finally realize the magnitude of the situation and want to re-visit every aspect of this case. I don't want you to volunteer any information but, in turn, you are to answer any questions they ask you directly, but with the least information you can get away with providing. Additionally, I want every employee to be reminded that they are not to speak with anyone, including the police. Instead they are to direct all enquiries to you. It is not my intention to hamper the police but, in turn, I don't want them impeding our progress. I honestly feel that they are not going to be able to definitively link the four deaths to the actual person or persons behind this mayhem because the key to solving this lies somewhere in an enormous pile of documents that must be deciphered by people who intimately know the people to which the documents refer. For that reason, I don't want the police to learn of the documents prematurely and seize them, thus preventing us from getting to the bottom of this."

"I completely understand, sir," Règinè smartly replied.

"Also, over the next few days, I'll probably require a number of our field personnel to carry out some investigative work. I'm not sure, at this point, how many and for how long but I'll let you know."

"In the meantime, I'll continue to watch closely the workings of the police and coroner's office and keep you informed."

With nothing further to say, the two of them, in their usual fashion, hung up the phone.

Faison was more convinced than ever that a professional assassin had been hired to kill Andrew; the fact that sarin was apparently involved was proof. One of the deadliest poisons, it was not easily obtained. Formerly used very effectively by the KGB to eliminate foes of the former Soviet Union, it had only been used in gas form since then and then only several times. Faison instinctively knew that the sarin must have somehow come from Russia and was linked in some fashion to Marislav Anatole. That conclusion was not random fantasizing but basic reality. Never had Faison believed that Anatole was acting on his own but Faison had originally felt that Anatole was working directly for the person or persons attempting to take the life of Andrew Poyntz. It would now appear that an individual who was much more sophisticated that Anatole was involved and had not only been behind Anatole's involvement but, if his senses were correct, probably responsible for Marislav Anatole's death.

Andrew and Fortunato had neatly stacked as many files as could be accommodated on every available surface in the office area of their suite. The remainder were left in the original cardboard file boxes Andrew had received, as his legacy, from his father's lawyer, Roland Witherspoon. Faison and Stark, followed by David Granpré, entered after gently knocking. David immediately opened his green-covered steno book and awaited instructions.

Now That I'm Gone

"Before we get started, I think it is necessary for me to outline what I feel has actually taken place, including why Andrew and Fort are involved and what we should be looking for while we search these files. Granted most of what I'm going to relate is conjecture on my part. Given the way this all seems to connect, I feel it is safe to say this is more fact than fiction."

Faison continued, "On the evening of October 24, around seven-thirty, Monty Fitzpatrick, of 36 Sycamore Square, called his usual tow truck driver, Marislav Anatole, and asked him to come over and give his car a boost. Approximately fifteen minutes later Anatole arrived and set his deadly plan into motion. Having driven by Andrew and Fort's home on the way to Sycamore Square, he noticed the lights were on and could observe the movement of at least one person moving about the house. After jump-starting Mr. Fitzpatrick's car, I think he suggested that Mr. Fitzpatrick follow him over to a gas station on lower Parliament Street so that he could better check the battery. As he led the way along Spruce Street, he turned down Lilac Lane, suddenly stopped the truck, alit and approached the driver's window of Mr. Fitzpatrick's car and, once the window had been lowered, quickly reached inside, grabbed the back of Mr. Fitzpatrick's head and slammed his forehead against the steering wheel, knocking him unconscious. He then took a stick that he had concealed down his left side, threaded it between Mr. Fitzpatrick's legs to the gas pedal, slipped the gear selector into drive and then pressed full force onto the gas. The car lurched forward, crossed the lawn and crashed into the gas junction at the side of the house. Quickly realizing that the impact hadn't ignited the gas, he rushed up the side of the car, lit a match, tossed it and ran like hell. With the explosion effectively blowing the house to smithereens and the resulting inferno taking care of the remainder, he raced from the scene, waited until later and then drove by, pretending to be a curious passer-by."

"Fortunately for Andrew and Fort, they weren't at home, but, unfortunately, Dardi McIntyre was in the house watering the plants and feeding Max and Sadie; she became the second victim. Once we learned about Marislav Anatole's existence, through interviews with Mrs. Hermione Tilsbury and Mrs. Clova Horst-Schilling, and told Detective Sergeant Gregor Ferguson, Marislav Anatole became a liability and had to be eliminated. Thus, on October 30, Marislav Anatole became the third victim."

"Still no closer to silencing Andrew, and possibly Fort, the person or persons behind this persisted in their quest by directing the same person whom I think killed Anatole to stalk Andrew and Fort and, as soon as they could, kill one or both. That's what happened yesterday in Yorkville, except Mrs. Margaret Palgrave became the fourth victim instead of Andrew or Fort."

The deafening silence overwhelmed the room, leaving everyone momentarily speechless. Finally, Andrew asked, "But why? What could be gained by killing me? As far as I know I don't have any enemies, especially ones that would hate me to the point of wanting me dead."

"Andrew, personally, I don't think the motivation behind these acts is one of revenge, per se," Faison clarified. "I sense the secret to these vicious deeds lies in the files your father willed to your safe-keeping and that are spread around this room. Once we carefully study them, it is my hope we'll be led to the individual or individuals willing to kill to prevent you from revealing their secret. The challenge for us is that we have to be thorough so as not to miss the minutest clue, able to piece together information that may not seem to be related and do so rapidly enough to prevent any more deaths.

"You will have the pivotal task in this quest, Andrew. You are going to have to initially sort the files into piles designated 'Personal Friend', 'Business Acquaintance', 'Patient', 'Family' and 'Not Sure'. Don't worry about the contents, just to which pile they belong.

"Fort, I'd like you to use your vast knowledge of 'Who's Who' and sub-sort the piles into 'Famous' and 'Not Famous' for each category. In this situation, 'Famous' will encompass well-known, infamous, star-status, mover and shaker, and prominent member of the community and position of authority. If you are not definitely certain, please don't hesitate to ask each one of us until you have a positive decision."

Interrupting Faison, Andrew asked, "Why can't I do both; wouldn't it be easier for me to just make both decisions?"

"Possibly, Andrew, but I'm afraid that you will start to spend too much time trying to do both tasks and slow the entire proceedings. For the time being, I would appreciate it if you just tried it the way I've suggested."

"Stark and I are going to carefully study each file that is placed in any of the 'Famous' stacks. I suspect that it is more likely that someone of position has more to lose than an ordinary citizen; ergo, they are willing to risk more in order that their status doesn't change. Given the prurient dimensions and traits you have indicated your father possessed, I am quite certain that we will discover he didn't miss a thing, especially if it came to the slightest item that might have been incriminating or against 'community standards'.

"David, I would appreciate it if you would establish a system that will handle the files and diaries that we've examined and conclusively feel are of no further interest. At this juncture, there is no way to know whether we'll have to go back to them in order to re-scrutinize their contents. In addition, would you please contact Règinè Ouellette and ask her to assemble several pairs of our best investigative detectives and have them await directions. Once we start to decipher information of a curious nature, I'll want them to follow-up to determine if there is any substance to it and if there could be any possible connection to the events surrounding the present series of deaths. After that, I would like you to be here to assist us and to take notes."

Faison hadn't finished his assignments before Andrew started to sort the stack of files piled to his right on an end table. For the first time in days, Andrew's visage reflected a calm exterior denoting his newfound confidence that the enigma was going to be unravelled and their lives would soon be back to their regular peaceful existence.

Blurred were the next four days. On Wednesday, the fifth day, around three-twenty, Andrew finished the massive initial sort. Having experienced every emotion he thought he possessed, plus some that were new to him, he finally leaned back in his chair, closed his eyes and allowed the tears to quietly flow. He needed the cathartic pleasure they brought; he felt cleansed. Minutes passed before Fort broke his concentration long enough to notice Andrew.

"Are you alright, darling?"

"You know, I think I am, strangely enough," Andrew responded. "I've been dreading doing this but now that it's done I feel that an enormous load has been lifted from my shoulders. I don't know whether it has accomplished anything but at this point I'm relieved that part is over."

"You should be," Faison added. "While the rest of us continue, since we still have quite a lot to go through on the initial effort, why don't you take the rest of the day to just relax? It would be good for you."

"I appreciate your kind suggestion, Fai, but I honestly don't feel that I could sit by while the three of you pressed forward. Instead, I want to start to de-cipher Father's diaries. Most likely, it will be extremely difficult to glean anything from them and will be the most emotional part of this entire undertaking. The sooner I start it, the sooner I'll be able to put it behind me and start to heal."

"I fully agree with both thoughts," Faison added, "and feel the diaries are going to be of prime importance in helping us solve our conundrum. The most difficult aspect of analyzing the contents will be that items may not immediately appear to be linked to anything else, but given the cryptic style your father used in notating his files, it would be a safe assumption that his diary entries are even more enigmatic."

David Granpré had been efficiently sorting the many notes and postulations offered by the other four since they initiated the unravelling of the secrets contained in the files. Suddenly it was eight days later and he found himself amazed at the scandalous, amusing, upsetting, gruesome, pathetic and pedestrian way so many people obviously lived their lives. At the end of the session the preceding day, Faison had requested David to prepared his notes and have them ready for Faison's perusal before he retired that evening. Long after Stark had fallen asleep; Faison relaxed on his chaise lounge across the room from the king-size bed and carefully reviewed David's work. Contrary to his original assumption, Faison discovered there were not as many noteworthy morsels nestled in the files as he had originally conjectured. Even then, several stood out and one theme was featured in numerous files leading Faison to conclude that it could lead to an additional item if they could only discover more details.

With breakfast over, Andrew, Fortunato, Stark and Faison headed for Andrew and Fort's suite where David met them with coffee and tea. Once settled and served, Faison began, "Incredible as it may seem, I feel that at this point, there are only four items that stand out as potentially damaging enough that someone may have been willing to do harm in order to suppress them."

"The first folder of importance, which David has titled 'Holy Smoke', features The Reverend Hartwell Bradley Wells and his, apparently, dysfunctional family. Reverend Wells, his wife Bethany, oldest son Marshall, their middle child and only daughter, Sharon, and the youngest son, Oliver, all seemed to have enjoyed unusual proclivities that would have proven most embarrassing and professionally devastating had his brother-in-law, Bethany's brother, the Bishop of Toronto, been informed. According to their file, the

Now That I'm Gone

Reverend had a very strong desire to seduce extremely rich, over-weight, elderly, women who would reward him with rather large 'donations' for services rendered. Mrs. Wells, on the other hand, seems to have had a strong desire to test the physical prowess of most of the young choirboys, servers and assorted male members of the church youth sport leagues. Marshall, their first born, apparently, constantly liberated Sunday offertories before the church treasurer could deposit them at the bank. In addition, he enjoyed checking out and, oft times, removing the contents of parishioner's coats found hanging in the vestibule during service. Sharon, the Wells' angelic-looking daughter, it seems, enjoyed every recreational drug available to man or beast and sold them to support her ever-hungry habit. Oliver, the baby of the family, apparently felt that designation meant that he should return the favour to every female he could find and help them make a baby. Generous as that seemed to him, the file indicates many of the girls' parents were not as thrilled as he was. As far as the file is concerned, the family dog is not credited with any unusual activities, so one must conclude that either Andrew's father wasn't privy to his actions or the dog was too worn out keeping track of the other members of the family to bother doing anything errant himself."

At that point everyone present, including David, broke the seriousness of the past number of days with hearty laughter. Once all had calmed, Faison continued, "The second file, titled by David as 'Mix 'N Match', which I think is worthy of study, is actually a dual one. At first it would appear that each of these would stand-alone; however, after studying them, I feel they must be looked at as one. Two prominent members of the Beach, and their wives, it appears, were inextricably joined in a manner most unusual for the time. Alderman Raymond Linstrom and his wife Jennette were, according to their files, both in excellent physical shape, stunningly attractive, personable, and suffered from insatiable sexual appetites. Happily married, with two teenaged daughters, they decided that monogamy was much too limiting and that it was unfair of them not to spread their sexual prowess around to deserving friends, neighbours and fellow politicians. Today they would just be known as swingers and would probably go unnoticed; however, in the fifties and sixties, people in their positions comported themselves quite differently than today.

"The other file features Maurice Aukland and his wife Doris, who lived two doors away from the Linstroms. Maurice, originally a teacher, moved fairly rapidly, as men did in those days, up through the ranks of the Toronto Board of Education, to first become a Principal, then Supervisor and eventually Chair. Not being satisfied with those achievements, he let it be known to the governing provincial Progressive Conservatives that he would like a political appointment. Thus within a span of less than fifteen years, Maurice found himself Deputy Minister of Education. During that time, the neighbouring Linstrom and Aukland families became very good friends. Quickly they discovered a common thread woven through their lives. Both men loved power and loved to dominate everyone with whom they came in contact. Similarly, their wives loved to be associated with power and felt tremendous stimulation when dominated. At first the two couples restricted themselves to discrete wife swapping; that rapidly evolved into larger and larger gatherings. The modus operandi for each event was always the same; potluck dinner, lots to drink and then the women would go to the master bedroom where all the coats were piled and randomly retrieve a man's coat. Whomever the coat belonged to was their sexual partner for the rest of the night....no ifs, ands or buts. The couples could either stay at the host house, be intimate with everyone else viewing, or go back to the home of either participant. The only rules were: confidentiality had to be maintained; and, all partakers were there voluntarily and had the right to say no at any time. Over the years these weekly events became laced with heavy sadomasochism and were the most sought after invitation in Toronto's political and educational circles. People desperately, but discreetly, manoeuvred for invitations or, once having attended, dared not to cross either Alderman Linstrom or Deputy Minister Aukland politically or personally; that, ultimately, led to Linstrom and Aukland wielding unbelievable power, for that time."

"I knew both the Linstrom and Aukland families and never had an inkling of anything like that," Andrew sputtered. "I'm absolutely stunned that my father never spoke of it, especially as I got older. All residents of the Beach perceived these two as pillars of the community. It just goes to show you how little any of us know about the people around us, even the ones we think we know well."

"I agree, Andrew," Faison responded, "but that's why your father's files, I think, are considered so volatile by someone who's behind the arson and murders. His thoroughness in notating obviously is scaring them and forcing them to act in order to suppress their past being made public. My hope is we will be able to unravel this conundrum before anyone else is harmed."

"The third file, tagged 'Snow Flake' by David, involves Dr. Samantha Sterling, only daughter of Geoffrey Sterling, Esquire, Senior Counsel Emeritus of Bay Street's premier law firm, Sterling, McDormant and Winetraub. Samantha graduated magna cum laude and valedictorian from the University of Toronto, interned at St. Michael's Hospital and immediately went to work for Andrew's father at his clinic."

"I vividly remember her coming to work for Father," Andrew interjected, "but Father never explained why she suddenly left and just faded from his conversations and my awareness."

"Unbeknownst to you," Faison continued, "she couldn't stand the tremendous pressure of trying to please her rapidly expanding patient base. In order to cope with the fatigue, surreptitiously, she started to take amphetamines. Over the months, the quantity and frequency increased to the point she found she required a stronger and stronger boost, leading to heroin. At the same time she added sleeping pills to help her actually sleep during the few off-hours she allowed herself. It didn't take long for her to begin writing phoney prescriptions to accommodate her needs. One day the Royal Canadian Mounted Police appeared at your father's office and informed him that she was about to be arrested for abuse of her right to prescribe drugs and for presumed illegal possession of drugs. In order to spare her any public embarrassment, your father arranged for them to let her turn herself in while accompanied by her lawyer. Not wanting her father or his firm to know what had occurred, she requested that your father ask Rolly Witherspoon to act on her behalf and negotiate a plea bargain that would allow her to plead guilty and pay a very large fine, in exchange for letting her continue to keep her doctor's license but without the right to write prescriptions. Your father arranged employment for her with a major drug research company and everything went well for the next eight years. Shortly before her probation ended, she was apprehended selling a large quantity of an illegal synthetic drug. Even the power of Sterling, McDormant and Winetraub couldn't keep her from a prison term. The only concession was the Crown Prosecutor agreed to keep any names or details from the press. Samantha was sentenced to prison for a minimum of three years, maximum of ten. With good behaviour, she was out in three years. Barred from ever practising as a licensed doctor, she turned to drug counselling at a downtown street clinic and thrived helping others. The bliss lasted for nearly six years. Once the director of the clinic discovered her relapse, she was forced to fire her. With her still trying to hide her return to her addiction from her family, she became the drug dealer to the rich and famous; cocaine, heroin, E, K, GHB, whatever they wanted, she supplied it. That's where you father's file on Samantha Sterling ends."

Without waiting for comments, Faison opened the last file and began, "The fourth file, named 'Merchant of Venom?', involves an extremely delicate situation that surrounds a mercurial gentleman who may or may not be either a Canadian hero, and for that matter a 'free-world' hero, or a despicable traitor who deserves the antipathy of all."

Andrew looked puzzled and leaned forward in his chair, anxious to gain knowledge concerning the pariah about whom his father had written.

"Cyril Leaverage, the elderly, yet still active, international business mogul, apparently became a spy for the Canadian government in the late thirties, shortly before he made his first trip to the Soviet Union. Toronto born in nineteen-eleven, Cyril was the only child of the modestly successful importer Lester Leaverage and his wife Natasha, daughter of White Russian immigrants. Particularly hard-hit by the depression, Lester felt there might be some excellent opportunities for his business in the struggling Union of Soviet Socialist Republics; however, having developed a serious heart ailment, he decided to dispatch his twenty-six-year-old son. Having been raised with a full understanding of both the English and Russian languages, being mature beyond his age, and possessing an ingratiating personality, Cyril was a natural for the task that lay before him. Shortly after he applied for a passport, the Canadian government contacted him and asked the purpose of his trip. Once they learned that he planned to establish a rapport with the Soviet government and their exporters, the officials proposed that he become a spy for Canada and Britain. Being egotistical, he immediately pictured himself as a perfect agent, dashing and debonair. It took very little time for Cyril to ingratiate himself with many of the politburo's movers and shakers. In desperate need of grain to feed the starving masses, but lacking the hard currency necessary, Cyril shrewdly devised a plan by which the Soviets would pay with gemstones, gold and vodka, at a greatly depreciated exchange rate. Within two years, the U.S.S.R was plunged into a war with Germany and was allied with Britain, Canada and the rest of the

Empire. Although the United States of America, because they had not yet taken sides, was willing to sell armaments and much needed supplies to the Soviets, as they were the German axis, they preferred to trade with those who had been there for them prior to the outbreak of the war and that meant Cyril Leaverage. Needless to say, Cyril prospered, both financially and as a spy. During his numerous trips, the Soviets trusted him implicitly, to the point they constantly let their guard down and, in ataxic stupors, confided way more than they ever realized. Canada and Britain revelled in the information being relayed to them by this mercantile mogul. In fact, after a while both countries declined to pay him, since he was earning so much from his war-trading efforts.

"Cyril's life was the substance of stories and movies. By nineteen forty-five, both his father and mother had died and he, as sole owner of Can-Sov Mercantile Ltd., was the primary wholesaler of Soviet oil, gold, gemstones and, occasionally, fine works of art, which had surreptitiously disappeared from the Hermitage in Leningrad. His immense wealth became the talk of North America and Europe and he revelled in the knowledge that he could, seemingly, do no wrong; that all came to a screeching halt in September of that year. On the fifth of that month, Igor Gouzenko, a low-profile cipher clerk, who worked in the U.S.S.R.'s embassy in Ottawa, walked into the office of the Ottawa Journal and told them he had very damaging information about Soviet spying in Canada, and throughout the world, and he and his family would like to defect. Realizing they could not be directly involved with such an important situation, the newspaper's editor called the Minister of Justice, Louis St. Laurent, who insisted on verifying the substance of the information before he would agree to meet with Gouzenko. On September six, while waiting to hear back from the Minister of Justice, Gouzenko and his family were almost captured by the Soviets. The kidnapping attempt was all that it took for the government to act; on September seventh, political asylum was granted the entire Gouzenko family and, for the next several months, the Canadian government diligently crosschecked every bit of information Gouzenko provided. To the Canadian government, the most important information was the list of names of all the Soviet agents in Canada; under the letter 'L' was that of the very recognizable 'Leaverage, Cyril'. At first, the Canadian government just thought that somehow Gouzenko had heard his name so frequently in the cipher office because of the massive amount of trade documents that flowed between the Canadian office of Can-Sov Mercantile Ltd. and the Kremlin. As the months dragged on, many in the government started to think differently. Between September, nineteen forty-five and spring of nineteen fifty, Cyril Leaverage's passport was confiscated eight times. Each time he gained it back when he imparted more secrets garnered from the previous trip to the U.S.S.R. At one point, the government accepted that he must be a spy for both Canada and the Soviets and decided to use that to their advantage and force him to be a triple spy. Cyril, ever cognizant of the trading opportunities, played right along with the Canadian government and acted as if they had been correct. During the fifties and early sixties, the status quo remained; however, in nineteen sixty-seven, Canada's Centennial Year, the fifty-six year-old Cyril announced that he was retiring from active participation in the operations of Can-Sov Mercantile Ltd. and was handing over the reins to his son, Lewton Leaverage. Immediately, the Canadian government approached Lewton and pleaded with him to become a spy for them; without a second of thought, Lewton declined. From that moment, the RCMP, on behalf of a cynical Canadian government, who was convinced that he was merely assuming the role of counterspy his father had earlier established, carefully watched Lewton and, for that matter, Cyril. Even today, although the Can-Russ Mercantile Inc., as it is known today, is led by Lorne Leaverage, Lewton's son, the Canadian government continues to maintain a somewhat jaundiced view of its owners, and to a lesser extent, its employees.

"Lest you think that all of this leads us to a closed file, I must elucidate the reason why I feel it should be one of those that are pursued. Apparently, during doctor-patient meetings with the Leaverages, over the many years, each of them, on more than one occasion, mentioned 'the mixed feelings they suffered over what they were doing', that they 'regretted ever starting something they seemingly couldn't stop', 'no amount of money could salve their conscious', and other statements along those lines. Therefore, it is quite possible the Leaverages were, and maybe still are, involved in espionage. If that was, or is, the case, it would certainly be something they would not want to come out in the open."

At least fifteen or twenty seconds elapsed before anyone in the room moved; finally Andrew sputtered, "My poor Father. Imagine having to live with all of this and, because of professional ethics, be unable to ever discuss the details."

"How do we proceed? All of these files definitely contain volatile information, but I'm at a loss as to what we can do to determine if any are connected to the murders and our explosion," Fortunato added.

"Actually," Faison assured, "I honestly don't think either Andrew or you can do anything more at this time to assist the investigation. We are at the point where I feel we must call in Key Security's best detectives and let them clarify the information contained in each file, ferret out the status of each of the individuals, and determine if any of them could have been motivated to be behind these atrocities. Stark and I will work with them, take on the continuing study of the diaries, using the detailed notes Andrew has made over the last week or so, and keep you completely up-to-date."

"But, Faison, that's not fair for us to just sit by while you and your people do all the work. Please, isn't there anything we can do to assist the investigation and help speed it up?"

"Andrew, that's very much appreciated, but, no thank you. There is absolutely nothing more for you to do at this point; you've already, both of you, contributed immeasurably. Now just relax a bit and let the professionals do what they do best."

Continuing, Faison completely caught them off-guard when he said, "Anyway, you two are going to be very busy over the next few weeks. I've arranged for Allison Sung, Key Construction's Chief Architect to meet here with you tomorrow to show you some preliminary designs she has put together for your new home. Obviously, you are in complete control and can accept or reject anything she proposes. Once you have settled on the final design, I'll have it approved by City Hall and then Key Construction will build it before you know what happened."

Once again their dear friends had stunned them with their generosity, leaving Andrew and Fort without anything to say except, "Thank you from the bottom of our hearts".

"Don't even think about it," Stark added, "Fai and I are just very anxious to help the two of you get your lives back to some semblance of order. Hopefully, working on the rebuilding of your home will alleviate some of your present angst. As for us, we're just being selfish. The sooner the home is finished, the sooner you two will get the hell out of here. Then Faison and I can once again run around naked and hold orgies in the reception hall."

"You wish," Fortunato, laughingly concluded.

CHAPTER 8

Patience was not one of Faison's strong suits; in fact, he had often stated that 'if patience was a virtue, he'd be a whore'. For that reason, Faison had requested David Granpré, Majordomo extraordinaire, to scour the personal diaries of Andrew's father, Dr. J. Merreck Poyntz, in the hopes of deciphering his cryptic notes. David weighed whether to work on the earlier years of the over forty years of confessions, observations and minutia, or to work backwards from the more current entries, since they quite possibly would reveal more germane situations. Logic ultimately prevailed over random order; David started from the beginning.

Faison and Stark's meeting with Règinè Ouellette was, all three hoped, the beginning of the end of the quandary which even the police seemed not able to solve. Rather than waste time, Faison merely offered Règinè personal observations as to each of the files' contents and how she might wish to pursue the investigation. It was redundant to point out the delicate nature of their contents and the personages cited; Règinè had dealt with the tony world of celebrities from the beginning of her career with the RCMP, having been assigned to the VIP Protect Unit at a very early point. All three knew that her knowledge and life-long-developed contacts would hold her, and the investigation, in good stead. Of course, it did not hurt that Faison, and Stark to a slightly lesser degree, knew most of the notated people, either directly or indirectly. Their insight would, no doubt, also assist the investigation. Over the next three hours, strategy was frankly discussed, appropriate personnel debated and time frames decided. Expenses were not discussed; results were all that Faison and Stark wanted.

Moriyama Ito had been chomping at the bit, hoping that he would be allowed to work on bringing to justice the instigator behind the explosion at the Cabbagetown home and the subsequent murders that were seemingly related. When he got the call to report to Règinè Ouellette's office at Key Security's headquarters, he hoped it was to be assigned to assist in some manner; he could hardly believe his ears when Ms. Ouellette informed him Mr. Quay and she had selected him to be lead investigator for the 'Holy Smoke' file. Margery Worton, former Captain in the Canadian Forces, and new to Key Security, would be his partner; they would be given two weeks maximum and should exercise total discretion and tact, whilst not revealing any details of the investigation to anyone, from The Reverend Wells and family, to any Key Security employees, in order that the entire investigation remain untainted and not affected by anyone, including those investigating other aspects of the case. Ito was to report daily to Ouellette and more frequently if warranted.

Worton was awaiting Ito, outside Règinè Ouellette office, pacing back and forth, file folder tucked under her left armpit, having been through the instructional process just prior to Ito. Once dismissed, she had immediately headed for the canteen and a cup of tea, missing his arrival; that had been her plan. She would rather let him learn of her being assigned to him by Ouellette and have an opportunity to review the contents of the briefing file before they met. By being there when he emerged, Margery hoped to catch him somewhat off-guard. After all, he would not have been able to read the details; she liked to have an edge, especially when she had to assume the subordinate position on the team.

"Hello," Worton offered as Ito emerged, completely flummoxing him, "I'm Margery Worton, your new partner."

Quickly regaining his composure, he returned her smile and said, "Hi, Margery, I'm Moriyama Ito. Of course, you already knew that since you just introduced yourself to me and identified yourself as Margery Worton. It's great to meet you and to be able to work with you; I've heard good things about you since you've joined the company."

That went well, Margery thought. His babbling indicated she'd caught him off guard and a good start.

"Let's find an empty meeting room and review the case and then plan our strategy," Moriyama suggested.

"There's one at the end of the corridor, on the left; I scoped it out on the way back from the cafeteria, anticipating our next step."

Settling into armed, swivel, leather chairs opposite each other at the four-foot diameter leather-topped table, they each spread their copy of the file open. Moriyama opened his mouth to speak, but Margery bested him and blurted, "What do your friends call you? Mori? Yama? Mo? It's just such a mouthful to constantly say Moriyama. What's your preference?"

Pausing to take a breath, Moriyama grasped the opportunity to respond, "I never liked others taking the liberty to abbreviate my name; in fact, I always try very hard to listen to people introducing themselves. The name they use is what I then use. To me, that's just common courtesy. Anyway, what's wrong with Moriyama?"

"Whoa! Absolutely nothing. In fact I think it's a beautiful name. It has a very regal sound to it. I just thought that it would be nice if we just dropped the formality, since we're now partners. Would you mind awfully if I called you Mori?"

Breaking into a big smile and a laugh, he responded, "If you do, don't you think people will think I'm Jewish?"

"Probably, but you'll cope," Margery parried.

"Alright, it's Mori for me and Marg for you. Okay?"

Now Margery was caught off-guard; she hated Marg, but to tell him that would put her at his mercy. "Marg and Mori, it is," she rallied.

"Actually, since I'm the lead, it'll be Mori and Marg."

The laughter seemed to put them both at ease, which, in turn, allowed them to roll the ensuing two hours into a productive session; the planned approach was sensible and would, hopefully, bear rapid results.

Règinè Ouellette instinctively knew that Mason Barbetta and Jorge Estevan were the epitome of the ideally matched detectives; both possessing Mensa quality minds, bodies tuned to perfection, fluency in Italian and Spanish, respectively, they had successfully worked numerous cases. There was only one problem; the last time they worked together, they both asked to be reassigned to new partners, in the middle of the case. Their requests were denied but, once the case was concluded, they had never been assigned to the same case.

Responding to the knock on her office door, Règinè called out to enter. Immediately, the door swung open and Barbetta and Estevan skulked into the room and plunked themselves down on the two chairs opposite her desk. That was all it took.

"Let's cut the bullshit. Your attitudes for the last several months have been insufferable, and I, for one, am not going to put up with it any longer. I don't give a flying fuck what's behind it; it's not professional. Once you report for work, your private lives stay at home. You owe that to all of your coworkers, each other, and the clients who expect you to be the best in the industry. Key Security is the best and expects that nothing less than the best is acceptable. Rumour has it that you two had been lovers and now you're not."

Barbetta and Estevan snapped out of their pouts, appearing as if Règinè had clubbed them with a two-by-four. Before they could say anything, she continued, "As you know, normally, your personal life would never, ever, be discussed. Everyone at Key Security always treats it as exactly that, personal; but, when it interferes to such a degree, rather than let you harm your careers, I feel you must be made to focus on your harmful behaviour. Whatever caused this change in attitude, between the two of you, must stay separate from your work. Mr. Quay has personally selected you to work a case that is very important to him. The honour is immense, succeed and your careers will benefit, fail and you might as well resign. Here is the complete file, labelled 'Mix 'N Match', including background notes from Mr. Quay. You are expected to complete this case within a fortnight and, as usual, I expect daily reports and immediate communication should you encounter any obstacles. That's all, for now. You're dismissed."

Robotically, the two seasoned detectives stood and made their way from Règinè Ouellette's office, closing the door as if they were in a trance. They found themselves halfway to the elevator bank before Mason grabbed Jorge's elbow and stuttered, "Did what I think just happen, happen, or am I having a really bad dream?"

"No, you're not dreaming, Mason. We just got the shit kicked out of us by the boss. The damn thing is, she was right. We have been acting like assholes ever since we broke-up."

"I just couldn't bear to be around you anymore. It just brought back too many wonderful memories and made it much too painful."

"Let's get the hell out of here, get some lunch and talk this thing out; because, quite frankly, I don't want to be without you or the job and if we don't get our shit together that's exactly what's going to happen."

For the first time in months, Jorge Estevan and Mason Barbetta were smiling. The word would probably be relayed to Règinè before the two of them drove out of the parking lot.

Unless she had a luncheon appointment, Règinè usually had the cafeteria kitchen prepare a salad for her and deliver it to her office, where she would dine alone while reviewing reports. She loved her work and found it to be the best therapy since her husband had died and her only child, Cecile, as a single mother, had gone to McGill University in Montreal, much against her urging, to attend the

University of Toronto. Cecile was as stubborn as her mother and Règinè loved that and many other qualities in her.

With some salad still remaining, the telephone rang, snapping Règinè back to the here and now. More and more, she found herself drifting off the work at hand and harkening back to the days when her husband was alive, work with the RCMP sublime, and her world was functioning like some feature article in Chatelaine, Canada's leading woman's magazine. That was then and the reality of now was that if Faison Quay had not offered her the position she now held, she knew she probably would have gone mad. Instead, except for the momentary lapses, she was handling her life better than she had ever expected. Grasping the receiver from the telephone on the small conference table at which she sat, she listened for a second and then instructed her secretary to please show her next appointment into her office. Wondering how could it already be one-fifteen, she grabbed the files from the table and relocated to her desk across the room.

The door opened, Règinè looked up, smiled and instructed Pauline Goodson and Yvonne Asselstine to be seated. She knew this choice was a risk, given that both of them had only been with Key Security for less than three months. Fresh out of university, Pauline with a master's degree in economics and Yvonne one in psychology, superficially neither would appear as a potential investigative detective, yet Règinè Ouellette instinctively felt it the instant she met them. It was that innate ability that led her to select the best people; she just hoped that was the instance with these two, since she had personally recommended them to Faison Quay and she didn't want to let him down, especially when it came to this case.

"I have selected you to work together on a very important case, labelled 'Snow Flake'. As with all of our work, discretion is of paramount importance, as is speed, not haste. You will have a maximum of a fortnight, with no minimum. Daily reports are expected and I will be available to you at all times and expect you to make use of that should the slightest blip occur in the investigation. Any questions?"

"No, ma'am. Thank you for your trust in us; we'll not let you down," Yvonne Asselstine offered before Pauline Goodson had a chance.

"Glad to hear. That's all for now. On your way out would you please ask the next two to come in?" Ouellette requested.

Busy making notes, Règinè was aware the door opened and two men had entered and were moving toward the two chairs opposite her desk, but she didn't stop until completed. When she finally placed her pen back into the holder and looked at their faces, Règinè Ouellette almost passed out. Stammering to the point of nearly turning her teeth into castanets, she clambered to her feet, thrust out her right hand to the taller of the two and said, "Mr. Quay, Faison, what a surprise. Stark, Mr. Redfearne, how nice to see you both," as she shook Stark's outstretched hand. "To what do I owe the honour?"

With a slight chuckle, Faison responded, "Calm down, Règinè, Stark and I have decided that we'd better investigate the 'Merchant of Venom' ourselves. After you and I spoke, I realized that some very cautious steps will be needed with, quite probably, numerous political contacts called on. For those reasons, we're the natural choices. Lest you worry about us, as always, we'll have our Key Security body-guards nearby at all times."

Slightly dazed by their announcement, Règinè tried as best she could not to outwardly show her surprise, and to a somewhat lesser degree, her concern. For a split-second she queried their motive; were they afraid she and her staff were not competent to handle such a file or were they using this as an opportunity to observe her leadership style? Fortunately, reason won out over her initial fears and she smiled and said, "That will be superb. Quite frankly, I was somewhat concerned that our people would encounter some insurmountable hurdles in trying to access information held by the government. Now that won't be a problem."

"Don't be so certain of that, Règinè. When it comes to government secrets, especially if they involve bureaucrats, even my connections might not be enough to shake loose the information we need. That said, I assure you that I won't hesitate to go all the way to the PMO, if push comes to shove. It wouldn't be the first time I required a gentle word from the Prime Minister to scare the shit out of the recalcitrant members of the civil service."

Stark continued, "Of course, we'll stay in constant communications and keep you fully informed."

"As I will with both of you," Règinè assured.

CHAPTER 9

Beaufort Road was one of two s-shaped streets weaving their way up through the up-scale Glen Manor area of The Beach, in east Toronto. Bounded by Woodbine Avenue on the west, Victoria Park Avenue on the east, Kingston Road on the north and Lake Ontario on the south, The Beach originally was a summer cottage area for Torontonians, and consisted of seven beaches with amusement parks strung along the lakeside. The Glen Manor area, or 'The Glen' as locals called it, was the toniest part of The Beach and was only two blocks wide by four blocks long. Cleaving up through the middle was a series of groomed parks and a natural ravine that featured a stream, trails and small animals such as raccoons and skunks. Stuccoed and timbered Tudor houses and cut-stoned domiciles lined the east and west sides of Glen Manor Drive, with a delightful swath of valley-like parkland dividing the sides and a wooden footbridge crossing it mid-way. Genuine 'Beachers' knew to call the overall area 'The Beach', whereas the parvenus insisted on jarring those in the know with 'The Beaches'; and, of course, 'The Glen' was always 'The Glen'.

Moriyama Ito and Margery Worton had done their homework prior to heading for Beaufort Road and the home of the Hartwell Bradley Wells family. Having both wondered how a retired minister could afford to live in 'The Glen', they had checked out the Land Registry Office, located in The Atrium, at twenty Dundas Street, West, a block from City Hall, to determine who actually owned the house, when was it purchased, how much was paid and what were the yearly property taxes. The records showed that the good Reverend's church built the house way back in the late thirties for the then parish cleric. During his tenure as vicar, Reverend Wells and family were provided the house as part of the perquisites of the job. Where the records got quite interesting was nineteen eighty-six when the title of the home was transferred to Reverend and Mrs. Hartwell Bradley Wells for the ridiculously low figure of one hundred and twenty-five thousand dollars. Considering three houses within a two hundred metre radius sold for a minimum of three hundred and fifty thousand, within four months of The Reverend's purchase, at minimum it would appear a sweetheart deal had been reached between him and the church. One of the questions that needed to be answered was why, especially since in today's market the house would be worth well over seven hundred thousand dollars.

Mori and Marg parked the Crown Victoria near the bottom of the street and started to walk up the inclined sidewalk. It had been a late autumn, thus explaining the piles of brown and red leaves mouldering in the gutters, awaiting removal by the city's Works Department. The smells emanating from the fallen foliage reminded Mori of his childhood and the wonderful times he and his playmates had spent mounding the leaves and jumping into them, only to rush to the curb and the protection of the sidewalk each time an automobile was heard approaching. About one hundred metres along the east side of the street, just where Beaufort opens to intersect with Glen Manor Drive, West, they crossed to the other side and continued to wend their way up the hill and their goal, the Wells' house. Barely had they made it onto the sidewalk when they heard an elderly man's voice huskily cry out, "Basodee, get your sorry ass back in this yard, now."

Just to their left, lunging down the narrow mutual driveway, so typical of most urban Toronto neighbourhoods, was an Irish wolfhound the size of a small pony. Mori and Marg froze, realizing the rapidly approaching beast might misconstrue any movement. Quickly picking up on the shrieks from the apparent owner, Marg calmly cooed, "Hello Basodee, what a good boy. Aren't you the pretty fellow?"

Mori stood in stunned amazement as the dog rushed right up to Marg and started to rub his head against her hip. All it took was for her to tousle the top of his head for him to drop to the payment, roll onto his back and lift his leg, hoping for a tummy rub.

"He always did have a soft spot for a pretty lady and I see today is no different," the winded owner gasped. "I hope he didn't scare either of you too much."

"Not at all. To the contrary, we think he's beautiful, don't we, Mori?"

"Oh, yeah, a real beaut," said Mori, adding under his breath, "if you like shitting your pants from fright."

"We were just enjoying a walk through your gorgeous neighbourhood, have you lived here very long," queried Marg.

"Sixty four years. Bought this place, with the help of my dear mother and father, and moved in when it was brand spanking new, with my beloved bride. Barely had a year in it before that bastard Hitler started acting up and I enlisted so that I could proudly serve king and country. If my parents hadn't taken care of my wife and the new home we would have never been able to keep it, but we did and been here ever since. Absolutely love the neighbourhood. All seasons are beautiful and it's so quiet here you can hear the snow and ice crack and crunch in the winter and the crickets chirp at night during the summer. What more could you want? My wife and I say we're going to have to be carried out of here in our coffins, because we're not leaving for any other reason. Mind you, if this damn dog gets loose too many more time and makes me have to chase him, I'll be leaving sooner than I want to."

By the end of his spiel, Mori had regained his composure and realized that the happenstance of meeting Basodee and his owner just might be the best thing that could have occurred.

"I guess you've seen just about everything over the years; the good, the bad and the ugly," Mori coyly pried.

"Now I want you to know that the wife and I pretty much keep to ourselves, but that doesn't mean we don't notice what's going on. Over the years we had some wonderful neighbours come and go; on the other hand, there've been some real miserable wastes of flesh and, unfortunately, some of them never seem to move away."

Playing along with Mori's initiative, Marg continued, "Yeah, I know what you mean. My mother always said that the pious ones are the ones you've got to watch the closest. She certainly was proven right when you see what's going on with all the accusations being levelled at some of the priests and brothers in the Catholic Church and the denials coming from a few of the Bishops. It's enough to make you give up religion."

"By god, one would think that you and your folks had lived in this neighbourhood from what you just said. We got this holier than thou bastard who's lived up the street for longer than I care to remember. Until he retired a few years ago he was an Anglican priest who pranced around acting like he could walk on water. The only thing was the rumours were always flying about the son-of-a-bitch and how he'd do most anything for money. I even heard that he was screwing a lot of the widows in his parish just so he could squeeze money out of them. And the irony about that was that while he was cheating on his wife, she was seducing all the young boys in the area that she could get her legs around, if you'll pardon the expression. It turned out that, rumour has it, the youngest of their kids was actually fathered by a fifteen-year old boy who lived across the road, over there, and would do odd jobs for them because he went to their church." Sniggering, he added, "Odd jobs alright. I think any decent soul would certainly call getting the pastor's wife pregnant an odd job."

"Gee, I wonder how they were able to keep that quiet and not lose their church posting?" Marg fished.

"I heard from a friend of mine who was the Church Warden about fifteen or so years ago, when the goings on was really bad, that he and the Rector's Warden tried to do just that; but, the Bishop just sloughed it off and said he'd have a word with Wells and his wife. Of course that was a lot of bullshit 'cause I'd heard a long time before that that Mrs. Wells was related to the Bishop and you know damn well that he was going to protect a member of his family. Of course, around the same time, there was the disgusting way he got his house; real Christian act on his part if you ask me."

"Why, what happened about them buying their house? I'm confused. I thought you said he'd been here for years," Marg queried, continuing to play dumb.

"You didn't hear this from me, mind you, but my Warden friend told me that the parish priest had come to him and the Rector's Warden and announced that he wanted to buy their rectory and had the nerve to tell them how much he would pay. Seems the offered price was way below market value. When they tried to reject his offer, the conniving bastard told them right to their faces that they didn't have any choice. He wanted the house in his name so that it was fully paid for before he retired and he didn't want to pay any more for it than what he offered."

"I'm amazed they did it; sell it to him, that is; especially after him being so bold as to basically demand it and then going further and setting the price. I wish I could tell my boss that he had to sell me his house and at what price."

"Well, miss, that probably wouldn't work the same way, unless you're a priest incognito. You see, he just came right out and told them that he had so much poop on all the big shots in the parish, including them, that if he didn't get what he wanted he'd start to spill the beans."

Chuckling, Mori jested, "I guess it's fitting that he wore black; it symbolized the blackmailing he was practicing."

"You got that right. Once he made those threats, my friend got real scared and knuckled under. From then on, Wells did whatever he wanted and nobody dared to stop him. When some of them stopped going to church, he told them for their own good they better start attending again. He was always guaranteed a full church until he chose to retire. Now if you go by the church you'll find the place nearly empty most Sundays."

"You mentioned the kids," Mori questioned, hoping to keep the information flowing. "Do they still live at home?"

Basodee's owner flung his head back and let out a roar of laughter, "Those kids were real lovelies; I wouldn't trust any of them with used toilet paper. In fact, the oldest got into some big trouble for stealing from his work. It seems the bishop got him a job in the office of some big time cathedral supporter and he thanked the guy by embezzling nearly a million bucks over a six-month period. The only way I know anything about that is because the cops came around here to check all of us neighbours to see if we knew anything about the kid's personal life. I got into a conversation with the cops and that's when they told me what he had done. Of course, nothing ever appeared in the newspapers. All hush-hush, you know."

"What happened to him?" Marg asked.

"Don't know. He just disappeared and I've never seen him around since."

"And the other children?" Mori urged.

"Actually, that's a good question. The middle kid was a real pretty girl until she got into her early teens. Then she started to dress in all dark colours, got very thin and started to look like the cat dragged her in. The wife told me that she'd heard from some of the folks who live next to them that they thought she was into drugs. Wouldn't surprise me the way that she looked. Now that we're talking about her, I realized that I haven't seen her since Hector was a pup."

Stupidly, Mori asked, "Who's Hector; your other dog?"

Furrowing his brow, the old man responded, "Good god, you must be awfully young or you've lived a very isolated life. There is no Hector; it's just an expression."

Attempting to save face, Mori quickly added, "I knew that, I was just pulling your leg."

Kidding right back and not missing a beat, the man laughed and winked and said, "Actually, lad, thanks for the offer but I leave that type of thing to the wife, if you know what I mean."

Mori blushed and Marg roared. Quickly gaining his composure and trying to get back on track, Mori persisted by asking about any other children, knowing full well there was only one boy left not discussed.

"If you mean the love-child from hell, all I know is the neighbour told my wife that Mrs. Wells had mentioned something one day about the boy was sick and she was real worried. He's not been around here for quite a while."

Just then, the front door swung open and a voice from the shadows of the front hall yelled, "For god sake, Jack, get the hell in here, you're going to catch your death, you've been gabbing so long. And bring Basodee with you."

With that the door slammed and he sucked some air through the right corner of his mouth and said, "Sorry about that. Before I go, can I ask you if you are Jehovah Witnesses?"

Caught off guard, Marg and Mori stood there for a few seconds and then Marg asked, "What would make you think that?"

"Oh, I don't know; maybe the fact that the two of you are strangers walking through my neighbourhood and chatting me up in such a friendly way. I just thought maybe you were trying to catch me off guard and convert me. Of course if you are, go up to the door and bother the wife. She just hates it when Jehovah Witnesses come to her door. I'd enjoy her reaction and you could count her as one more attempt for the day."

"Actually, sir," Mori explained, "We're not Jehovah Witnesses, were just out exploring the neighbourhood to see if we like it enough to consider buying a house."

"Oh, I hope you weren't offended."

As Marg started to assure him that they were not, his front door squeaked ajar and another bellow ordered him in.

"Absolutely not. We had better let you go before you upset your wife any further. We've certainly enjoyed our visit and the conversation."

"Me too. Hope you buy close by so we can visit lots then. Come on Basodee, back to the house."

Jack grabbed the Irish wolfhound by the collar, waved with the other hand and headed back up the driveway. Once he closed the front door, Mori turned to Marg and suggested, "We've gathered enough information for the moment and seriously doubt that we could add much more by attempting to cross-examine any more neighbours, especially today. If Jack were to see us poking around for much longer he might come after us to check out how we're doing or we might run the risk that someone has seen us talking with Jack and would start to get suspicious if we then tried to pry further."

"I agree, Mori. With what we've already got from him, I suggest we not discuss this any further until we get back to the car and write down our individual recollections of our entire conversation with Jack. Then we can set about following up on all the information."

Turning to face down the street, Mori said, "I concur and by the way, don't look now but I just noticed out of the corner of my eye that Jack and his wife are peeking out from between their Venetian blinds in the front window."

The two detectives smiled at one another, remaining silent until they had returned to the Crown Vic and each had notated their observations. Remarkably, when compared, both sets of notes were almost identical. Several items stood out from the rest. They had to find out where each of the Wells' children were presently, what they were involved in, and, hopefully, somehow get to speak with Reverend and Mrs. Wells, so that they could determine if they were the ones behind the events that initiated the investigation.

Without hesitating, Mori dialled Règinè Ouellette and, upon hearing her voice and letting her know to whom she was speaking, asked her if she could arrange to have the police search their records to see if any of the three Wells children had any records since they had become adults. Agreeing to get it carried out and have a report back to them within twenty-four hours, Règinè hung up. Their next act was to drive several blocks north in order to visit Malvern Collegiate Institute. According to Mori's logic, the three children probably attended Malvern, since their home was in that school's catchment. Having recently read in the Toronto Star that Malvern was going to be hosting a celebration in the spring of two thousand and three for its one-hundredth anniversary, Mori used that to explain to the principal's secretary that they were researching an article for the upcoming fete. It only took a few minutes, once they were given access to the yearbook archives, that they located all three children. Photocopying the homeroom class pictures of each child was a quick and easy way to get a list of all those who had attended the school with the Wells. The hard part, he feared would be to track any of them down.

What neither Mori nor Marg had focused on was the stoic manner in which Beachers lived. The district was fraught with families that had been there for three generations; people simply didn't move out of the Beach, it was too much in their blood. By ten in the evening, they had been able to make appointments with fourteen classmates of the three, to be held over the next three days and evenings. They knew they were going to be running flat out, but there was no alternative. A consummate profile of Marshall, Sharon and Oliver was going to be invaluable in tracking them and determining if they were in any way involved with the mayhem and murders.

Telling each former classmate that they were conducting an investigation, the nature of which had to remain secret, seemed not to surprise any of the interviewees. Whether they claimed to be just a casual acquaintance or an intimate confidant, all seemed to feel it was just a matter of time before any of the three would end up behind bars. It was so tempting for Mori and Marg to grasp the first pieces of information they received during the first day of interviews and conclude that they knew all that was necessary, but that would not be professional and deep down they knew. Over the next two days a clearer picture emerged along with a few complete shocks. By the end of the third day, Mori and Marg felt they were ready to attempt to meet with the Reverend and Mrs. Wells.

Sometimes the direct approach works best; in this case, that was all it took. Of course, Mori told the slightly quavering voice at the other end of the telephone that they were looking to buy a home in the area and had been told that they were especially knowledgeable about property and which houses and owners would be the best to contact. Mori's flummery was all that was necessary for Reverend Hartwell Bradley Wells to extend an invitation for afternoon tea the next day.

At precisely four o'clock, Mori pulled up in front of the Beaufort Road home, slipped the gear selector into park, turned the key to off, got out and went around in order to assist Marg from the car. They had both felt it would appear more authentic if they pretended to be a devoted, happily married couple, thus explaining the fake rings on their left hands. As Mori lifted the heavy doorknocker, the door opened and they were greeted by Reverend Wells, who was primly garbed in his white collar, black shirt and suit, with a large gold cross dangling down his front. He reminded Marg, an avid movie buff, of a cross between Sir Cedric Hardwicke and Dame May Whitty. With pursed lips and an unctuous, slightly British, accent, he pulled the door back and asked them to enter. The good reverend offered his hand, shook Mori's in a perfunctory manner and lingered over Marg's hand, stroking it like he was admiring a mink coat. Marg wanted to slap him; instead she smiled and graciously thanked him for allowing them to interrupt his busy day.

"Oh, not at all," he responded. "I have plenty of time on my hands since I retired. Please, come into the living room. I've got tea waiting."

They followed him into the musky room, crossed the fairly worn ersatz Persian rug and settled onto the chintz-cover chesterfield that was place in front of the lead-paned windows that overlooked the serene streetscape.

"If you'll excuse me for one minute, I'll go get my wife. She is waiting in the sunroom."

He disappeared, with his creaking passage echoing through the house as he trod the aged, dried-out, hardwood floors. A minute later he re-appeared in the gumwood framed doorway pushing a wheelchair before him. Ensconced in it, with a crocheted lap rug draped over her legs, was a frail, grey-haired lady, whose head tilted slightly to the right, revealing a drooping right eye and mouth, symptomatic of a stroke. Mori and Marg immediately rose and Reverend Wells quietly announced, "I'd like you to meet my wife."

Caught off guard, having expected some vibrant strumpet guised in the garb of a demure rector's wife, the reality was totally the opposite.

"How do you do, Mrs. Wells? This is my wife, Margery Worton and I'm Moriyama Ito."

Bethany Wells nodded slightly and attempted to speak, to no avail.

"My wife suffered a stroke several years ago, and has been struggling with her therapy ever since. It has been very difficult for her, having been such an active person up to that moment. To make matters even worse, our beloved family doctor, Dr. J. Merreck Poyntz, retired, leaving us to cope with a new doctor."

"We're very sorry. I'm sure it has been very hard on both of you," Marg sympathized.

"That it has, but, you know, God works in mysterious ways. Both of us had, truly, gotten lost over the years in lust, greed and ungodliness. Maybe it was his way of telling us to slow down, re-prioritize, and take some time to enjoy the simpler things in life that we had overlooked for so long. As a matter of fact, we've taken several cruises since Bethany's illness and actually enjoyed them. Mind you we don't go ashore at any of the ports but we've so enjoyed the ships we've been on, the fresh salt-air and the vistas from our balconies. As a matter of fact, we just got back from a cruise a couple of weeks ago. We flew to Vancouver, visited some old friends for two weeks and then boarded the Crystal Symphony for a back-to-back cruise to Alaska and back; almost three weeks of extreme pampering for both of us."

"So you were gone at total of five weeks, that's amazing," Mori concluded.

"Bethany and I, at first were very apprehensive about being away that long but then stopped and realized there was no reason not to be. We have no responsibilities and no way of knowing how much longer God is going to give us, so we might as well make the most of it.

"Listen to me. I've been babbling on about us since you arrived; I'm so sorry. Please forgive me. Now what was it you wanted to know?"

Actually, Mori thought to himself, absolutely nothing more, but he realized he had to pretend that he had come for information about the neighbourhood. As they sipped tea, Reverend Wells alternated between offering Bethany tea through a straw, sipping his own, circulating the biscuit plate loaded with his favourite, Peak Freans Dark Chocolate coated Digestive Biscuits, and information about his area of The Glen. Once the tea had been consumed and the conversation seemed to be ebbing, Mori and Marg took the opportunity to graciously thank the Reverend and Mrs. Wells for their hospitality, asked if they could call again if they had any additional questions and then departed.

Back in their car, Mori pulled around the corner, stopped, and without any conversation, both of them opened their notepads and proceeded to make their notes of what had just transpired. Once that was done, they drove back to headquarters and, for the next several hours, revisited every aspect of the investigation to that point. Concluding they had all they required in order to prepare their final report, Marg opened her laptop computer and started keyboarding their inclusive report including all germane information gathered, their recollections and observations of their multitudinous interviews, conclusions, and recommendations. It had taken less than a week, but they felt their finished report was a true and accurate reflection of the "Holy Smoke" case, at least from their point of view and professional ability.

CHAPTER 10

The remainder of the first day Mason Barbetta and Jorge Estevan had received the case had been spent expostulating, accusing, forgiving, admonishing, crying and finally experiencing a night of the most romantic and passionate sex the two had ever encountered. Apologies had been accepted; clothing had been torn from aroused, sweaty, bodies; never before positions had been tried; finally the two, dementedly ecstatic detectives crumpled into an exhausted embrace and plunged into a deep and requited sleep.

'Mix 'N Match' almost seemed like a misnomer to Mason and Jorge, after they had carefully reviewed the file over breakfast in Jorge's kitchen. Who would dare speak to them, even after all these years; where would they even start? Neither of them had ever heard of either Alderman Raymond Linstrom or Deputy Minister Maurice Aukland but they felt that common sense would have them leaning toward pursuing the Linstrom investigation first, since it would probably be the least contentious.

Having resorted to the detective's greatest source, the telephone book, and discovering Maurice Aukland still resided in The Beach on Pine Glen Road, Jorge suggested they tackle the case head on and attempt to talk with him, without him realizing they were actually conducting an interrogation. Twenty minutes later, their black Crown Victoria arrived at the former alderman's home only to discover an elderly gentleman out in front attempting to rake the leaves on the lawn into a pile. Exiting the car, both of the detectives were struck by the quiet of the neighbourhood and the charming feel the area exuded. Although the houses were situated close to one another, there was no feeling of crowding. The street was actually fairly short, with only eight or so homes on the south side and only three or four on the north side, running from midway up the east side of Glen Manor Drive to join with the central bend in the second s-shaped street in The Glen, the brick-cobbled, exclusive, Pine Crescent.

"Good morning, sir. You wouldn't, by any chance, be the famous Alderman Raymond Linstrom?" Mason called out.

Pausing in mid stroke of his raking, the tall, white-haired, ruggedly handsome figure lifted his head, looked directly at the two intruders to his gardening reverie, slightly smiled and said, "I haven't heard that in a long time. How nice of you to remember."

Waving to beckon, he continued, "And who might you two be? Come a little nearer; my eyesight isn't what it used to be."

Extending his hand, Jorge introduced himself, followed by Mason, both conveniently omitting where they were from and why they were there. They spent the next few minutes making small talk; discussing the beautiful autumn day, the difficulties taking care of large treed lots and the pleasures of the peaceful ambiance The Beach, and Glen in particular, offered. Sensing from his demeanour and conversation style that he was suffering from early symptoms of Alzheimer, they carried on the casual conversation, slowly segueing to the neighbourhood of the fifties and sixties, the mores of past and present and the politics of then versus now. Lindstrom kept harkening back to the old days and the fact that his title of Alderman had been usurped with Councillor; he preferred Alderman. Over the next hour and an half, Mason and Jorge were stunned at how open and forthcoming Raymond Linstrom was about the power he had wielded, the people he had manipulated and the fun he had experienced. It was at that point they casually asked him if he'd ever heard about the wild parties some people in the area had participated in throughout the fifties and sixties. He let out a hoot of laughter, became more animated than he'd been up to that point and firmly stated, "Heard about them? Hell, I created them. You wouldn't believe the wild things that went on in those days. The kids today think they're such swingers and we were just boring squares back then. Boy, are they wrong. We had orgies that would have even shocked Hugh Hefner; sometimes they even shocked me! It seemed the more liberated the participants got, the further they would push things, the more uninhibited people got. There wasn't a fetish that wasn't explored by partakers of the hospitality my wife and I extended. We even built a dungeon down our basement to be used by any and all. The only difficulty we ever had was trying to get babysitters for our dear daughters, Lorna and Garnet, who would mind them at their own house. We were apprehensive about leaving them with teenagers and any adult that we would trust wanted to attend the parties rather than sit at home tending to our kids."

"Weren't you afraid of getting raided by the police?" questioned Jorge.

"You've got to be kidding. The off-duty cops used to attend and sometimes even the on-duty ones. That was always a big hit with the women and men who were uniform lovers who got off being ravaged by some big burly cop in his motorcycle boots and tailored uniform. Of course, in those days it was traditional to rent your x-rated films from Number Ten Police Station, up on Main Street; that way they wouldn't raid you."

Before either Mason or Jorge could interject, he continued, "Given the terrible car accident that befell my dear wife, when she was sixty-eight, in nineteen ninety-two, and her death the following year, I'm so glad we took advantage of all the opportunities that came our way. We lived, made the most of every day and had no regrets. Of course now, at eighty-two, I'd consider myself lucky if I was able to even get an erection never mind be able to participate in an orgy. Thank god I've got an active imagination even if my libido and memory don't work anymore."

"From the sounds of it, you really did live; I'm envious," offered Jorge. "You must have wielded a hell of a lot of power through all those connections, especially since no one would dare cross you once they had attended one of your parties."

"You've got to be kidding. Some of those fucking ingrates would come and screw their brains out, eat our food and then act like they didn't even know us when they saw us at some civic function. Real pricks, some of them and the one that became the biggest one was that smuck, Maurice Aukland."

Playing along, Mason added, "You mean the former Deputy Minister of Education?"

"Yeah, that's the one; Mister Big, or at least in his own miserable, shit-filled, mind. That son-of-a-bitch was nobody when we started playing around screwing each other's wife. It was Jennette and me who initiated it, hosted it and eventually expanded it to the level and fame that it grew to become. He was so fucking tight, unlike that hose-bag of a wife of his who was the loosest whore you could ever find, that he sponged off us over the entire time we did it. Mind you, he loved to pretend that he was one of the hosts so that he could act big with his weaselling, tight assed, egotistical, friends from Queen's Park. It wasn't any of them that got him all of his promotions and appointments, it was little old me, but god forbid he ever once thanked me or acknowledged my help and in the end, when I wanted some help with a couple of pet projects, he turned his back and pretended that was inappropriate. A real fucker he was, and still remains. Not that I'm bitter, much; I just hope Maurice, and Doris for that matter, rot in hell."

"I can certainly understand how you feel. It would be very disappointing to have done so much for someone only to have them turn their back afterward," Jorge sympathized.

"I knew you'd understand. It's too bad you guys weren't around for the orgies, you'd been really popular; could have had any woman in the place, I bet you."

Chuckling to themselves, they winked at each other, then both thanked him for the compliment and Mason continued, "It's been wonderful having the honour and opportunity to speak with you and hear about those amazing days. We best get going and let you get inside to warm up a bit."

"I've really enjoyed talking with the two of you; it brought back some wonderful memories and few I'd rather not recall. Drop by again anytime; we'll have a few beers and talk some more."

Mason and Jorge shook Raymond Linstrom's hand, got into their car, and drove away. Former Deputy Minister Maurice and Doris Aukland wouldn't be as easy, of that they were certain.

Contrary to the general public's commonly held belief that all bureaucrats are lazy, useless, leeches just putting in time until they can retire on huge, cushy pensions, the majority are diligent, caring and frustrated that they have to answer to politicians and their hacks. Given the opportunity, most are more than willing to squeal on their elected bosses and are thrilled when afforded the opportunity. Mason and Jorge were banking on it; the trick was to find the right ones. Herta Huber, former Trustee for the Toronto Board of Education was the entrée Mason knew would be able to assist them. Herta had been a long-time friend of Mason's mother and father and had resigned when the governing Progressive Conservative government at Queen's Park had appointed a Commissioner to run the Board in reaction to the Trustees' refusal to cut important educational programmes, in order to balance the budget. Being a woman of principle, Mason felt she was, probably, the most qualified to furnish them with an inside picture of the Ministry and the former Deputy Minister, who, in effect, ran the day-to-day operations of the ministry, on behalf of the Minister.

Dr. Herta Huber, after resigning, resumed her practise of Clinical Psychology and, for the most part, was enjoying it immensely. At age fifty-six, she knew that she didn't have to prove her capabilities to anyone; she could just enjoy applying her knowledge to help others. It was with mixed feelings that she agreed to speak with Mason and Jorge about her experiences with the Ministry, since she had, honestly, put it all behind her and had, successfully, moved forward.

The first few minutes were spent catching up on the latest family events, followed by her intuitive questioning as to Mason's present level of personal happiness, knowing full well that he and Jorge had once been lovers. At that point, it was Jorge's turn to interject, before Mason could respond, and inform her that everything was back to where it always should have been. Herta was delighted for both of them.

Rumours, innuendo, surmises and facts filled the next three hours. Herta Huber was a font of information; she knew each and every wart of those with whom she had had to work; it had been the only way she had been able to hold on for so long. She had hated that was what it took, but she had made a commitment to her electorate and herself at the very beginning and she wasn't going to let the egomaniacs, sycophants and those lacking in vision, sabotage her efforts; she, therefore, learned every weakness of her opponents and used her knowledge to accomplish her goals, whilst avoiding, for the most part, the slings and arrows most in her position suffered.

Copious notes were taken; little had surprised Mason and Jorge. Not surprisingly, after their conversation with former Alderman Raymond Linstrom, they were expecting a fairly lurid summary of Maurice Aukland and his antics while Deputy Minister of Education; they weren't disappointed. Herta Huber recounted the rapid climb Maurice Aukland had made from principal to the lofty pinnacle of Deputy Minister of one of the largest provincial ministries, using deceit, blackmail, bribery and political savvy. He was despised by Toronto Board of Education officials, in particular, and other municipal Boards throughout the province, by most ministry employees, politicians and almost anyone who had ever had the misfortune to cross his path. Nothing was too sinister to be considered in his scheming ways and no one was out of reach of his vengeance and wrath, if they dared to attempt, or actually achieved, crossing him.

When asked if she had ever met Doris Aukland, Herta allowed that she had been introduced to her on several occasions over the years and each time had observed she had become more common, less polished and more brazen; describing her as being as 'common as a gutter snipe' and 'so tough one would be able to bounce crowbars off her without her even feeling the impact'.

It was imperative they determine the present day mindset of Maurice and Doris Aukland, whether they were capable of arson and murder, if they were, could they be linked to the actions, and where were they during the illegal events? Complacent because their investigation had been so straightforward and relatively simple to that point, Mason and Jorge were jolted by the next phase in their quest.

There was no use continuing to gather hearsay testimony from former or present acquaintances given what had already been learned about them, therefore, Mason and Jorge decided to go right to the source and attempt to interrogate the Auklands.

Running north from St. Clair Avenue, Dunvegan Road, in the heart of old-money Forest Hill, was a bastion of movers and shakers, lined with two million dollar, and up, homes, featuring cut-stone or timbered Tudor, each edifice a masterpiece of refinement and good taste; gardens and lawns manicured and driveways cobbled, some with porte-cocheres. Even on a brisk fall morning, approaching noontime, nannies pushing prams and butlers walking dogs could be observed as Mason and Jorge searched for the home of Maurice and Doris Aukland. Records had indicated they had paid cash for the mansion in nineteen eighty-two and had never required any mortgage or other financing over the intervening years. Manoeuvring half way around the circular drive and coming to a halt directly in the front of the main entrance, Mason parked and the two of them alighted, approached the leaded-paned oak door, rang the doorbell and, in unison, adjusted their ties and jackets. Momentarily, the door opened and a woman, who appeared in her early sixties, and attired in a formal maid's uniform, asked if she could be of assistance. Jorge introduced Mason and himself, explained that they were detectives who were investigating a criminal event and asked if they could speak with Mr. and Mrs. Aukland. After being courteously invited across the threshold, they were asked to wait in the reception hall whilst she checked to see if they would be received. The maid disappeared up the long curved staircase, leaving Mason and Jorge to fidget and ogle the finery of the hall that was larger than their two apartments put together. In the centre of the room was a five by seven marble-topped gilded table stolidly standing atop a magnificent Persian carpet. Radiating from around the carpet was intricately inlaid mahogany flooring that featured a crested pattern just before it reached the wainscoted walls that in turn were adorned with large oil paintings and niches each holding marble statuary.

Crowning the foyer was a magnificent crystal chandelier holding several dozen faux candles, each with miniature lampshade.

In a somewhat mesmerized state, the two of them found themselves four or five steps farther into the hall, gaping at the artwork, when the maid reappeared, this time from a doorway that was partially hidden by the base of the staircase. Waiting until she had reached them before she spoke, Mason and Jorge were informed that Mr. Aukland was not at home but Mrs. Aukland would be pleased to assist them and would be with them in a few moments; in the meantime, she requested they follow her to the drawing room and wait there for Mrs. Aukland.

High-heels clicking on hardwood floors preceded the white silk-swathed apparition that appeared in the oak-framed doorway. Marabou encircled the ends of the flowing sleeves, the neck and the floor-length hem of the peignoir, and the tops of her 'come-fuck-me' slippers; the equally long silk gown clung to her body like Saran Wrap on a Jell-O mould. More bleach had been used to blonde her hair than the bleach used by the vestal virgins to keep their robes pristine; a trowel had obviously been used to apply make-up over the apple-doll-wrinkled face; more plucking had been employed on her eyebrows than at a factory preparing a batch of Colonel Saunder's chickens; a straw coat whisk had been sacrificed to create her eyelashes, and a paint roller used to finish off her collagen inflated lips. All in all, she was a vision not to behold on a newly filled stomach.

"Hello, boys," Mrs. Aukland cooed with a voice that would etch glass. "You both look much better in person than on the security camera. The only thing better would be if you were wearing your dress uniforms; they always look great piled in a heap next to my bed."

Jorge started to correct her that they we're not police detectives, but a subtle nudge of Mason's elbow stopped that from going any further. The self-perceived ever-lovely Doris sashayed across the drawing room, stopped only when Mason and Jorge could determine that it was vodka and not mouthwash on her breath, and grabbed them both by the crotch, squeezed, moaned slightly and purred, "Nice badges, mind showing them to me?"

Startled, they both lurched backward, freeing their crotches from her grasp and Mason blurted, "Mrs. Aukland, we're investigating a series of crimes and would appreciate it if you could assist us by answering a few questions."

"Honey, I'd love to assist both of you, but answering questions isn't how I would prefer to do it."

"Yes, I'm sure, but that's the way it's got to be," Jorge proffered with a doer facade.

"Well if it's going to be that way, I guess you better put your tight little asses down on the chesterfield and I'll order you some coffee, unless you'd prefer some booze."

Quickly scouting the room, they spotted a two-seater loveseat, at least two metres from the nearest single chair, and headed for it, sitting immediately, not waiting for her to attempt a different arrangement. Realizing she'd lost that opportunity, she slumped onto the closest eider-stuffed chair, kicked off her high-heeled slippers and placed her feet onto the marble-topped coffee table. Next, she pulled a sterling silver cigarette case from the pocket of her peignoir, extracted a cigarette, placed it between her lips and then rasped, "So which one of you brutes is going to light it for me?"

"Actually, neither of us smoke and, since I have asthma, I would deeply appreciate it if, while we're here, you didn't either," Jorge said with a polite but serious tone.

"Shit, you two are about as much fun as a kick in the box. Don't you two ever crack a smile, or fuck around, or fart, or, I don't know, do anything other than sit there like two old farts?"

"As I said a minute ago, Mrs. Aukland, we're here on a very serious case," Mason reiterated, "and time is of the essence, so may we please begin?"

"Oh, for fuck sake, lighten up. I'll answer your goddamn questions just to hurry it up and let you get back to your Aunt Bee and Cousin Opie."

Wanting to laugh, or at least smirk, both Mason and Jorge suppressed their inclinations and began the questioning. Over the next two hours, they questioned and Doris Aukland, out of defiance, because the two detectives had eschewed partaking in her mid-day libation, polished off a bottle of chilled white wine, having been brought in an ice bucket by the maid. The more she consumed the more forthcoming she became.

After a series of general questions, Mason pointedly asked, "Mrs. Aukland, how do you and your husband handle individuals who either directly or indirectly pose a threat to you and your lifestyle?"

Doris shifted in her chair, finished what was in the wineglass and responded with a sneer, "My husband and I have scratched, and slept, our way from a piss-pot existence living on a teacher's salary to the financial position we presently enjoy and we're not about to let anyone destroy our results."

"Do either of you know a Russian émigré by the name of Marislav Anatole?" Jorge continued.

Doris blithely responded, "I know lots of Russians but rarely bother to find out their names since I never plan to be with them longer than it takes to reach orgasm. Actually, they usually make lousy lovers; the saving grace about them is they have big, uncut, cocks and like it rough, which really turns me on. In fact, my definition of eternity is the time between when I orgasm and the doorknob gooses the Russian, who just brought me, as the door slams closed behind him. As for my husband and Russians, he doesn't like most of the Russian women he comes across because they are either pros, and of course, he will never pay, or they are newly arrived and haven't learned to shave; he can't stand hairy armpits, legs or pussies."

"Do you personally know of any reason someone would have a vendetta against the family of Dr. J. Merreck Poyntz," Mason bluntly probed?

"Are you kidding? He saved my ass and that of nearly everyone else in The Beach so many times everybody loved him. He was a saint, never condemning, always willing to listen, making notes so that he could remember and always indicating sincere concern. We should have continued going to him when we moved up here from The Beach, but Maurice thought it would be better for us socially to go to a doctor in this area. That was a big mistake, as far as I was concerned, but my asshole husband insists he knows everything."

"What about his son? What do you think of him?"

"Show me a picture of him and I'll tell you."

Persisting, Mason added, "I meant do you feel about him as you did about his father?"

"Listen, I don't know where you hope to go with all this and quite frankly I don't give a shit, but as far as his kid is concerned, I vaguely remember seeing some photos on his office credenza but I couldn't tell you whether they were of his kids or a pet chimpanzee. Now, unless either or both of you have changed your mind and want to spend a little time using your handcuffs to restrain a wild and horny Forest Hill nymphomaniac, I'm afraid this interview is over."

With that, Doris Aukland arose, slipped her feet into her fur-trimmed slippers and headed for the drawing room door. Turning, she applied a broad smile and finished with, "Really too bad that you're both so business-like. I think we really could have had a great roll in the linen. Goodbye, boys."

With that she pivoted and sashayed into the reception hall, leaving a fading clicking of her heels on the hardwood to echo in the bemused minds of Mason and Jorge. Almost immediately, the maid once again appeared and offered to show them out.

Back in the car, their professional training kicked in and they silently and carefully notated their latest investigational experience. The challenge was to truly capture the event without being confused by the diversionary tactics of Doris Aukland and her contrived commonness that was craftily employed by her to simultaneously attract, addle and repel.

After what seemed like hours and had actually been slightly less than forty-five minutes, Mason broke silence, "Keep writing, I'll be right back." With that, he leapt from the car and rang the doorbell. As soon as the maid opened the door, Mason blurted out, "Mrs. Aukland started to tell us the name of her travel agent but got diverted with something else and we forgot to go back to it. Who is it?"

Caught off guard, the maid dithered for a second then said, "Oh, I'm not supposed to give out any information about anything to anyone. It's up to Madam to do that. You'll have to step inside and wait while I go and ask her."

Before she could swing the door back any further, Mason offered, "It's not necessary to bother Mrs. Aukland with such a minor item, especially when she had started to tell us. I'm certain she wouldn't want to be interrupted over such an unimportant thing. In fact it would probably upset her and neither you nor I would want to do that, would we?"

"No, I suppose your right. I for one wouldn't want to do that. Now, what was it you wanted to know?"

"Just the name of the travel agent the Auklands use. It's just a formality."

"Well, I suppose it's all right." She lowered her voice, leant forward until she could almost whisper in Mason's ear and said, "They use 'Artois and Maynard' in The Colonnade for all their travel arrangements. Now, I best be going. Please don't tell Madam that I told you anything; just let her think she told you. Goodbye." With that, the door closed and Mason turned back to the Crown Vic with a pronounced smirk emanating from his mouth.

"What was that all about?" Jorge quizzed the moment the car door opened.

"Just thought that I'd try to get the name of their travel agent from the maid since I figured there was no way we would have ever gotten it from the Floozy of Forest Hill."

Before Jorge could ask which agency they used or where they were headed next, Mason slipped the gearshift into drive and they were off, around the curved driveway and barrelling back down Dunvegan Road. Within ten minutes they were pulling into the underground parking entrance of The Colonnade. Once parked, they took the elevator to the second level, where they found the ultra-exclusive 'Artois and Maynard – Travel Advisors'. The instant they entered the thickly carpeted entry, they were greeted by a morning suit clad gentleman who stiffly bowed and asked, "To whom do you wish to be directed?"

"The manager, whomever that may be," Mason responded.

Without blinking, the implacable greeter enquired, "May I tell Mr. Artois the purpose of your visit?"

Reaching in his pocket, he retrieved his badge, quickly flipped it open and closed and said, "We're detectives and we'll tell him ourselves."

Sniffing once, as if his nose was running, he sneered, "Very well, please wait here," and he disappeared through heavy dark-green velvet curtains.

Within thirty seconds, the curtains parted and an impeccably groomed gentleman, wearing a dark-blue Armani suit, emerged smiling, with his perfectly manicured hand extended toward Mason and began, "Good afternoon, detective, I'm Louis Artois."

"How do you do? I'm Mason Barbetta and this is my partner, Jorge Estevan."

"A pleasure, Detective Barbetta."

After smoothly shaking Mason's hand, Artois turned and shook Jorge's hand and then asked, "And how can I be of service to you two gentlemen?"

"We'd like to ask you several questions and I think it would be better if we could do so in private," Mason suggested.

"Absolutely, please come this way."

Walking to the velvet curtain, he held it back and asked the two detectives to please enter. Once through the doorway, they found themselves being lead along an ornate, but tastefully decorated, passageway at the end of which was a large oak door with a brass plaque that read 'M. Louis Artois, Owner'. With a grand gesture, he flung the door open and requested them to enter and be seated. Once the door was closed, he navigated around the sheared French-velvet covered chairs and his hand-carved oak desk and regally settled onto his high-backed leather executive chair.

"Now that we have some privacy, how may I help you?"

"We understand that your company is the exclusive handler of all travel requirements for Mr. and Mrs. Maurice Aukland. Could you please provide us with a detailed list of all their travel for the last year as well as any future trips they may have booked."

"Oh, my. You really have caught me off guard. You see, Mr. and Mrs. Aukland are very, and I stress very, good clients. They have referred many of their friends and business associates to Artois and Maynard and, personally, use us extensively. Consequently, I feel somewhat awkward discussing them and their dealings with you. I'm certain you can see the predicament in which I find myself."

"Actually, I don't, since this investigation involves the death of four people. You can either cooperate or you can refuse and suffer the consequences of having the court issue a search warrant and the police closing your business down for a number of days while your files are slowly, and I do stress the word slowly, examined, along with every square millimetre of the premises."

"Hmm, yes, I understand what you are saying. Under the circumstances, we at Artois and Maynard would be more than pleased to assist you gentlemen."

Louis Artois turned to face the computer sitting on a small desk to his right, punched a few keystrokes, scanned the screen for several seconds, then clicked the mouse and awaited the HP Laserjet 5P next to the computer to start whirring. In less than two minutes Artois was handing Mason a sheaf of paper that reflected all of the details of the travel activities for the Auklands over the last year as well as several upcoming sorties.

"We deeply appreciate your assistance, Mr. Artois and would appreciate it if you kept this completely confidential. Given the nature of the crimes being investigated and the possible people involved, you can appreciate the delicateness of this investigation. Nobody other than the three of us should be allowed to know anything about this meeting. Agreed?"

"Oh, absolutely Detective Barbetta. Mums the word. After all, I wouldn't want to place Artois and Maynard on the wrong side of the law, would I?"

"Thank you Mr. Artois, you've been extremely helpful, discrete and very professional. But, of course, what else would one expect of Artois and Maynard," Mason pandered.

"Quite right, gentlemen, quite right."

"We'll see ourselves out. Thanks again and goodbye."

Shaking their hand, Louis Artois waited for them to close the door behind them, reached into his pocket and withdrew a fine linen handkerchief, wiped his moist brow and then slumped into his chair.

Mason and Jorge made it all the way back to the solitude of the interior of their car parked in the underground garage before Jorge burst with laughter and screeched, "My god you've got balls."

"Why thank you, you gorgeous hunk of male flesh. But what about my chutzpah?" Mason countered.

"You know damn well I'm not talking about your nuts; I'm talking about the brazen way you worked that poor bastard to give up confidential information. It was masterful. He was so scared, I thought he was going to shit his pants or pop a blood vessel. When you told him about the chance of a court order and closing down his business while his records were scoured, he damn near went into full-blown apoplexy."

"Yeah, but you were witness to the fact that I never said we were police or any official; he just assumed it and we got what we needed."

"True enough, but both the way you handled Doris Aukland and Louis Artois was brilliant."

"Why thank you, sir, now let's go back to my place and you can tell me again about my wonderful balls."

Jorge leaned across to the driver side of the car and gave Mason a long and passionate kiss. When finished, he sat back up, adjusted his tie and jacket and said, "First, we'll go back to your place and go over everything that occurred today, review all the travel records, plan tomorrow's strategy; then, and only then, we'll have a long sensual soak in the whirlpool, make mad passionate love on the fur rug in front of your gas fireplace and then a nice cozy dinner pour deux. How does that sound?"

"My dear, it sounds so good, I've already got a raging hardon."

The rest of the day went as exactly as planned, except for one surprise. After reviewing their entire collection of notes and the computer printout provided by Louis Artois, Mason and Jorge were stunned to discover they were ready to file their report and the serious conclusions they had determined. The next day would be spent doing just that.

CHAPTER 11

Claude Boisvert, the managing partner of Sterling, McDormant and Winetraub, seemed to be expecting Pauline Goodson and Yvonne Asselstine; maybe not them per se, but someone, sometime, prying into things that he and the firm felt best left alone. After greeting them at the reception desk, Claude led them to a small but very sharply appointed conference room and asked them to be seated.

Without wasting time on niceties, he opened with, "So who sent you and why do they want to dredge up a subject that has been put to rest for many years?"

"As I said in my telephone call, we work for Key Security and are investigating a series of murders and arson on behalf of our client," Pauline firmly but respectfully responded. "We are certainly not accusing anyone of anything; instead we are attempting to determine the whereabouts of individuals and their possible involvement in aspects of the case. It was for those reasons that we requested today's meeting with you."

Assuming a rigid posture and an extremely frigid demeanour, Boisvert snapped, "I'm afraid you have wasted your time, not to mention mine. As barristers and solicitors, Sterling, McDormant and Winetraub will not divulge any information about any client, period. We don't have to and, therefore, won't. I couldn't give a fig what the circumstances surround. Furthermore, we wouldn't collaborate with the police, nor would we have to, so why do you think we would cooperate with you and your private investigation?"

"Given that you haven't even been told whom we're investigating," Yvonne chided, "I think it might behove you to refrain from making such a precipitous decision. Once you've done so, and been fully informed, even then, I seriously doubt that you will be the one empowered to decide whether or not your firm cooperates with us. Most certainly, it will be your board of directors. Therefore, if you will, please restrain yourself from pontificating long enough for us to apprise you of the details."

Chastened to the point of being speechless, Claude Boisvert's face swiftly went from ashen to beet red. He was not used to being spoken to in such a tone of voice or manner by anyone and thus found it particularly grating to be reprimanded as if he were a recalcitrant schoolboy. Yvonne, on the other hand, had drawn on her psychology education to assess that Boisvert was an egotistical, bullying, misogynist who would be cowed if confronted by a strong adversary proffering a position that called into question his authority.

Attempting to regain some level of control, Boisvert weakly parried with, "I'll be the judge of that. Now get on with whatever it is you've come here for; my time is valuable and I'm certainly not going to waste it debating with the two of you."

Pauline took the initiative and whacked him in between his eyes with a verbal two-by-four, "Is your firm presently representing Samantha Sterling? If so, is she an actual client or are you merely representing her because of her father's relationship with this law firm? Where is she presently residing? Is she employed? If so, by whom? If not, how does she support herself? Do her parents presently assist in maintaining her? Is she presently using drugs and if not can she provide character witnesses to attest to that fact?"

There was a long moment of complete silence following Pauline's barrage. Finally, Boisvert mumbled, "Good god, I had no idea that you were here to enquire about Samantha Sterling. I sincerely thought you wanted information about a client from long ago."

Before he could continue, Yvonne piped in, "We do; her. She was once a client of this firm and we want the answers to those questions and a number of others."

"As far as I know, she has never been a client of this firm, as long as I've been associated with it. Granted her father, Geoffrey Sterling, is Senior Counsel Emeritus of this firm, but he has very little to do with us on a day-to-day basis. Furthermore, he was never one to mix his personal life with the business of this firm. I actually only know about Samantha Sterling through rumours provided by a few old-timers. I can honestly tell you that as far as I know, this firm has not had anything to do with her in at least a decade. Furthermore, I, and I'm certain everyone else on staff, hasn't a clue where she is or, for that matter, whether she's still alive."

"If requested, would you be willing to attest to that via an affidavit?" Pauline tested.

"Most assuredly. In fact, I'll have one drawn and signed and then courier it over to your office," Boisvert readily offered.

Tones of voices had, by this time, changed on the part of the three present. Yvonne immediately accepted his offer by offering him her business card and politely directed, "That would be very much appreciated. You'll find our address on the card. Thank you very much for your time and cooperation."

With that, Goodson and Asselstine each shook Boisvert's hand and departed.

Samantha Sterling had to be located. Geoffrey Sterling resided in an up-scale condominium at the southeast corner of Avenue Road and Lonsdale Road, overlooking the park-like setting of Upper Canada College, the most exclusive private boys' school in Canada and one of the most sought after schools in the world. Pauline Goodson and Yvonne Asselstine had waited until three-thirty in the morning to pull into the circular drive of Sterling's condo, park, and enter the lobby. The rotund gentleman, in his mid fifties, struggling to clear his bleary eyes and appear awake, wiggled his way out of his chair, straightened his askew tie and blustered, "Good evening, may I help you?"

Dressed in the most official looking attire they could muster, they briskly approached the concierge desk adorned with a faux bronze plaque that read, 'Allan Venables – Concierge', flipped their badges open and closed and introduced themselves as Detectives Goodson and Asselstine.

Pauline led, "We require your assistance in a very important matter and insist that, in doing so, you keep this confidential and completely to yourself. Do you understand?"

"I think I do," he meekly responded.

Yvonne pursued, "Either you do or you don't. Possibly we misunderstood your position. We just assumed that as a professional," and she stressed the word professional, "you would want to assist us and realize that investigations often require complete and unequivocal discretion and secrecy. Maybe we should return when we can speak with a more senior staff person?"

"No, no, that won't be necessary. I'd be more than happy to assist you. This is the most excitement I've had since I started working in this mausoleum. What do you want to know?"

"Does Samantha Sterling live in this building and, if so, with her father?"

Looking directly at Pauline to answer her question, he shook his head and said, "The only person who lives in that condo is Mr. Sterling. Mrs. Sterling, bless her dear heart, passed away several years ago, leaving Mr. Sterling a very sad and lonely soul. The only visitor he ever has is his maid who comes in three days a week and the odd visit from some stuffy, tight-assed, lawyer from his old law firm, who is in and out faster than a priest in a whore house." Being somewhat old-fashion and realizing what he had just said to two women, his face immediately went red and he stammered, "Oh, please excuse me, that was quite rude."

"Not to worry, we hear much worse when we're out for an evening with the girls," Pauline assured. Continuing, she re-asked, "And his daughter, Samantha Sterling, how frequently does she visit?"

"Until now, I didn't even know he had a kid, and I've worked here for ten years."

"Is it possible that she might visit during the day, thus making it impossible for you to be aware of her?" Yvonne asked.

"Oh, you don't understand. All of us are on rotating shifts of days, afternoons and nights. Every week we change which shift we work. It's hell on the body, but what are you going to do? If you want the job, you've got to accept that your sleeping habits are always topsy-turvy. Anyway, getting back to Mr. Sterling's daughter, I don't see how I would have missed her. If she had ever come here and asked to be announced, I would remember. As a matter of fact, I can't ever remember anyone ever arriving and mentioning they were a relative of his, even around the time Mrs. Sterling died."

"Well, if that's the situation, I guess we don't have any further questions to ask," Pauline said smilingly. "We'll be off, then, but remember, this is between us and not to be entered into your overnight log or mentioned to anyone, including the building manager or Mr. Sterling. Got it?"

"Yes, ma'am. Mum's the word."

"Goodnight, Mr. Venables," Yvonne and Pauline spoke in unison, and then headed for the door.

As they were about to push the two brass-trimmed plate glass doors open, the concierge called out, "Goodnight and thanks for the excitement. Come and see me anytime." With that, he sat down, leaned back, folded his hands and rested them on his protruding stomach, sighed and smiled, then closed his eyes.

By mutual agreement, Pauline and Yvonne agreed to not get started until later in the day, at noon, when Pauline would pick up Yvonne and they would continue their hunt. That said, once home, Pauline had been unable to sleep; the whereabouts of Samantha Sterling was gnawing at her to the point she decided to email Règinè

Ouellette so that it would be waiting for her when she arrived at her office. In it, she requested a police check be conducted to determine if Samantha had been involved with the police since she was last released from prison and, in turn, had she conducted her parole without incident. With that accomplished, she finally felt like she could sleep. As she drifted off, she hoped there would be an emailed response in the morning that would supply information that would nudge the case forward.

Her optimism was only slightly rewarded, the next morning, by Règinè's response. According to the police, Samantha Sterling successfully completed her probation and had no further conflict with the authorities. After Yvonne had been picked up and read the report, Pauline suddenly recognized the inconsistencies between the police report and that of Dr. Poyntz. Nowhere did the police mention her relapse while on probation and working at the street clinic and her subsequent firing. Before she could enunciate her finding, she had executed a u-turn and headed downtown. Filling in Yvonne on her observation, they both showed renewed excitement in their quest.

Locating a parking place only two storefronts away from the clinic, Pauline quickly parked the car and the two alighted. Junkies, elderly street people and dazed drunks filled the chairs packed around the periphery of the room immediately inside the door. As Pauline and Yvonne entered, only two people even bothered to raise their heads long enough to react to their presence. Approaching the woman sitting at a desk on the other side of a divider, Pauline flashed her badge and forthrightly requested, "We're here on a very urgent and important case and need to see the clinic supervisor."

Without altering her demeanour an iota, the beleaguered worker droned, "So which one of our lovelies is in shit this time?"

"We must discuss it directly with the supervisor. Is he or she available," Yvonne participated.

"She's with a client but should be through in just a few minutes. I'd offer you a chair but there aren't any." Lowering her voice, she sneered, "Lucky for you, otherwise you'd have probably caught fleas."

Several minutes had elapsed when the door to the right of the reception desk opened and an elderly man, clad in tattered clothes emerged, followed by a rotund, shortly-cropped white haired, woman who appeared to be in her mid to late sixties. Before she could say anything, the receptionist barked, "These two are undercover and need to talk with you."

"Good bye Mr. Simone, don't forget to come in next week and let me know how you're doing." Then turning, she smiled, extended her hand to Pauline and said "How do you do. I'm Prudence Potts, and," slightly chuckling, "if you laugh at my name I'll flatten you, even if you are cops."

"It's a pleasure to meet you. May we have just a moment of your valuable time?" Pauline requested.

"You sure can, but hold the bullshit; I'm too old and grizzled for that crap. Come this way."

With that she retreated through the door and led them down a short hallway to a sterile-looking office with a battered desk, two vinyl chairs and a dented four-drawer file cabinet with two drawers permanently ajar.

"Now, what can I do for you?"

"We are investigating a series of murders and are trying to locate an individual who might have information concerning the crimes," Yvonne said, cutting to the nub of the situation.

"Okay, who are you seeking?"

"Samantha Sterling," Yvonne continued.

"My god, that's a name from the past. She hasn't been associated with this clinic in years. In fact, I doubt whether she's still alive, given her horrific record with drugs."

"We know that she got fired from here but haven't been able to track her once she left here," Pauline offered.

"It was one of the hardest things I've ever had to do as director of this clinic. She was kind, caring and effective and then I found out she had started back using drugs. For almost six years she had stayed clean, and then she met some asshole who got her using again and that was it. I had to let her go."

"Why didn't you inform the police?" Pauline queried.

"Because I wouldn't call them for any of our clients so I sure wouldn't call them for a wonderful staff member like her. She tripped, but I sure wasn't going to kick her while she was down. As it was, once I let her know that I knew, I really didn't need to push too hard; she went pretty much on her own."

"Do you know where she went or what she did after she left your employment?" Yvonne pried.

"Not for certain, although, I did hear from a new client that he had been turned into a junkie and fallen from a fairly high position by someone who sounded like her, but the names didn't match."

Pauline pressed, "Do you have any thoughts on where she might be or what she is doing? I persist only because of the importance of the case."

"Honestly, I haven't a clue. That said, I'll put out the word on the street and get back to you if I receive anything that I think might be of assistance. Do you have a card?"

Realizing that producing a business card would give away that they were not police detectives, Yvonne quickly covered by saying, "Given the secrecy surrounding this case, it is better that we get back to you in a few days. I'm sure you understand and will respect our request that this conversation remain completely confidential."

"Listen, honey, everything that goes on in this place is confidential and I'm so old and worn out I can't remember most of what I hear. The good thing is that I'm still able to help the majority of poor bastards who come here looking for guidance or a friendly ear. That, I can still provide, and damn effectively."

"We're sure you do and deeply appreciate the time and assistance you've given us. Take care and thank you," Pauline said as she extended her hand, as did Yvonne.

Over the next several days, Pauline Goodson and Yvonne Asselstine called on all of the downtown street clinics seeking Samantha Sterling or information as to whether she was alive or dead. They had, reluctantly requested guidance from Règinè Ouellette and had received a photograph that she had obtained from one of her many contacts at the RCMP. Using that, even though it was quite dated, a number of people at the clinics, primarily client, but not exclusively, indicated that they recognized the person in the photo but no one was able to put the face with a name, including when the name of Samantha Sterling was mentioned. All that changed late in the afternoon on the fourth day, when by chance, while checking at the Hassle Free Clinic on Church Street, in the heart of the gay community, a somewhat well-dressed client, waiting to be seen, recognized the person in the photo.

When pressed, he bitterly said, "That's the bitch that got me addicted, which, in turn led me to using hard drugs and dirty needles, which led me to contracting HIV."

"Are you certain you recognize this person?" Yvonne pressed, to confirm his assertion.

"You don't forget someone who ruined your life, even if she looked much older than how she appears there."

Pauline joined the questioning, "Do you know her name and where we can find her?"

"Her name is Sheila Spellman and she used to live in the Manulife Building at Bay and Bloor. I'm not sure if she still lives there because she stopped granting me access once I lost my job and ran out of money to support my habit."

"How did you meet her?" Yvonne followed up.

"She used to host very chic cocktail parties where very wealthy up and comers would congregate under the guise of partying. In actuality, the only reason someone took a new person to the party was so they would receive a discount on that evening's personal drug buy. It was like a posh pyramid scam. It just kept building and the beautiful thing was she didn't have to hustle to build her business; her clients did it for her. All she had to do was provide the venue and some wine and the business just expanded exponentially. She went from once or twice a week to hosting parties every night and the damn thing was, she knew that she wouldn't get busted because all guests must have been previous clients in order to get past the concierge desk and no one could get upstairs for the first time without being brought by a previous guest. In addition, no one risked bringing anyone who might not be completely discrete for fear that they would screw up such a great way to obtain their drug requirements."

"Sounds like she really had a smooth set-up." Yvonne continued, "You stopped dealing with her because you ran out of money?"

"Yeah, I got so far into the scene and was using so much cocaine and heroin that I lost my job, that paid over a hundred thousand a year. Then when I ran out of my savings, I had to sell my condo just to keep up my drug habit. That went rapidly and when that was gone, so was my access to her and her supply. I tried calling her and leaving messages but the bitch never returned one of my calls. If it hadn't been for the 519 Community Centre and their counsellors, I'd be dead. At least now I'm getting my life slowly back together, no thanks to her."

"You've been an enormous help to us. We sincerely hope that you continue on your journey back to a good life. Thank you so very much," Pauline genuinely extended.

Finally, the break they were seeking. After all the searching, in all the seedy locales, it turns out she was probably no more than a few blocks from them. Within ten minutes they were standing in the lobby of the Manulife condominiums asking for Sheila Spellman. When informed that Ms. Spellman had taken her dog for a walk and would probably be back any minute, they thanked the concierge and said they would wait. Stepping slightly to the side of the main part of the desk so as not to impede the steady flow of people coming and going, Pauline waited for an opportune moment and then asked the concierge, "I hope we've got the correct date. She is having a party tonight, isn't she?"

"I presume she is. She usually has one every evening. Ms. Spellman is a very popular hostess. I never cease to be amazed at the people she invites to her nightly parties. There's hardly an evening that I don't recognize scads of visitors. The amazing thing is how often they visit her."

He had barely finished when the door to Charles Street West opened and in breezed Samantha Sterling, a.k.a. Sheila Spellman.

"Ms. Spellman," the concierge called, "these ladies want to speak with you."

"Sorry girls, but I don't personally add anyone to the nightly guest list. You've gotta be introduced by one of my regular guests."

By the time she finished her admonition, she was parallel to Pauline and Yvonne, the latter who corrected her with, "You've misread our intentions. We're not here to get on your guest list; we're here to speak with you. Do you have a minute?"

"I don't do interviews, sorry."

Yvonne pressed, "We're detectives, not reporters, and we need to discuss a very important matter."

"I don't give a shit whether you're the chief of police, I don't give interviews; so either arrest me or fuck off."

"Does the name Dr. J. Merreck Poyntz mean anything to you?" snapped Pauline Goodson.

Sheila reeled around, glared at Pauline and Yvonne for a minute, as if she was trying to get her bearings, then in a weary tone replied, "What does he want with me after all these years? I've put him, and all those painful memories, far behind me."

"Actually he doesn't want anything of you: he's dead," Pauline punched.

"Oh, shit." For a minute her eyes went glassy, as if they were going to start to shed tear, then she snapped out of it and directed, "Come with me, I not going to talk about private things in public."

She led the way through the double glass doors, straight ahead, into the adjacent Manulife Centre and a coffee shop directly opposite. Without looking back to see if they were following she headed for the table by the railing, pulled out the chair and plunked herself down. Pauline and Yvonne sat opposite her and Pauline asked, "Would you like something to drink?"

"Yeah, a double cappuccino with extra foam and a dusting of cinnamon."

While Pauline was buying the coffees, Yvonne decided to sit mute and observe their temporary captive. Once the coffees were in front of the correct places, Yvonne dove in with, "You're a difficult lady to find. Why do you use the pseudonym of Sheila Spellman; are you afraid that people will recognize you if you use your birth name of Samantha Sterling?"

"Samantha Sterling is dead. She's been dead for almost twenty years. She died in prison. I'm Sheila Spellman and have no family and no responsibilities. I do what I want, live better than most of my friends and don't want to change a thing about my life. As a matter of fact, I like my life so much, I'd do nearly anything necessary to make sure it doesn't change."

"Does that go as far as murder?" Yvonne bluntly challenged.

"Possibly," Sheila responded without any hesitation.

"You acted surprised when we told you, in your lobby, that Dr. Poyntz was dead. I take it you didn't stay in touch with him. Why was that, since he gave you your first job and helped you when you initially got into trouble?" Pauline probed.

"For the same reason I didn't stay in touch with my parents. I'd done some pretty stupid things and hurt a lot of people who meant a great deal to me; I didn't want to keep hurting them, yet, at the same time I had to survive, so I allowed Samantha to die and created Sheila Spellman. That way I protected those who meant the most to me and went on with my life, at the same time. It was the best way to handle a shitty hand that was dealt me. Now that I've spilled my guts to two broads I don't even know, I want to know why the hell you are after me. It can't be because of my parties since you know damn right well there are too many important people, including cops, involved in my little party scheme, to allow the likes of you to fuck it up."

"Do you know a fellow who goes by the name of Marislav Anatole?" Yvonne bluntly asked.

"Why?" Sheila fired back.

"We need to find him and we have been told that you might know him," Yvonne countered.

"Well I don't know which son of a bitch told you that; but, I can bloody well assure you that I don't know anyone by that name. I'll admit to knowing a hell of a lot of Russians, in fact some of my new regular partygoers are very successful Russians. When they first started attending my parties, I thought they were trying to muscle in on my concept, if you get the drift; but, it turned out they couldn't give a shit about that, they just wanted the entrée I could provide to all the prominent people who usually attend. Actually, they've been wonderful to me and I've made a lot of good friends through them."

Pauline continued to probe, "So you want us to believe that even though you know a pack of Russians that you can specifically remember, you have never met, or don't know, a Marislav Anatole?"

"Quite frankly, I don't give a shit what you do or don't believe. Furthermore, I don't even know why I'm continuing to talk with you and answer your fucking questions. You caught me off guard when you invoked Dr. Poyntz's name, but now that I realize that he was only mentioned because, somehow, you learned that he held a soft spot in my heart and exploited it, I don't think it's prudent for me to continue."

With that, Sheila Spellman suddenly stood, stepped away from the table and warned, "If I were you, I'd go back to the station and ask the desk sergeant for a new assignment. You're barking up the wrong tree and tangling with the wrong bitch; I don't bark, I bite, and it's a deadly bite."

With that, Sheila flounced off through the double doors and disappeared back into the security of her condominium.

After pausing long enough to watch the doors close behind her, Yvonne moued in Pauline's direction and said, "So, do you think we hit a nerve or did you pee in her double cappuccino, with extra foam and a dusting of cinnamon, when I wasn't looking?"

All it took, after the request by Pauline to Règinè, was a telephone call to Integrity Patrols, the security company holding the contract at the Manulife Condominiums, and copies of Sheila's guest list for the following four days was made available to Key Security and, thus, to Pauline Goodson and Yvonne Asselstine. In the interim, they continued to pursue questioning Sheila's condominium neighbours and staff, as well as cross-checking all information about Marislav

Anatole they could garner from Key Security computers and staff, with what they had obtained about Sheila Spellman. Once they had received the guest lists, it took Goodson and Asselstine another three days to scour them and compare them to the entire mass of information gathered thus far. Time was running out; conclusions had to be made; their reports had to be submitted.

CHAPTER 12

Faison Quay knew the only way to get to the bottom of the Leaverage dynasty's perceived perfidy was to travel to Moscow and redeem as many IOU's as need be. All it had taken was a simple mention to David Granpré and everything had been taken care of, down to the minutest detail. Faison had informed Andrew and Fortunato they would be accompanying them, since he didn't feel comfortable leaving them in Toronto, even if they were under twenty-four hour protection. Predictably, he received absolutely no complaint. They had never been to Russia and thought, even though the trip would probably only be for two or three days, they would still get the opportunity to see some of the principle sites.

Realizing they would be stopping in London, England, in order to refuel, Faison thought of a simple way to protect Mrs. Hermione Tilsbury, a key witness to the original crime, while keeping her at arm's length from the police. David was dispatched, shortly after nine, with a letter, personally signed by Faison, inviting her to be his guest on his private jet for a trip back to London. Included would be a suite at the Key Palace Hotel and a chauffeur-driven limousine at her disposal for the entire time she was there. When Hermione read the letter, she couldn't believe her eyes; after all, she had not been back since she left in 1934. At first she declined the generous invitation, feeling that she did not possess a wardrobe adequate to the trip. Her fears were allayed when David assured her they would be going on a shopping spree that afternoon to acquire all her clothing and personal travel requirements. Additionally, the first item on the outing was to get her photograph taken so that it could be immediately taken to the passport office where they were awaiting its arrival, in order to assemble her passport, so Chester, their driver for the day, could pick it up, while he was waiting for David and Hermione to finish the shopping.

In typical Faison Quay fashion, everyone around him stayed in a state of awe and astonishment, as their world was turned topsy-turvy and completely reorganized. Hermione savoured every minute of her queen-for-a-day tour of Holt Renfrew, including a stop at their beauty salon for a complete spa makeover and pampering. By the time she stepped back into the limousine for the trip directly to the airport, she felt as if she had died and gone to heaven.

Basil had taken care of all of the packing for Andrew, Fort, Stark, and Faison, and, because of the abruptness of the decision, David, who would be accompanying them.

It was exactly seven o'clock when Ernie went through the security gate, pulled the Rolls-Royce onto the tarmac and came to a stop just next to the steps leading to Faison and Stark's Bombardier Global Express. Marcel Trembley, valet, was standing at the top of the stairs awaiting their arrival; David and Mrs. Tilsbury were already on board, as was the luggage for the entire group. Once Ernie's four passengers were safely ensconced in their luxurious seats, Marcel closed the plane's door, went to the galley and returned with champagne flutes on a sterling silver tray to serve everyone, including a cooing Hermione Tilsbury, who was over the moon to see Andrew and Fortunato again. Almost immediately, Captain Vinita Rialto revved the engines and the plane moved away from the terminal. Within minutes, the jet was airborne and twenty minutes later they had reached their cruising altitude. Background music played, pre-prandial drinks were served with hot and cold hors d'oeuvres and Hermione kept pinching herself to make certain she wasn't dreaming. Chef Marcel Bocier had prepared cold poached salmon, cream of fresh asparagus soup, roast rack of lamb with duchesse potatoes, pencil-thin green beans and carrot sticks, artichoke vinaigrette, fresh peach bombe and an assortment of perfectly aged cheeses with biscuits that complemented the aged port. By the time Marcel had removed the last of the china and cutlery, a total of three hours had elapsed since they had left Toronto, finding the jet almost mid-way to London. Lights were dimmed, chairs reclined and everyone, except for David, closed their eyes for a nap. Two hours later, Marcel raised the lights and brought around the sterling tray, this time piled with warmed, damp, towels spritzed with essence of vanilla. Once collected, a breakfast of Faison and Stark's favourite orange juice, omelette au fromage, fresh sliced peaches, strawberries, raspberries and blueberries lightly sprinkled with Grand Marnier, croissants, muffins, coffee and tea was seamlessly served by Marcel. Everything had barely been carefully stowed when Marcel came around and asked everyone to adjust his or her seatbelt and prepare for landing in London. Within minutes, Captain Rialto was pulling up to the private aviation terminal at Heathrow and Marcel was lowering the stairs.

Now That I'm Gone

Everyone disembarked: first to see Hermione Tilsbury safely transferred to the limousine that had pulled up to the Global Express jet; then, once she had departed, the others entered the terminal, in order for the plane to be refuelled, for the next leg of the journey to Moscow. Within forty-five minutes, everyone was back on board and the plane was taxiing down the runway. Moscow was slightly less than four hours away, with the time being filled with Stark and Faison suggesting the many historic sites available to Fort and Andrew. The fact they would have a limousine available the entire visit, with a translator and special permission to access any and all venues without waiting, whetted their appetites even more than they had originally thought.

During the nap time over the Atlantic, again while waiting in the London private plane terminal and again from take off from London until a light lunch was about to be served, two and one half hours after leaving London, David Granpré had been unobtrusively pouring over the diaries of Dr. Poyntz. At that point, David unbuckled his seatbelt and discretely motioned to Faison to join him at the back of the cabin.

Looking more serious than usual, he spoke in a low voice, "Mr. Quay, I've come across something in the diaries that I feel requires being brought to your attention. Throughout the diaries, in the margins, and beside specific dates, each carefully circled, is the single word 'THANE'. At first, it really didn't imprint on me; but, when I realized that it appears over and over, I came to the conclusion that it must have been important at least to Dr. Poyntz, if not to us. For that reason, I feel you should notify Ms. Ouellette and ask her to include the word in her briefing notes to each of the duos investigating the other cases. In their quests they may come across something that may relate to the word and, thus, unlock a critical aspect of the puzzle."

"Thank you, David, for bringing this to my attention. However, before I call Règinè, I think it would be prudent to ask Andrew if the word means anything to him."

Returning to his seat, Faison leaned toward Andrew and enquired, "Andrew, David has noted that throughout your father's diaries, the word 'THANE' constantly appears. Does it mean anything to you; do you recall your father ever mentioning the word?"

Looking puzzled, Andrew paused for a minute, attempting to recall anything and then responded, "Fai, I honestly can't remember ever hearing him use the word. Could it be a name or do you think it could be a code word?"

"Andrew, I don't have a clue what it could mean and since you don't either, I best inform Règinè Ouellette and ask her to include it with the information the other teams are using in their pursuits."

Faison picked up the telephone on the table next to him, pressed several buttons and within a few seconds he was speaking with Règinè. Once done, he sat back in the seat and made a mental note to include it in his search.

Barely had the lunch been finished when Marcel announced they would shortly be arriving at Sheremetyevo-2, Moscow's international airport. Pre-clearance had been arranged by the President's office, thus enabling the limousine to come right to the foot of the plane's stairs. Less than half an hour later the thirty-five kilometres had been covered and the five weary travellers arrived at the Hotel Metropol Moscow, on Teatralmy Road, directly across from the Bolshoy Theatre and only a stone's throw from Red Square and the Kremlin. Designed by William Walcott in 1898, in Moderne Style, the Hotel Metropol Moscow had been the site of numerous historical events from Lenin speechifying to the Second House of Soviets from the balcony in the Metropol Restaurant, to David Lean shooting scenes for his nineteen sixty-five classic, Dr. Zhivago. Thoughtfully restored between nineteen eighty-seven and ninety-one, it remains one of the truly magnificent international hotels.

Registration having been taken care of before their arrival, the party merely went directly to their suites. Andrew and Fortunato were given the Deluxe Suite adjacent to the Presidential Suite that would house Faison and Stark, with David in an adjoining suite on the other side. Nothing had been scheduled for the remainder of the day, thus allowing them an opportunity to rest until dinnertime. For that, David had pre-ordered an appropriately light dinner to be served by the hotel in the Presidential Suite's dining room, to which Faison had insisted he attend. Brandies and ports were savoured by all, in an especially pleasant and relaxed atmosphere and then all opted for an early night under the fine linen-clad duvets.

Had it not been for the concierge calling to awaken the soundly sleeping travellers, all would have over-slept. Once ablutions were complete, all re-convened for breakfast in Faison and Starks private dining room. Over a Canadian-style breakfast, having eschewed the need for a Russian breakfast, the two couples and David discussed the joys of Moscow and what Andrew and Fort would want to see; given this was their first visit. Of course, as David explained, unless they wished otherwise, he had already given instructions to their chauffer and guide as to what they should be shown. Accepting that he knew best, Andrew and Fort finished their breakfast, kissed Stark and Faison goodbye and headed for their limousine, accompanied by David.

Faison and Stark barely had enough time to finish their tea when David reappeared and tactfully reminded them that their appointment with President Putin was less than one-half hour away. After the traditional quick trip to the loo and the brushing of their teeth, Faison and Stark were helped into their coats by the already-to-go David. A quick trip down in the waiting elevator and a scant few minutes car ride found the party of three emerging from their limousine and being guided through the maze of corridors that eventually led to the President's office.

Putin and Quay had known each other since 1991, when Vladimir Putin was appointed by the Mayor of Leningrad to be his head of external relations. Quay's companies saw the trends occurring within the last days of the USSR and wanted to position so they would be in the forefront of the new Russia. Having left the KGB in 1990, Putin was the intelligent, personable type of personage Faison knew would be required to move the country into the international arena of respectability and away from their ideological quagmire to which they had confined themselves since 1917. In 1996, the new mayor of Leningrad recommended Putin to the Presidential Service, where he was rapidly appointed Chief-of-Staff. Two years later, he was named Head of the new Federal Security Bureau, followed in rapid succession to the head of the nation's Security Council. Barely a year later, President Boris Yeltsin named him Prime Minister and on the last day of that year, and the eve of the new millennium, Boris Yeltsin handed Vladimir Putin the reins of Acting President of Russia. Barely three months later, Putin was elected President, with his inauguration on May 7, 2000, attended by his personally invited guests, Faison Quay and Stark Redfearne.

Vladimir Putin, along with his personable and intelligent wife, Lyudmila, had developed an affinity for Faison and Stark from the start and that had grown to a considerable depth of respect over the years. Originally, their contact and friendship had been based on the need for each other to work within the restriction of the archaic Soviet system. Key Holdings International wanted to expand its operations to the USSR and the USSR was eager to attracted companies of that calibre. Faison felt that it was important to personally conduct the initial groundwork in order for the officials to see firsthand that he and his companies operated with a different set of ethics than most other large international companies. Faison's word was his absolute bond and he expected nothing less from the people he dealt with; that held true with the Politburo of the USSR and all officials who would be working with his companies. Any deviation from that high standard and he would personally call the leader in charge of that area. They, in turn, knew that if they didn't correct the problem, he would not hesitate to call the President, whoever that was at that moment and heads would roll. Putin had admired that modus operandi and had worked very hard to build an open and, for that time, a very honest relationship. Faison only needed to let Putin know he was coming and the red carpet was immediately rolled out, all restrictions were relaxed and business was always successfully accomplished to the benefit of both sides. Provided the Putins were in Moscow, Faison always made time to spend at least one evening with them and their two daughters, Masha and Katya, and of course their much-loved white poodle, Tosca.

As the entourage approached the ornately gilt-trimmed doors, the two armed sentries, in tandem, smartly reached for and turned the large gold doorknobs and press back to reveal the lavishly decorated office of the President of the Russian Federation. Vladimir Putin immediately moved from behind his desk, broke into a wide smile, extended both arms and began to move toward Faison.

"My dear friend, Fai, how are you doing?" Putin asked in flawless English, as he hugged Faison.

"Extremely well, Mr. President, and you?" Faison responded, always using the correct address each time they met, then reverting to their more intimate and personal form.

"Not bad…nothing that the cessation of the rebellion in Chechnya wouldn't cure." Turning to Stark, he repeated his inquiry and hugs and then extended his hand to David Granpré and cordially welcomed him.

"Let's sit down over here," Putin said while indicating an ornately gilt and brocade seating area, consisting of two two-seaters and four matching chairs.

Faison Quay sat in a single chair immediately beside Vladimir Putin, with Stark and David seated to Faison's right. They had barely seated when a side door opened and a butler entered carrying a large silver salver adorned with an ornate silver samovar and four crystal and silver teacups, in the classic Russian style. Once the tea had been served, he retreated and the pleasantries began. Over the next twenty minutes, they caught up on the principle events that had occurred in each other's family, including Putin kindly enquiring as to how Veetwo was doing. When he learned of the pending marriage between Veetwo and his fiancée, Felicia Pomeroy, he insisted that they honeymoon in Russia as his guests. Faison promised to relay the very generous, and much appreciated, offer.

Finally, Vladimir Putin enquired, "Faison, you've piqued my curiosity when David called my secretary and asked if you could visit with me on a very confidential matter. It seemed so formal, not your usual notification that you were coming to Russia and wanted to get together over dinner and some good conversation. What's up, Fai, as you say in North America? How can I help you?"

"It's very gracious of you, Vlad, to be so kind as to see us on such short notice and to be so perceptive as to our requirements. If this weren't such an important situation, I hope you know, I would never presume on our dear friendship to bother you with such matters."

Politely interrupting, Putin reassured, "Fai, you know by now that we can say anything to each other and know that we'll always hear the truth in response. Please don't ever feel restricted in how you converse with me. Outside of here, I may very well be the president of Russia, but when we are together in private, I am merely your friend, Vlad. Now what do you need from me?"

Over the next ten minutes, Faison laid out the details of the explosion and subsequent murders and then the contents of Dr. J. Merreck Poyntz' file. As soon as he mentioned Cyril Leaverage, Putin adjusted his seated position and re-crossed his legs. Further into Faison's retelling, Putin became even more noticeably restless by adjusting his shirt cuffs, straightening his tie and, eventually, coughing slightly. Faison had obviously raised a delicate matter and, now, their friendship was going to be put to the test.

Before he finished, and before Putin could speak, Faison added, "Vlad, I know that I have raised issues that, for many reasons, are better left buried. In fact, they don't really need to be actually brought fully to the surface. All I really need to know is whether there is any reason why the Leaverage's would be so nervous that any one of them would resort to murder? In order to ascertain that, I need to know if they are still spying for Russia and if not, when did they stop?"

Faison had caught everyone off guard with his blunt and non-equivocating questions. Stark and David sat transfixed, fearful to look toward Vladimir Putin. Finally Putin cleared his throat and said, "Fai, I honestly don't know how to respond. You've put me in a very difficult situation. As a dear friend, I would do anything for you, but as the President of Russia, I am afraid I'm being asked to betray my oath of office. I fully understand the gravity of the situation and how difficult it has been for you to come to me with your request, but you must appreciate my situation as well."

"Vlad, I can assure you, I do. This has been one of the most difficult decisions I've ever had to reach. Were it not that so many innocent people have died, I wouldn't think of imposing on our deep and treasured friendship; unfortunately, I could not afford the luxury of not coming directly to you for help. That said, I want you to know that neither I nor Stark or David would ever, and I stress ever, betray your friendship by revealing any details of our conversation or any information you might impart. For that matter, I don't require the details, just whether there may be justification for us to suspect that one or more of the Leaverages had reason to make certain that their past or present activities were not what they seemed."

Usually a very decisive person, Vladimir Putin sat silent and resolute for the longest thirty seconds of Faison's life. When he did speak, Faison saw a side of him that he had never seen.

"Fai, I am going to ask you to leave this with me," he said in a somewhat removed and distant tone. "I will discuss this with a few of my close advisors and meet with you again at the same time tomorrow, here, to give you an answer."

With that, Putin rose, indicating the appointment had reached its conclusion. Faison immediately stood, shook hands with Vladimir, as did, Stark and David, then turned and headed for the door. As if like magic, the doors opened as they approached, revealing the two guards on the other side being in control of the large gold knobs.

Just as they passed through the portico, Putin called out, "Don't forget dinner is at eight o'clock, Lyudmila, the girls, and, of course, Tosca can hardly wait."

Looking over his shoulder, but not breaking stride, Faison called out, "Until then, thanks so much for your time."

David had scheduled the balance of the day, before he had left Toronto. Meetings in the Presidential Suite of the Hotel Metropol Moscow with Key Holdings International employees stationed in Russia had been planned, with luncheon reserved for just the three of them; he instinctively knew Faison and Stark would want some quiet time.

From six to seven, David had not scheduled any meetings. On the dot of seven, however, he appeared in Faison and Stark's suite to assist with their toilette and dressing, in tuxedos, for their dinner with the Putins. Promptly at seven forty-five, David led them to the waiting elevator and down to the limousine primly parked at the front door of the Metropol. A quick retracing of the morning's route and they found themselves at a different entrance of the Kremlin, this time to be led to the private quarters of the President.

Throughout the casual and friendly evening, absolutely no business was raised by either Vladimir or Faison. The digital camera Stark produced, causing quite a stir for most of the hour before dinner, enthralled Masha and Katya. After dinner, the girls kissed Stark and Faison goodnight and Vlad deferred to Lyudmila and her conversation. By eleven o'clock, Faison and Stark realized everyone was in need of a good sleep so they offered their thanks for a wonderful evening, hugged and kissed all around, and bade Lyudmila and Vladimir goodnight.

The morning found the three of them, Faison, Stark and David, retracing the ritual from the day before and then, once again, sitting in the same places in the President's office. After a few warm and genuine comments about how wonderful the previous evening had been, Putin assumed a more formal tone and declared, "Fai, I, and my staff, have given your request a great deal of consideration. In essence, we are in an untenable, no-win, situation. If we admit that the Leaverages were once, or presently are, working for us, we compromise our security; on the other hand, if we don't admit to it and they were, or are, working for us, one of them may get away with four murders, and, quite possibly, even more. That said, I know you and trust you implicitly and fully accept your word as your bond. Of all the westerners, and for that matter everyone, I've ever known, you are the most trustworthy. For that reason, and the fact that my advisors also agree that it is the correct thing to do, I am going to respond to your request with the actual facts. In checking our records, your assumptions about Cyril and Lewton Leaverage were on the mark. In fact, they were working for Canada and the USSR; both sides knew from the beginning; and, both sides used them to try and fool the other side. When Lorne Leaverage assumed the mantle from his father, Lewton, he presumed things would stay the way they had been; but, the old regime quickly discovered that Lorne wasn't up to the job. Quite honestly, they found he had the brains of a brick and told him so. He pleaded to let him continue but they decided he just wasn't fit for the job. In turn, our sources in Ottawa discovered the Canadian government had reached the same conclusion. Poor Lorne was, truly, left out in the cold. From then on, we didn't communicate with him, although he tried on numerous occasions to re-establish contacts and activity. By the time I got involved, he was long gone."

"Is there any way that he could have continued in some minor manner, given that he's in Russia so frequently on business? In other words, could he now be spying for industry and not the government?"

"It's faintly possible, but highly unlikely. We know with whom he's dealing and I can assure you, except for very straightforward transactions, the people and companies who deal with him, and Leaverage's companies, think he's an idiot. From what I can determine, Grandfather Cyril was the smartest and most conniving, Lewton the most manipulative and Lorne just a fourth-generation idiot wielding a fortune, and for the most part, grossly mismanaging every aspect of it, along with the opportunites that goes with it."

Faison persisted, "Do your people feel that he is capable of murder?"

"It's strange that you would ask in such a direct way, because I asked the very same question when confronted with the report. The answer I received was 'possibly'. Dumb people do dumb things; and, he is certainly dumb. In order to maintain the status quo, he might have felt that he had to prevent anyone discovering what the family had done. The irony is neither the Canadian government nor ours could care less, since we've both known from the beginning. The only damage that could have resulted would have been within his business circles and, quite honestly, you and I both know businesses are not going to stop doing commerce with someone just because there is some espionage going on, since they all carry out some, whether it's spying on competitors or the countries they visit."

"I concur with your analysis. The unknown factor, of course, as you put it, is just how dumb is Lorne? Of course, the other factors are Cyril and Lewton and just how desperate are they to conceal their pasts. Even if they are astute enough to have determined that both governments knew of their perfidy, their friends and business associates didn't and they, quite likely, wouldn't wish for them to discover the truth."

"Just one last question," Faison added, "does the word 'THANE' mean anything to you? Could it have been the code name given to one of the Leaverages or have some other meaning within your espionage operations? You don't have to provide the details if it is, I just need to know if the word can be linked to one of them."

Putin chuckled and said, "Actually Fai, that's an easy question to answer because I specifically remember their code names, having just read them this morning, in my briefing papers, and thinking how humourous they were. Cyril was code named 'Rabbit' since his last name, Leaverage, was close to the English word, leveret, which means a young rabbit. Lewton's code name was 'Bunny', since he was the child of 'Rabbit', and Lorne was gifted with 'Cottontail', because he was bringing up the rear."

Faison and Stark burst into laughter, while David tried his very best to stifle his, since he felt that he was only there in a non-participating position.

Regaining his composure, Faison persisted, "Since it wasn't any of their code names, what about the possibility that it had some other function in your espionage undertakings?"

"As far as I know, it means nothing, but that doesn't mean that in the past it didn't. I'll check with my people and let you know if it did have any importance. If you don't hear from me, it means it didn't."

"That's very kind of you, Vlad; I really appreciate your help in this matter."

Putin concluded, "I'm sorry, Fai, that we couldn't be more definitive, but at least you've been able to learn the truth from our side. I just hope you are able to use the information to your advantage and solve this sad situation."

"Thank you, Vlad, I hope you know how very grateful I am to you for your incredible frankness and transparency. I'm also deeply aware how difficult it was for you to discuss this matter; but, I know you did so, knowing what we have discussed remains with us and will never be divulged," Faison concluded.

Standing, Putin smiled and said, "I know that, Fai. I'm just glad that I could help you and completely trust you or I wouldn't have cooperated."

Faison, Stark and David immediately stood and Faison extended his arms to embrace Vladimir as soon as he finished speaking.

"Goodbye, Vlad. Thanks so much. I'll let you know as soon as we know when our spring visit will be, so that we can schedule a little more time together. In the meantime, I'll be sure to tell Veetwo of your generous offer regarding his honeymoon."

The two embraced, as did Vlad and Stark, followed by a warm handshake between Putin and David. As the three made their way toward the door, Vladimir Putin called out, with a slight smirk on his face, "Bye the way, have your friends, Messrs. Poyntz and Fortunato enjoyed their tour of Moscow, short though it has been?"

Knowing that nothing had been said about Stark and Faison's travelling companions, Faison smiled back and joked, "I appreciate your men looking out for them and making sure they are safe. It's also good to know that some things never change, they just get slightly altered."

Putin smiled broadly, shrugged his shoulders and ended with, "You're right, Fai, some things never change. Have a safe trip home. See you in the spring."

By then the three had cleared the doors, they turned slightly in order to bid one last goodbye with a wave then continued on their way, hearing the doors to Vladimir Putin's office being closed.

The rest of the day Faison spent back at the Metropol calling the heads of companies who conduct business with Leaverage's firms in order to clarify their dealings. Knowing who Faison Quay was, and his links with the President's office, everyone whom Faison contacted demonstrated no qualms in being forthcoming, being all too aware that to do less would be the kiss of death, as far as future trade deals were concerned. In the evening, David had arranged for the five of them to enjoy a lavish dinner in the Metropol Restaurant, with its spectacular vaulted stained glass ceiling, exquisite Russian and international cuisine and impeccable service. The conversation consisted almost exclusively of Andrew and Fortunato detailing their adventures over the previous two days, making special note that no matter where they went it seemed that they were expected and didn't have to wait in any queues, nor pay for entry into anything. Being careful not to illuminate their naiveté, Faison merely explained President Putin had been pleased to facilitate their visit, omitting the fact that they had actually been under the watchful eye of the President's security staff from the minute they first left the hotel.

Following a hearty Canadian-style breakfast, Fort and Andrew went out for a few hours to visit Lenin's tomb and several other last minute places of special interest, while Faison and Stark concentrated on Key Holdings International business while David packed suitcases and made ready for their departure.

Leaving in the late morning allowed them to enjoy a leisurely lunch on board the private jet before arriving in London to refuel and pick up Mrs. Hermione Tilsbury, who was so excited to see them, she couldn't contain herself and got so flustered she tried to kiss and hug all of them at once.

David, seated next to Mrs. Tilsbury, couldn't avoid noticing the tears streaming down her face as the jet lifted off and soared over the English countryside. Patting her hand, he offered, "It must be very difficult for you having to leave after such a short visit."

"Oh, no deary, the tears aren't about leaving, they're about coming back in the first place. You see, when me 'arold and I left 'ere in 1934, England, and for that matter, London, was beautiful and all me family and friends were young. Now, that Thatcher woman 'as buggered up London to the point parts are a tip, me old neighbour'ood got bombed to smithereens so none of that exists anymore and all me family and friends are nearly all dead. All t'at said, it was bloody wonderful seeing me dear sister, Anoria, face t' face. 'cause of the big age spread, I left England before she was very old, so's I have really only known her fr'm our letters. 'opefully, we'll get a chance to see each tuther again be I croak.

"Also Mr David, please don't get me wrong, I'm much appreciative to Mr. Quay for 'aving givin' me the trip, but between y'u and me, I'd rather 'ave the sweet memories than the reality, if y'u knows what I mean."

Comforting her, David softly assured, "I certainly do understand, being a firm believer in getting the most out of each day so that I don't have to spend much time remembering the past."

Fortunato and Andrew, on the other hand, couldn't stop talking about their experiences over the last few days and how wonderful they thought Moscow was. Whether they completely forgot the real purpose of the trip, or whether they were just being discrete, electing to leave it to Faison and Stark as to when and how much they would divulge, Andrew and Fort failed to inquire as to the results of Stark and Faison's discussions with President Putin. Decidedly, Faison was relieved since he could not, nor would not, discuss any part of their meeting.

Two limousines waited for the planes arrival at Toronto's private terminal, one to whisk Mrs. Tilsbury back to reality, and the other, the stretched Rolls-Royce, to take the balance of the party to Key Mansions. Little was said as they glided through traffic, enjoying the experience of Ernie's chauffeuring skills and the classical music softly wafting through the car.

There was little daylight left by the time they reached home and Faison felt fatigued from it and, of course, the long trip. In spite of that, he didn't want to wait until the next morning to speak with Règinè Ouellette, so he excused himself and headed directly for his office.

Règinè answered after the first ring and welcomed Faison home.

"It's good to be home, but I must say I'm knackered," Faison confirmed. "Just wanted to let you know that I'll, hopefully, be dictating my summary of the trip to David first thing after lunch tomorrow and he'll have it ready shortly thereafter. How are the other cases proceeding?"

"One is finished, the second is almost wrapped up and the third one will be another day or so."

"What is your take on them so far; anything definitive that could link any of them to the murders?"

"I think it would be premature, at this point, to draw any conclusions. I'd rather wait until all the reports have been submitted. That said, from your question, I get the distinct impression that you have determined, even before you assemble your report, the Leaverages are in the clear."

"You assess incorrectly, I'm afraid, Règinè. I haven't reached any conclusion; however, I will after one or two telephone calls first thing in the morning. After that, I'll wait to hear from you as soon as the others are completed."

Before he called it quits for the day, he made one last call. The phone rang twice, "Gregor, how the hell are you? I'm sorry I haven't been in touch with you in the last few days but we've been out of the country on business. How did the canvas go of Anatole's neighbours?"

"Actually, not that well. It seems that for the most part, the neighbourhood watch motto must be 'see no evil'. One of the old reprobates who lives on the ground floor recalled that Anatole had the occasional visitor, especially in the last several weeks before his death. When pressed, he couldn't remember too much, except that he thought it was the same person each time, they were well dressed and drove a fancy car. They asked him to describe the car but it wasn't clear enough to be definitive. I took the information and checked to see what kind of car Gino Esposito drove, and then took a photo of a similar car around to show the witness. He said it might be, but couldn't be sure because, to him, most cars looked the same. I then showed him a press photo of Esposito; but, he said he never really got a good look at the visitor's face. After getting a whiff of his breath, I figured we weren't going to get anywhere with him, especially when it came to providing testimony at a trial. Sorry it didn't produce something solid."

"Not to worry, Gregor, I'll let you know what's going on from our side in the next day or so and, in the meantime, stay in touch with me if you have any breakthroughs."

CHAPTER 13

Thank goodness for friends in high places, Faison mused as he dialled Marleena Czahnivsky's Ottawa office.

"Good morning, Faison Quay speaking; is the Minister available, please."

"One moment Mr. Quay, she'll be right with you," the receptionist answered.

Faison was barely able to take a sip of tea when he heard, "Good lord, Faison, Ziam and I were just talking about you and Stark last night at dinner. We thought you'd fallen off the face of the earth. Usually by this time in the fall we've heard from David about scheduling a trip to whatever exotic island you're ensconced on that year."

"Well, my darling, so far not this year. We've been involved with trying to solve the terrible circumstances surrounding the explosion of Andrew and Fortunato's home. As a matter of fact, that is why I'm calling you. I do hope you won't mind."

"Why would I mind; isn't that what being a friend is all about?"

"Unfortunately, I require some information that, I'm sure, is classified. That said, you and the Prime Minister know that I would never ask such a favour if it wasn't extremely important. Furthermore, the information will not directly be used and no one will ever know that we have spoken about it, never mind actually having received information from you."

"Fai, enough already, both the PM and I know you well enough to not even think twice about any request. You have never, nor would you ever, abuse a friendship or a confidence. What do you require?"

"Marleena, during our investigation, the names of Cyril, Lewton and Lorne Leaverage arose. I need to know if any of them are presently acting on behalf of Canada as a spy, especially with Russia and, for that matter, any other country. In addition, I need to know if any of them were ever assigned a code name of 'THANE' and, if not, does the word hold any special meaning in Canadian espionage circles."

"Shit, Faison, you don't want much. You must know how sensitive that entire area is and, when combined with the Leaverage name, how explosive it becomes? Even though everyone in the

Ministry of Foreign Affairs and International Trade think the Leaverages are conniving, money grabbing, lowlifes, they are still the heads of one of Canada's, and of the world's, largest conglomerates. If anything ever got out that we were assisting you, being the owner and Chair of Key Holdings International, all of our heads would roll. That said, leave it with me and I'll feel out the PMO and, if I have to, the Prime Minister himself. I'll get back to you as soon as possible."

"Thanks so much, Marleena. You know that if it weren't absolutely imperative that I have the answers to those questions, I would never impose on my friendship with you or the PM. Also, it is very important that you reassure the PM, while you reassure yourself, that I will never misuse the information or release it to anyone. It is merely so that we can determine whether any of them could be involved with the explosion and the subsequent murders of four people."

Faison knew that he had just pushed his friendship with Marleena to a limit that most people would eschew, but he honestly had felt there was no alternative; after all, he had done the same thing with his friendship with Vladimir Putin.

Within thirty seconds of Faison pressing a button on his desk, David appeared carrying a green-covered steno book and a ballpoint pen.

"Yes, sir, how may I be of service?" he said while remaining standing in front of Faison's desk.

"Please be seated, David, I need to go over what you have been able to glean from the diaries."

"Actually, quite a bit and not a lot. Concerning the latter, there does not seem to be anything definitive in his diaries that would lead me to conclude that anything in them would reveal the monster who is responsible for these dastardly events. Regarding the former, I feel the diaries are rife with clues, innuendo and probably the comprehensive reasons that would lead someone to commit such crimes. My problem is I am unable to find the thread that would allow me to focus in such a manner that would lead me to successfully solving the enigma."

"What of the constant use of 'THANE', have you been able to link it with a specific person or events," Faison probed.

"It's interesting that you should pose such a question. This morning, I finally realized although 'THANE' is written next to a broad assortment of nasty, and often completely illegal, deeds outlined in detail, most frequently appearing near the very sad series of notations and memos detailing the life and death of someone encoded with the name 'POP'. He or she is mentioned throughout many years of Dr. Poyntz' diaries, with the last mention being a suicide. The strangest part of the entries is 'THANE' is written in red ink and, apparently, from the same pen, even though the time frame is over many years, as is POP, except that is written in a shade of blue that doesn't appear anywhere else in any of the diaries. The rest of the entries are written in a myriad of inks and pencil, with hand writing varying, indicating aging."

In other words," Faison extrapolated, 'THANE' and 'POP' were added all at once, whereas the events connected to 'THANE' and 'POP' were written by Dr. Poyntz over many years and not all at once."

"Precisely," David confirmed.

"I think it's time we ask Andrew for some insight." Lifting the receiver and pressing two buttons, almost instantly, Basil lifted the receiver at the other end and responded, "Yes, sir."

"Basil, would you please ask Mr. Poyntz to join me in my office and include Mr. di Palma if he is available."

Given the size of the two-floored penthouse, it took several minutes before there was a knock at the door, evoking a call from Faison to enter.

"What's up, Fai?"

"Come on in and we'll move over to the seating area where we can all be comfortable."

Faison and David sat on one chesterfield with Andrew and Fort seated opposite. They had barely gotten settled when Basil appeared with a silver tray featuring a sterling silver coffee and tea service. After pouring everyone their choices, Basil retreated and Faison began, "Andrew, do you know anyone that your father treated as their doctor, or was a friend of your father, who was named or nicknamed POP?"

"Pop?" Andrew sank into deep thought for a moment, finally smiling slightly and saying, "There was old Mr. Rabinovitz, who owned the corner convenience store. Everyone called him Pop. We all loved him. He would be so patient as we pondered which candies we would spend our allowance on; three of one kind for a shiny copper, two of something else for another copper, finally filling the wee paper bag with a grand assortment of wonderful candy. During the summer on a really hot day, I would request a Mello-Roll and admiringly watch him retrieve the vanilla ice cream, paper-wrapped, cylinder from the freezer and deftly, without touching the ice cream, peel the paper just so and then place the cylinder of ice cream upright on top of the cone. It was masterful and always thrilled all of us children."

"Good god, Andrew, I'd forgotten all about Mello-Rolls. I loved those damn things," Faison extolled.

Returning to the focus of the discussion, Faison explained, "That said, I don't think your father had Mr. Rabinovitz in mind when he made all the entries since he clearly used capitals for each of the letters instead of just for the first letter if he was referring to a specific individual who was usually called Pop. David has told me they are spread over years and involve someone your father obviously cared about. Could it be your grandfather?"

"Absolutely not. Grandfather died a long time ago and when he was alive Father would never have referred to him, either directly or indirectly, as Pop. To do so would have resulted in my Grandfather give him a smack up the side of the head. It just wasn't done in our family, even by the time Marsha and I came along."

Turning to David, Andrew requested, "David, would you mind getting my father's diaries and let me look at what you're talking about. It might help jog my memory."

"Absolutely not; it was silly of me not to have gone and gotten them, when Mr. Quay asked for you to join him. I'll be right back."

While David excused himself and went to retrieve the diaries, Faison queried, "Andrew while you were reading the diaries, did you happen to notice the use of the different coloured inks whenever your father had written POP?"

"Not only did I not notice the different coloured ink, I really didn't take note of any of the notations, choosing instead to concentrate on the substance of the actual diaries. It just never occurred to me that anything else would be of importance."

"Not to worry," Faison reassured, "we'll get to the bottom of this; it's just a matter of time."

Just then, David re-entered the office, crossed directly to Andrew and handed him his father's diaries. It was evident to all present that he was somewhat hesitant in accepting them, although he tried to conceal his reticence from everyone. He first attempted to put them in the order his father had created them, followed by a quick scanning until he came across the first sign of the strange blue 'POP'. He was well into his third diary when he froze, blanched and then slowly stammered, "Oh my god, I think I know what, or should I say who, 'POP' stands for."

"Who, Andrew?" Fort blurted out.

"The facts don't mesh with what I remember, but it appears that when Father penned 'POP' in the strange blue ink he meant his brother, my uncle. His full name was Preston Oliver Poyntz. That has to be what 'POP' stands for."

"I've never heard you mention an Uncle Preston," Fort reacted in a stunned tone. "Where did he get to? How come you've never told me you have an uncle?"

"That's just it, I don't; at least not anymore. He died of a heart attack when I was very young. As a matter of fact, he died on my twelfth birthday. He was only thirty-two when he dropped dead. After his death, Father was absolutely devastated since it was his baby brother and he had such high hopes for him."

"What do you mean by that?" Faison continued the probe, initiated by Fort.

"Uncle Preston had graduated from the University of Toronto's School of Medicine with honours. Father was thrilled and invited him to join him at his clinic. Instead, Uncle Preston decided he wanted to gain some experience first and travel at the same time, so he enlisted in the Royal Canadian Navy and soon became a Lieutenant Commander in the medical branch of the navy. From what Father said, when asked, the navy would allow medical officers the opportunity to work four years and then spend one year in civilian life in order for them to stay current with the latest technology and developments. It was while he was on the year's leave, and assigned to St. Michael's Hospital, in charge of interns, that he suddenly died. I honestly don't think Father quite recovered from the shock; never forgiving himself for letting Uncle Preston go into the military instead of joining him."

"David, would you be so kind as to pass the diaries over to me? I'd like to peruse them for a moment," Faison requested.

For the next half hour, Faison scoured the diaries from first to last, during which he made copious notes. Finally, he placed his pen back into its holder and calmly said, "Andrew, either your father lied to you about your uncle, and how he died, or he is playing some cruel joke with you now."

"What do you mean, Fai? I don't understand. Why would my Father lie to me about Uncle Preston, he loved him?"

"On that, I have no doubt. In fact he loved him so much, he systematically concealed the fact that your Uncle Preston committed suicide."

"He couldn't have," Andrew responded in typical reactionary fashion. "Father could never have kept that from Mother and she would have told Marsha and me."

"Not necessarily, Andrew. Of course, I may be completely off base. Therefore, let's review the evidence that your father conveniently left for us to discover."

Faison then proceeded to start at the very first entry where 'POP' appeared in the diaries and carefully pointed out each and every one up to and including an entry describing a suicide. Each detailed a different activity involving the nameless individual. In essence, it detailed the life of a very talented professional who lived a double life in order not to let his prominent family down or, for that matter, negate his chances to further his career, which was then in the military and afterward, hopefully, in civilian life. For many years he was very successful in diffusing suspicion by squiring around beautiful women, driving fancy cars and, in general, being a bon vivant. His world suddenly came crashing down around him when he refused to pay a street person who had tailed him for days and who then tried to blackmail him into giving him several hundred dollars to keep quiet and not tell his employer what he had discovered. The gentleman refused to succumb to bribery but soon lived to regret the decision. The next day, two plain clothes police officers arrived at the hospital where he worked and asked him to accompany them to the station. He agreed and quietly went with them in order to avoid any embarrassment. Once at the station he was told he was being charged with soliciting for the purpose of sex, attempted buggery and sexual assault. It seems the vagrant had claimed that the man had propositioned him and, when he was refused, grabbed his crotch and threatened that he would rape him if he didn't agree to accompany him to a dark alley. He further claimed he was able to break away and outrun the man, whom he then watched, from a distance, return to the hospital. It wasn't too difficult for him to ascertain the name of the individual and the fact he was a doctor on staff. 'POP' was placed in a cell and left there for several hours. Without having contacted anyone, he was suddenly released and told that an anonymous individual had paid his bail and not to worry because the record would be made to disappear. Deathly scared to ask any questions, he left, returned to the hospital and never told a soul. Less than three days later, he received a letter stating that he had been bailed out by a benefactor who expected to be compensated for his efforts, to the tune of two thousand dollars. Without hesitating, he followed the instructions and went to the bank, withdrew the money in tens and twenties, placed it in an envelope and mailed it to a post box at Postal Station A, in downtown Toronto. He thought everything was back to normal until a month later he received another letter, this time asking for five thousand dollars. Stupidly he paid it and each and every request that came to him; the amounts varied, the lowest being five and the highest ten thousand dollars. Eventually he ran out of money and started to ask your father for the money. At first, your father just thought he had lived a bit above his means and gave him the money, but when it continued, he pointedly asked him if he were in difficulty. When the answer came back in the negative, your father declined to give him any more money and admonished him to stop living such a lavish lifestyle. The next day, POP went over to Eaton's department store, wrote himself a prescription, returned to his office at the hospital and took the entire bottle of sleeping pills. He was found dead by an intern and your father was called. Not wanting to have him refused a Christian and military burial, your father cited heart failure as being the cause of death, thus averting a scandal. Unless I'm completely wrong, that man was your Uncle Preston."

Silence permeated the room for a few seconds following the completion of Faison's summary; Andrew's soft sobbing then drowned it out. Tears streamed down his cheeks and not even the caress of Fort could stem the outward show of his internal suffering and pain.

After a respectful interlude, David gently offered a box of Kleenex he had picked up from the credenza behind Faison's desk, then poured a fresh cup of coffee and placed it on the glass-topped table situated between the two chesterfields.

"Why didn't father tell me, us? Do you think my mother knew? I can't imagine she would have kept that from me, especially after I came out to her. She mustn't have known. My god, how could he have kept that to himself for so long? It must have been devastating for him to have had to deal with the fashion of his brother's death, only to have me come out to him. No wonder he was so instantly accepting; he must have feared that I might kill myself."

He took a sip of coffee, and then continued, "It all makes so much sense now. I never really knew my uncle but I always had an affinity for him. As I grew up, whenever I met someone who had known him, I pried and asked question after question about him, never really getting answers that filled the gulf. If I'd only had the chance to really know him, we might have been able to help each other deal with our sexuality, during those days of no information and ignorance."

"Andrew," Fort interrupted, "nothing can change what has happened and certainly time wouldn't have been on the side of preventing what occurred. He was a victim of the times and you were just fortunate to have been born when attitudes had changed to the point that blackmail wasn't a threat by the time you had become aware of your sexuality. In addition, sad though it may be, his death probably helped change your father's opinion so that he would embrace, rather than reject, you."

Turning to Faison, Andrew asked, "Why didn't father just write what was actually happening and include Uncle Preston's name?"

"Andrew, I think you already must know the answer to that question. As Fort just said, it was a different era when this occurred and your father was actually ashamed and fearful of people discovering the truth. He couldn't have imagined how quickly Canadian mores would change; therefore, he couldn't risk having his diaries read and people learning of your uncle's secret. Much later, I believe he realized that attitudes had changed and one day you might read the diaries and figure out about whom he was writing, especially if he added your uncle's initials beside the annotated events. You just didn't catch on because it happened so long ago you weren't used to seeing his initials used in such a manner."

Having regained his composure and finding comfort in Faison's explanation, Andrew asked, "All that makes so much sense, but I'm still at sea over what 'THANE' stands for and why did Father write it in red ink?"

"Well, Andrew, one half of the answer is clear but not the other part. I think he was indicating that whomever 'THANE' stood for, danger was involved, thus the red ink, and I really do believe he knew who it was and was saying so by using 'THANE' over and over in direct relationship to the events surrounding your uncle's tragic death."

"Do you really think that 'THANE' is behind the murders and the explosion of our home?"

"There can be no other conclusion, Andrew and, unfortunately, until I receive the reports from Règinè Ouellette I don't really feel we can add the next pieces to the puzzle. All of the cases that have been investigated are all possibly able to lead us to 'THANE'. We'll just have to wait."

Several days passed, each one starting with a telephone call from Règinè Ouellette assuring progress was being made. Each day, Règinè asked if Faison would like each case as it was completed and handed in and each day he declined. Finally, instead of a phone call, David entered Faison's office carrying a large expandable file case and asked where Faison would like it placed. Anxiously, Faison directed him to place it just to the side of his desk; and, once there, he quickly unfastened the ties and pulled out the top report. For the next three hours Faison pored over the reports, constantly highlighting in yellow marker items of special interest and recording other items on a foolscap tablet just to the right of the report.

Precisely at one o'clock, Faison closed the last report, stood and stretched, called David and asked that he let everyone know that it was lunchtime, and then quickly attended to his toilette requirements in the washroom adjacent to his office. Stark was already waiting in the Garden Room when Andrew, Fort and Faison all arrived. Anxiously, they all awaited some news as to what Faison may have discovered. It was Stark who finally broached the subject with, "Can we expect you to seal yourself in your office this afternoon or are you waiting for dessert before you let us in on your conclusions?"

"Actually, I don't think either is likely. You see, at this point I'm no further ahead than I was before I received the reports. I must have missed something when reading them because I was so certain that at least one of these cases would lead us to the murders; yet, I still haven't been able to make the link."

"You mean that after all the investigative work you and your detectives have put into this, we're still no further ahead?" Andrew said in a depressed tone.

"Actually, we're light years ahead in the sense that each of the reports indicates a deep possibility each of the individuals had solid reasons for wanting to silence Andrew and not wanting their pasts to catch up with their present. Of course, I realize they are not all guilty, so now I must revisit each analysis and look more closely for what, obviously, I have overlooked the first time. The answers are there; I'm just misinterpreting them. Personally, I think I've been allowing my emotional involvement in the case to cloud my judgement. This time I have to step back and look at everything with a more jaundiced eye. No matter how clever a felon is, clues are always available, it's just up to those seeking the miscreant to find them."

After lunch was concluded, Faison returned to his office and spent the rest of the afternoon studying in minute detail each of the reports, including his own on the Leaverages. As he proceeded, 'THANE' kept cropping up; where did that fit in; what did 'THANE' have to do with the suicide of Andrew's uncle; is 'THANE' possibly connected to any of the investigated cases; and what the hell does 'THANE' mean?

It was almost five o'clock when David knocked gently on the office door and then entered.

"Excuse me sir, a courier just arrived with an envelope addressed to you and marked 'Top Secret'," David announced as he crossed to Faison's desk.

"Thank you, David, you may open it."

David removed the letter opener, sitting on the credenza, from its leather sheath, slit the top of the envelope, pulled the message from the wrapping and immediately handed it to Faison, discretely avoiding actually seeing its contents. He then stepped around to the other side of the desk, affording complete privacy for the reading.

Barely a few seconds were required before Faison snapped, "Shit, god damn it," and then threw the paper onto the desk in front of him.

"I presume the message is regarding your enquiry about the Leaverages?" David cautiously pried.

Picking it back up, he read,

"Dear Fai:

Further to your questions regarding Cyril, Lewton and Lorne Leaverage, none of them are working on behalf of the Crown and haven't been assisting the Crown in any manner for some time. In addition, there are no records of the Crown ever using the code name 'THANE' for anyone, especially the Leaverages. Sorry this was a dead end.

Much love,

TH MAC."

It barely took several seconds for both Faison and David to realize the importance of what had just been read. Looking at each other with their eyes gaping, Faison shouted as if he'd just discovered the Ark of the Covenant, "That's it. Bloody hell, that's the answer to the puzzle. The 'TH' in 'THANE' stands for The Honourable. Whoever 'THANE' was, or is, they are known as The

Honourable; that means at onetime they were, or possibly still are, a cabinet minister."

"Should I ask Messrs. Poyntz, di Palma and Redfearne to join you or do you wish to go to them?" David instinctively enquired.

"We'll go to them, and on the way, please ask Basil to bring us a bottle of champagne and five flutes; you're joining in the celebration."

Grabbing Marleena's note, Faison led the way with David in close pursuit. While David detoured to request the bubbly, Faison made a beeline for the Grand Salon, burst through the arched entrance waving the 'Top Secret' message and announced, "Ta da; we've done it; we've cracked the code."

All three remained seated for a few seconds, in stunned silence, with Stark the first to jump to his feet and rush to embrace Faison, rapidly followed by Fort and then Andrew.

"Are you certain, Fai?" questioned Andrew, "Do you mean the secret behind 'THANE' or who the actual culprit is?"

"For now, what 'THANE' partially stands for, but I'm certain it won't take us too long to solve the last little bit of the puzzle," Faison reassured.

"Honey, don't keep us in suspense any longer, fill us in," Stark pleaded.

Just then, David and Basil entered the room causing Faison to dramatically gesture toward Basil as if he were a traffic policeman and issue the faux command, "Stop, right where you stand. There shall be no further levity until the grand announcement has been made."

Shaking Marleena's message as if it were a rumpled linen serviette, he grandly took hold of it with both hands and triumphantly announced, "In my hands I hold the solution to 'THANE', delivered to me just a few moments ago. I am going to give you three," broadly passing his hand in front of them, "the opportunity to prove your perceptiveness. Who can correctly tell us the complete name, with title, of Ziam Ngout's partner?"

Sniggering at his antics, the three quizzically looked at one another, as if there was a hidden trick to the question, and then Andrew piped up and offered, "Marleena Anastasia Czahnivsky, MP."

"Partially correct, but you don't win the grand prize of a sleep over with Gino Esposito."

Andrew quickly responded, "Well thank god I didn't, if that was the prize."

Stark picked up on the challenge and tentatively offered, "The Honourable Marleena Anastasia Czahnivsky, Minister of State for Eastern Europe."

"And the winner is the hunky man with the gorgeous face, Dr Stark Redfearne, who wins the grand prize of a hot night of sex with a very happy man by the name of Fai."

Rather than get the reaction he had hoped for, everyone in the room just stood staring at one another. Finally Andrew cautiously asked, "Fai, you're not trying to tell us that Marleena had anything to do with the explosion and murders?"

Issuing a loud hoot that echoed throughout the room, Faison replied, "Good god, no, man. I'm sorry if I gave that impression with my little game. No, no. Actually it was Marleena who essentially helped solve the enigma, without even realizing it. You see, when she sent me this note responding to a request I made of her the other day regarding some very important facets of the case, she inadvertently partially revealed what 'THANE' is all about. When she signed her name, she did so in the intimate manner she often does with all of us; that being MAC. However, this time, I presume because it was somewhat official, she added TH, indicating The Honourable, in front of MAC. At first, when I read it silently, it didn't click, but when I read it aloud to David, it struck us both at the same moment that the 'TH' part of 'THANE' stood for The Honourable. Now all we have to do is figure out whom Andrew's father knew with the initials 'ANE' and we'll have discovered who is 'THANE.'"

"You're brilliant," gushed Stark.

"He's right, you are brilliant," added Fort. "Andrew, can you think of anyone with the initials 'ANE'.

"Not off hand, but let me recover from this bombshell and then I'll don my thinking cap."

"In the meantime," Faison interjected, "Basil, would you be so kind as to pour the champagne? I do believe a celebration is called for."

The balance of the evening was enjoyed relaxing over an elegant dinner and warm and witty conversation; enjoyed by all except Andrew who, although he ate and conversed, appeared slightly distant and somewhat pensive, in spite of being urged by Faison to relax and enjoy the evening, since they could wait until the next day to concern themselves with finding the solution to whom the initials 'ANE' belonged.

Upon awaking, Stark could hardly wait to tell Faison of the idea that had come to him just before going off to sleep and was even more excited when Faison concurred. As soon as the meal was completed, Stark excused himself and rushed to his office, quickly grabbing his personal telephone directory and thumbing down the side index until he reached the letter E, at which he flipped it open and fingered down until he reached, Easton, Christopher. Dialling the number beside the name, he was rapidly connected to a voice at the other end saying, "The Ontario Legislative Library, Christopher Easton speaking."

"Chris, it's Stark Redfearne. How are you doing?"

"Just great, Stark, but totally surprised to hear from you at this time of the year. Where are you calling from?"

"Actually, you won't believe it, but we're still in TO."

"Are you both okay?"

"Fine, except we've found ourselves caught up trying to solve this mess surrounding the explosion of Andrew and Fortunato's home and I need your help."

"That was terrible, what happened. We had just been to their place a few weeks before Andrew's birthday party; it's so difficult to believe that it's now a pile of rubble. I'd be happy to help you, no matter what it concerns. What do you need?"

"Christopher, I need to know if there has ever been a cabinet minister with initials 'ANE'. Can you check the records, when you get the time, and let me know?"

"I'd be happy to look. Is it alright if get back to you a little later in the morning? I'm presently conducting a computer search for the Speaker of the House and I don't want to piss him off with any delays."

"Not a problem, Chris, I'm just so appreciative of your assistance. I'll be here; you have my number."

"I'll be calling as soon as possible. Ciao."

"Thanks and bye."

Not wanting to have Fort and Andrew sitting around stewing, waiting for Stark to get a response, Faison insisted they accompany him for a quick trip to the Four Seasons for a round of morning coffee or tea. He'd missed going as of late and felt it would be a good tonic for the three of them. Stark, on the other hand, stayed close to the phone and attempted to read the day's edition of the Toronto Star. Finding that his mind was wandering, he went to the kitchen and made himself a cup of coffee, much to the chagrin of Basil who entered just as Stark was exiting the kitchen with his coffee. Next he wandered into the Garden Room, the translucent roof having been closed weeks earlier, thus continuing to provide an amiable setting for the multitude of tropical and semi-tropical plants, checked on the Koi slowly swimming around the pond and counted the number of different colours of hibiscus blooming. Coffee finished, he slowly made his way back to his office, turned to the crossword puzzle in the newspaper, still spread across his desk, and speedily polished it off. Time seemed to be stalled, the morning taking forever to pass.

It was approaching noon when David knocked and entered.

"Sir, Mr. Christopher Easton of the Ontario Legislative Library just called and asked me to extend his apologies for being so slow in getting a response back to you. Figuring that you would like the information in hard-copy form, he has emailed it to you. Would you like me to recover it for you?"

"No, thank you, David, I'll get it right now. However, please let me know as soon as Mr. Quay and Messrs. Poyntz and di Palma get home."

"Absolutely, sir," and with that David left the office and closed the door.

Any other time Stark would have turned his computer on the very first thing upon entering his office; but, he hadn't wanted to bother with email and had, therefore, left it closed down. Tapping his fingers on the desk in an agitated state didn't speed the start-up process, but it helped him to cope. Finally the desktop appeared and he impatiently clicked on the small white envelope icon with 'e-mail' under it and almost instantly the 'In-Box' of Outlook Explorer appeared. There, at the top of the list, was the email promised from Christopher Easton and in the window below the actual message.

It simply stated:

> Sorry for the delay. Unfortunately, I was only able to find three who matched the requested combination of 'ANE'.
> They are:
> Arthur Nevin Endersby – 1898 - 1907;
> Alice Nancy Eden – 1958 - 1966;

Now That I'm Gone

Anthony Newton Earlton – 1970 - 1985
Hope the list helps.
Chris

Stark sat transfixed, the name Anthony Newton Earlton seemingly standing a meter high and flashing. It had to be a relative of Robert Earlton.

Startled by the telephone, he lifted the receiver to hear David report that the limousine had just pulled into the circle.

Excited to the point he could hardly contain himself, Stark rushed to the elevators and shrieked when the door opened and Faison, Andrew and Fort step out, "I've solved the last part of the puzzle and I guarantee that none of you will be able to guess who 'ANE' stands for and how they're linked to Andrew and the murders."

"You're certainly right with the first part of your statement, my darling. If any of us were able to figure out who belonged to the initials 'ANE' we wouldn't have been sipping coffee and tea at the Four Seasons. As for the second part, unless you want to be pummelled by the three of us, right here, you better cut to the core."

"'ANE' stands for Anthony Newton Earlton and, if I'm not mistaken, he must be a relative of Robert Earlton, MPP."

"Oh my god. Do you mean to tell me my life-long friend, Carlton Pankhurst's new lover, Robert Earlton, is behind all of this tragic mayhem?" Andrew slowly stated, in total disbelief.

"It certainly appears that way," Stark confirmed.

"But why? What have I ever done to him; I hardly know the man?"

Finally interjecting, Faison concluded, "Andrew, we have always been fairly certain your father's diaries were somehow the cause of all of this. Uncovering that Robert Earlton is more than likely behind these acts makes quite a bit of sense given that he is an up-and-coming star in the Tory government's firmament and, thus, would not want the contents of those diaries linked to him and his family. He was present at your birthday party and, I recall, very interested in the conversation surrounding your father's bequest to you. Do you remember how curt he became when he told you 'to get on with your life'?"

"Yes, as a matter of fact, I do, and how he queried me about who owned the patients' files. But I still don't see the connection between him and anything outlined in the diaries."

"I am certain that we will discover his relative was behind the blackmailing of your uncle and, ultimately, the cause of him taking his life. At the very least, blackmail, by a former prominent politician who belongs to the family of an aspiring politician, is not something most contenders would want publicized. Robert panicked when he heard you were going to thoroughly review your father's file; he knew what his family had been up to and was certain that your father had figured it out and meant the Earlton family when you cited blackmail by politicians. He couldn't risk having you unravelling the secret, especially since he didn't know how much dirt the diaries contained and what you would do with the revelation once uncovered."

"If that's the case, how do we prove the connection?" Fort asked.

"We are now going to have to go back in time and find out as much as we can about the Earlton family and, in particular, Anthony Newton Earlton and Robert Earlton," Faison declared.

CHAPTER 14

The fusion of newly acquired information, with Faison's dedicated persistence, created a volatile impetus that stimulated the two couples, plus David, into a vigorous whirlwind of activity. Although Faison was aware of the Earlton family, and the anecdotal rumours surrounding them over the years, he was not cognizant of the detailed machinations of the most recent scion, Robert, never mind his predecessors. With an open mind, he set out to reveal the intimate minutiae surrounding the basis of the family's affluence and influence.

Stark contacted Detective Sergeant Gregor Ferguson and asked him to scout around to quietly determine if there had ever been an arrest of Andrew's uncle, Preston Poyntz and if so, who were the arresting officers, when did the arrest occur and what was the disposition of his arrest? While Gregor proceeded to obtain the answers to those questions, Stark concentrated on speaking with politicians, past and present, which may have a story to tell, off the record, involving the misdeeds of the Earlton dynasty.

Being the most familiar with the vast collections of Dr. Poyntz' records, it fell to Andrew and Fortunato to re-scour each and every file with the goal of discovering references to any member of the Earlton clan or of activities similar to those surrounding the suicide of Andrew's uncle.

David volunteered to reread the entire collection of diaries, while applying the newfound knowledge of Uncle Preston and the Earlton family. It was hoped his reinterpreting of entries might bring fresh information to the surface and clarify the messages Dr. Poyntz was, obviously, attempting to convey.

Each evening, after dinner, the five sleuths would gather in the Grand Salon and listen to the concerns, disappointments, and accomplishments of each other's day. By the third evening, what had previously appeared as a blurred mosaic was taking shape as a clear and definitive photograph of a warped and corrupt family, totally lacking in morals or scruples.

As a result of numerous telephone calls to a number of Toronto's most politically and socially astute doyens, Faison confirmed his initial reaction to Robert Earlton and his most recent qualms regarding the Earlton family. Diabolical, scheming, ruthless, untrustworthy, shallow and dangerous were just a few of the negative adjectives used by the respondents concerning the Earlton lineage. During his quest, not once did Faison hear one person defend them or say something positive; to the contrary, he merely had to mention the name to evoke vitriol and disgust. When pressed, the universal response, when asked if any Earltons, past or present, had engaged in illegal activities, was an unhesitating affirmative. Loan sharking, blackmail, and bribery, both giving and receiving, were merely a few of the criminal activities on which the family had long relied. Applying that information to the encoded events Dr. Poyntz had notated, surrounding his brother's tragic demise, reinforced Faison's original assumptions; the Earltons had, and would, stop at nothing.

Detective Sergeant Gregor Ferguson had delved far beyond what Stark had expected and produced information that was not only vital in explaining how the arrest of Andrew's uncle was covered up, but also the scope of the operation employed in the process. Running a computer search of Preston Poyntz had been quick and easy and produced a truncated record; it listed his arrest and charge, but failed to list the disposition. The only clue there might be more to the file was a notation by Internal Affairs that they had reviewed the file almost six months afterward. Realizing the only way a charge could be made to disappear was with the help of someone on the force, Gregor went directly to Internal Affairs and inquired as to what their interest had been, way back then. At first, he was told there was no way anyone would be able to go back that far; when he pressed, they told him the files were sealed; when he continued to press he was firmly told he was treading on thin ice and should back off. That was the wrong thing to tell Gregor Ferguson. With hackles raised, he went directly to the Chief, whom he knew was trying desperately to bring about openness in the force. Once he explained that the information he sought was crucial to a murder investigation, the Chief agreed to speak with Internal Affairs and find out what was being withheld from Gregor. He would then determine if the information was germane to the investigation and hand it over if it was. To say the Chief was ashen when Gregor returned the next day would be an understatement, thus impressing on Gregor the gravity of the information before the Chief said a word. The files had revealed, long before the Chief or Gregor were associated with the force, that a Desk Sergeant working out of the old central downtown station had been caught accepting bribes in exchange for notifying a prominent politician each time a well known individual was arrested and brought to his station. One phone call by the Sergeant and the politician would send a flunky to retrieve copies of the arrest papers and pay the Sergeant for making the charges disappear and releasing the person who had been arrested. Those papers were then used as the threat in blackmailing the released individual. When confronted, the Sergeant denied everything, refused to reveal any information and then abruptly resigned. Rather than prosecute him, Internal Affairs decided to do nothing, thus avoiding a potential scandal; after all, had they pursued it, they didn't know where it would lead and they weren't willing to take a chance. When Gregor mentioned to the Chief his concerns that the Earlton family might have been behind the scheme, the Chief warned him that since they had no proof of any connection to anyone and it was too long ago to go back and investigate, he was forbidden to insinuate any connection between those events and the Earltons.

Fortunato and Andrew's re-examination of the files had been reluctantly undertaken, feeling it was a waste of time since they had already been closely studied the first time. Their attitudes changed quickly when they started to discover notations similar to what Andrew's father had made in his diaries concerning his brother. Threats of blackmail, reports of bribes, fears for their life, paranoia that they were being followed, insomnia brought on by numerous telephone calls in the middle of the night with no one on the line when answered, all appeared scattered through the files of famous patients. At the time of the original entries, his father had not discovered the commonality of the patients' concerns and after his brother's death had concentrated only on encoding his file, never going back to link the others to the despicable behaviour.

David applied the newly interpreted codes and awareness to the diaries and discovered similar entries throughout, much the same as had Fort and Andrew.

It was time to call Gregor Ferguson and have him fully briefed on what had been discovered, in addition to what he had provided.

Gregor happily responded, arriving within twenty minutes of receiving the invitation. Over the next hour, Faison concisely detailed everything that had been garnered, including the reports on each of the four cases. When he finished the recap, and before he could tie all of it together, Gregor declared, "I presume you've reached the same conclusion I have, that Robert Earlton is behind the murders and explosion?"

"Unequivocally. We all concur; however, you must agree that, although we have an abundance of anecdotal evidence, it remains just that. Our challenge is to now directly link him to the events and, with Marislav Anatole dead, that is going to be extremely difficult. Our only hope is to locate who killed him, attempted to kill Andrew and did kill Mrs. Margaret Palgrave."

"Unfortunately you are completely correct. Thus far, I have hit nothing but dead ends, as has Detective Ng."

"It's just a desperate stab in the dark, Gregor, but has Detective Ng checked on all of the security cameras spanning Avenue Road and Cumberland to Bay Street and Cumberland," Faison offered? "Depending on the angle that they are set, oft time they not only capture the entrances of buildings but the streetscape as well. Since we know the date and time of Mrs. Palgrave's murder, it's possible one or more cameras will show the white Caravan we believe was involved."

"Just hold a minute and I'll check with him."

Locating Ng's number in his cellphone's memory, he anxiously pressed call. "Hi, it's Gregor Ferguson. A quick question for you; did you happen to check the security cameras along Cumberland Street, after Margaret Palgrave's murder, to see if any of them caught the white Caravan?"

After a short pause, Gregor continued, "Would you get on it right away and let me know if you find anything? This is a long-shot but, possibly, our only chance."

Once Gregor had finished, Faison asked, "Have there been any additional clues emerge from the investigation into Anatole's murder that maybe you've forgotten to mention?"

"I wish there were, Fai, but honestly we've been over every possible aspect of his death, from the place where his body was discovered, to his truck, his apartment, as you remember, and even attempted to lift DNA from the murder weapon. Absolutely nothing."

"What about his cellphone records? Have you thought about checking his cellphone records over the last week of his life? There's a good chance he spoke with whoever it was who was paying him to kill Andrew."

Sheepishly, Gregor responded, "Shit, I didn't and I bet no one else has either. Let me check with the other members of the investigation team and, if they haven't, we will."

"We have to think very carefully to determine if there is anything else that we've overlooked. As you know, all too well, it's the little things that make the difference in solving a case and this one is only going to reach a satisfactory conclusion if we don't overlook anything. I, for one, will continue to approach the solution from the Robert Earlton angle, while you tackle these final aspects of Anatole's murder. Maybe from the dual tactic, we'll finally connect all the dots and put an end to this perpetrator's freedom."

"I totally agree. Stay in touch, as I will. By the way, thanks for trusting me enough to furnish me with all of the information you've uncovered thus far." Winking, he concluded, "Of course, I could arrest you for obstruction of justice and withholding information sensitive to a criminal investigation, but you and I know how far that would get and I much prefer working the way we do than in the official manner. Furthermore, you know you're much too sexy for me to sacrifice you to those miscreants in the penal system," Gregor concluded as he made his way to the door.

Laughing in response, Faison added, "Yeah, right. Of course I'd gag you with you know what, if you ever tried that, so you'd be unable to talk anyway."

As he passed through the door, he called back over his shoulder, "Promises, promises. That's your way of keeping me on your side; the promises of things to come."

Always enjoying a benign flirt, Faison blew him an exaggerated kiss as the door closed behind Gregor.

More than twenty-six frustrating hours passed before Faison again heard from Gregor. Nothing he had been able to probe connected Earlton to any of the murders. Therefore, when David announced Gregor was wishing to speak to him, Faison took a deep breath and hoped for a miracle.

"Gregor, I truly hope that you've got something, anything, for me. We've hit a dead end on our part."

"Actually, it is a miracle and one I never expected. When I ask Detective Ng to check the security cameras, I only mentioned

Cumberland Street, and at first that's all he checked. Apparently, there were fourteen cameras along that one long block between Avenue Road and Bellair, but there were five more in the short block between Bellair and Bay Street. Out of those nineteen cameras, three showed bits and pieces of a white Caravan driving that route at the exact time of Mrs. Palgrave's murder. Unfortunately, nothing that revealed anything more than the outline of a driver alone in the van. Try as he could, there was no way to bring up the licence plate. He then had a brilliant idea. As you know, at the bend several blocks up Bay Street, where it curves to the west, sits the Infiniti dealership. Ng took a gamble and checked to see where their security cameras were aimed. It turned out that one inside was aimed directly at the front door, with Bay Street in the background. After careful study by our forensic photographic section, one frame at a time, and digitally enhancing, we were not only able to spot the white Caravan but track it as it came up Bay Street and into direct vision. From that, we lifted the plate number and track it back to the owner."

"Gregor, that's tremendous. To whom is it registered?"

"None other than one of Leaverage's companies. When initially confronted, the manager of the division played dumb; but, when he was told that he was going to be charged with hindering a police investigation and withholding evidence, he spilled the beans like a nervous Boston cook."

"Alright, now that I'm on tenterhooks, don't keep me in suspense, what else?"

"Oooh, I love it when you talk dirty," Gregor dared to joke, "but not now; wait until this is over," he continued with a snicker.

"Ya, ya, and your dog too. Now what else do you have for me, and I don't mean what you'd like it to mean?"

"Very well, on a serious note, the manager allowed that he had been ordered by Lorne Leaverage no less, to provide a fellow with a thick Russian accent the loan of a vehicle and not to ask any questions. He did what he was told and hasn't seen the Caravan since."

Anxiously, Faison cut in, "Have you spoken to Lorne Leaverage yet?"

"No. I wanted to check with you first and strategize how you wanted to proceed, even though I know I shouldn't even be involving you in this."

"I appreciate your candour and your courtesy, but I can assure you, I will not allow you to be compromised during this investigation. Above everything, you represent the police and I merely want to do everything within my resources, both personal and financial, to assist you in apprehending the people responsible for what's happened. As for the next step, I do believe, from everything I've been told, Lorne Leaverage is a weak and spineless twit who will cave in faster than a hooker has an orgasm. I say cave in because I just can't believe that he is fully responsible for everything that's happened and, if I'm correct, will implicate who is really behind this desperate and pathetic chain of events. I honestly can't imagine how Leaverage is connected to Earlton, but in my deepest being, I now feel it. Of course, what I sense and what you can prove can be, and probably are, light years apart. To that end, I sense that if you confront Leaverage with the fact that you plan to charge him with the first-degree murder of four people and planting an explosive device leading to a death, he will capitulate and implicate Earlton."

"I'm glad that you have reached the same conclusions since I fully concur and had basically planned to conduct the next phase of the investigation exactly along that path. I'll be in touch as soon as I am finished bringing Leaverage to the station and informing him of my plans to charge him."

Smiling, Faison interjected, with a chuckle, "It will be very interesting which high-powered Bay Street lawyer he grabs to defend him."

"Doesn't matter who he gets, I'll nail that son-of-a-bitch so hard he'll think he's been to an orgy with a gay football club."

Faison so wanted to give Andrew and Fortunato some good news; but, he settled for merely telling Stark, since he didn't want to heighten their hopes, only to be dashed if Gregor was unable to make everything stick. That fear was proven unnecessary when the next morning, just after eleven, David announced that Gregor was waiting in the reception hall and would like to meet. After being quickly ushered in, Gregor gushed as he came through the door, "You were right, on every single aspect. Lorne Leaverage crumbled like a stale cake, claiming he was merely a dupe and implicated Robert Earlton as the mastermind behind the entire botched plan. According to Leaverage, Earlton convinced him that Andrew's father had amassed information that was detrimental to the Leaverages and unless he helped put a stop to the information getting out, their family would be ruined. For a while, Lorne Leaverage was so taken in, he asserts, he honestly thought Earlton was truly a lifesaver, thus he was willing to acquiesce to Earlton's bidding."

Elated, Faison rushed around his desk, embraced Gregor and whooped, "Halleluiah, finally a concrete breakthrough. Please, sit down and tell me to what he's admitted and to what he accredits to Robert Earlton."

"Basically, as I said, he blames everything on Earlton, but under strong questioning, he did admit that he had provided the thug who recruited Marislav Anatole and then killed him, in order to avoid detection."

Faison pressed, "What about the sarin; that's not something one can easily obtain? Did he admit to providing that?"

"As a matter of fact, he did. He said that he had smuggled some back on a recent trip from Russia, just in case things got out of control."

"It sounds like he was out of control, long before he went to Russia." Faison astutely added, "Did he tell you where to find the person who hired Anatole, murdered him, and in an attempt to murder Andrew, ended up killing innocent Margaret Palgrave?"

"Yes and yes," Gregor triumphantly added, "and Tomas Karparov is now under arrest and charged with the first-degree murder of Marislav Anatole and Mrs. Margaret Palgrave."

"That's the best news I've had in weeks. By the way, who's Karparov and how did he get involved in all of this?"

"It turns out that Lorne Leaverage used him as a body guard whenever he was in Russia on business. Eventually, he thought he might be of use to him back home, so he arranged a work permit for him and brought him to Canada as a very grateful émigré who was more than willing to carry out his dirty work."

"That's wonderful news, Gregor, but what about Robert Earlton, have you arrested him?"

"Actually, we're trying to locate him. I visited his home and discovered some very reluctant staff, which were obviously scared to death and kept saying they didn't know where he was. Just in case they tried to warn him, I've placed an officer there to make certain they don't place any telephone calls to him. In the meantime, we are trying to track him down."

"Why didn't you call me, I could have located him with one phone call?" Faison chided.

"Of course, I should have known that you'd know Carlton Pankhurst." Gregor said in a somewhat exasperated manner.

Picking up the receiver on his desk, Faison pressed Carlton's two-digit speed-dial and within several seconds was speaking, "Carlton, this is Fai."

After a slight pause, he continued, "Fine thank you. Sorry to be so terse Carlton, but I have a very important request to make and it requires your blind trust in me, and the utmost secrecy and discretion from you. Without providing any details until later, can you trust me unequivocally enough to allow me to proceed?"

Without hesitating, Carlton responded, "Fai, I've known you for years and have never had any cause to doubt anything you ever said; why would I at this point? If you need my assistance, I am more than willing to give it, and to do so without question."

"Carlton, I appreciate that more than you'll ever know. That said, I'm about to ask you something that will probably turn your life upside down, and for that, I'm truly sorry."

"My god, Fai, what could be so serious that it would cause that?" Carlton asked incredulously.

"Where is Robert Earlton?" Faison bluntly asked.

Without hesitating to realize the connection to the preamble Faison had provided, he offered, "At his chalet at Georgianview Estates, on top of Blue Mountain, just north of Collingwood."

Before Faison could respond, Carlton caught his breath and gasped, "Fai, what's going on? Why do you want to know where Robert is?"

"Carlton, I prefaced all of this with a warning that you'd have to trust me and, now that I've asked you, I'm going to insist that you trust me for several hours. In doing so, you must promise not to try and contact Robert. I promise you that I will be back to you as soon as I can. In the mean time, let me send one of my cars over for you and you can come back here and wait with Stark."

"Fai, for god sake, please tell me what's going on," he plaintively cried.

"Carlton, trust me, as your friend. My car will be there in a matter of a few minutes. Now, I must go and remember, I beg you, don't call anyone about this; it's a matter of life and death."

Hanging up, Faison dialled David and ordered a car to be sent to pick up Carlton Pankhurst and bring him back to Key Mansions. In addition, he asked David to have Ernie downstairs in ten minutes and the Key Security helicopter ready to rendezvous with them at the sports field of Upper Canada College in twenty minutes, to fly to

Collingwood's Blue Mountain. Faison, being one of the most generous benefactors of Upper Canada College, had long negotiated the privilege of being able to land and take off from the sports field of the college, as long as he gave enough warning that students and faculty could be cleared off the field. He used it very rarely, but always showed his deep appreciation afterward.

Turning to Gregor, Faison suggested, "Let headquarters know that we are flying by my helicopter to the meadow just to the north of Georgianview Estates, on top of the Mountain, next to the north ski run. Also ask them to notify the Collingwood police, as well as the Ontario Provincial Police, and have them meet us there. That way they will know what the hell they are there to do. I'll stay out of the way, but, you know how I am; you use my toys, I get to play too."

Moving toward the door, Gregor flipped his cellphone open, dialled and almost immediately started to issue instructions. Gregor and Faison were met by David at the elevator and furnished with their coats. While assisting Faison with his, David assured him Ernie was already downstairs and the helicopter would be arriving at roughly the same time they would be at the sports field.

The flight was just shy of forty minutes and was met by two cars from each of the Collingwood Police Department and the OPP. Upon alighting, Gregor explained in detail the nature of the situation and requested that he be allowed to approach the chalet by himself, while the rest of the contingent remain secreted. Once everyone was in position, Gregor emerged from behind a garden shed near the front of the property and nonchalantly made his way up the fieldstone path. As he neared the covered porch, he called out Robert's name and introduced himself as Gregor Ferguson, carefully avoiding the Detective Sergeant designation. When there was no response, he cautiously mounted the stairs, crossed the porch and rapped on the door. After several seconds, he rapped again and then called out Robert's name, once again. With no response heard, he sidled, with his back to the wall of the house, across to the window to the right of the door and gingerly bent his head so he could glance through the window. A full view of the living room afforded Gregor the opportunity to realize the reason for the lack of response. Spread on the bearskin rug next to the rustic chesterfield laid the body of Robert Earlton, a rifle still clasped in his right hand. Blood was splattered across the furniture behind him, as well as the wall and chest of drawers situated eight feet beyond where he must have stood when he had pulled the trigger.

Gregor slumped back against the chalet facing and beckoned the rest of the backup to come. Sensing what had occurred; Faison rushed to Gregor and put his arm around his shoulder.

"Damn, Fai, I hate it when things end in this manner. Usually, it could have been prevented and because of that, I always blame myself. As it is, because he took his life, there will be many questions that might never get answered."

"If anyone is to blame it is I. I trusted Carlton not to warn him; but, I have to presume that he disregarded my request and called him."

Gregor and the other police officer preceded Faison into the chalet; but, the instant he entered, Faison noticed the cordless telephone lying on the hardwood floor just to the side of the body. Carlton must have called and warned him.

Gregor arranged with the on-sight police to do all that was necessary at the chalet and then ship the body back to the provincial coroner's office in Toronto, in order that the autopsy would be quickly conducted there. He just wanted Robert Earlton and his trail of perverted horror put behind them.

Once in the helicopter, Faison called David and enquired as to Carlton and his demeanour. After a short conversation, of which Gregor was not privy, Faison, in a louder voice told David they were on their way back and would be home within the hour.

Little was said during the flight back to Toronto, but once the helicopter had landed, Faison turned to Gregor and pleaded, "I know you're pissed off that Carlton, more than likely called and warned Earlton; but, rather than acting on your instinct to charge him with interfering with a criminal investigation or something worse, please consider how distraught he was and how, in the long run, he did everyone, including the Crown, who now doesn't have to prosecute Earlton, a big favour. Let's direct our efforts in exposing the Earltons for all their past misdeeds and nailing Lorne Leaverage with the appropriate punishment, he so rightfully deserves."

"You're correct that I'm pissed off that I couldn't bring that bastard back and make him face the charges against him; but, I also really can't blame Carlton Pankhurst for being blinded by his new-found paramour. How could he have known what heinous crimes had resulted from the person he loved? I'm certain he'll be in enough pain to last his lifetime, once he learns of Earlton's duplicity."

"Thanks, Gregor, for taking the high-road," Faison conveyed with a smile and hug, which Gregor returned.

It was dark by the time Ernie discharged Faison and Gregor at the front door to Key Mansions. During the drive, Gregor had accepted Faison's invitation to join him in telling Andrew and Fortunato the reign of terror that had been forced upon them was now over. Gladly, Gregor had accepted.

David and Basil greeted them when they emerged from the elevator, with David explaining, "Sir, I haven't told Mr. Redfearne or the others that you were close to home, since I reasoned you would want to surprise them with, what I anticipate is, joyous news."

"It is, and I do appreciate your intuitive sensitivity. Are they in the Grand Salon?"

"They are, indeed, sir, and Basil has champagne chilled and ready. We'll give you a moment and then we'll bring it in."

Faison thanked David and proceeded, along with Gregor, to the Salon. Startling them with his loud greeting and wide grin, Stark was the first to jump to his feet and rush over to give Faison a big hug and kiss, anticipating that good news was about to be revealed. Andrew and Fort were somewhat more hesitant, preferring to cautiously wait to be informed, rather than hold out hope, only to be dashed. Faison quickly informed them of the afternoon events and assured them that it was finally over.

The only comment Andrew could utter through the, not unexpected, tears that followed was, "How ironic that the scion of the family that caused my uncle to commit suicide took his own life, rather than confront his and his family's scurrilous actions."

Fort followed closely behind Andrew with his own lachrymose purge. After what seemed like an eternity, their horror was over and they were free to start putting their lives back together.

It had been a wonderful day.

EPILOGUE

Over the next few months, an air of normalcy once again settled over the Quay/Redfearne home. Stark and Faison had departed shortly after the arrests and suicide for their winter escape to a luxurious villa David had secured for them on St. Lucia.

Weary from the past months and the ordeal his father's files and diaries had caused him, Andrew had decided not to wait the full year before reporting to Rolly Witherspoon as to the disposition of the bequest. Fort had accompanied him to the meeting, during which Andrew recounted everything that had occurred since he had been saddled with the accursed gift. Once he concluded his dissertation, Rolly smiled and told him he was now a very wealthy man. It turned out that Andrew's father had serious doubts about his son's ability to act in a positive fashion, when provided with an opportunity that could go either way. Had Andrew used the information contained in the files and diaries to blackmail or degrade the patients and friends mentioned, Rolly had been instructed to turn him over to the authorities. By acting in a positive and diligent manner, Andrew had been rewarded with a bequest from his father in the form of the entire balance of his estate, which amounted to two million, nine hundred and sixty-six thousand, eight hundred and three dollars and thirty-seven cents. Andrew was now, indeed, a very wealthy man. Needless to say, he and Fort required a few moments to recover before Andrew could muster the focus necessary to sign the requisite paperwork.

The very next day, Andrew and Fortunato telephoned their respective employers and told them they were taking unpaid leaves of absence. Following that, they approved the blueprints for their new home and then immediately left onboard the Global Express private jet, having accepted the invitation Stark and Faison extended to them, to join them on St. Lucia for the remainder of the winter.

It was a wonderful winter.

ADDITIONAL
Faison Quay Mysteries
By
Michael James Stewart

In The Absence Of Passion
~ Second In The Series ~

Paris Police Inspector Gilbert Beaubien's frustrated efforts to solve the murder of an odious, yet famous, Louvre art restorer, is inextricably intertwined with world-renown, multi-billionaire, Toronto-based, Faison Quay VI, and his quest to locate the missing award-winning photojournalist, Passion Pomeroy, mother of Faison's son's fiancée.

Utilizing his vast wealth of contacts and money, Faison travels across Europe in his attempt to unravel the deepening mystery of Passion's disappearance and an increasing number of seemingly unrelated murders.

Fast paced and, oft-times, humourous, the story presents the reader with an abundance of clues, while informing and challenging them to solve the deepening mystery, In The Absence Of Passion.

Narcissus' Reflection
~ **Third In The Series** ~

Accused of systematically killing his family, Neith Donacon turns to the only person who believes in his innocence, David Granpré, Majordomo extraordinaire to world-renown, multi-billionaire, Toronto-based, Faison Quay VI.

David's unwavering belief is all that keeps Faison pursuing the truth when every new clue points assuredly at Neith.

Faison's quest takes him on a twisted, international, path of diamonds and demons; and, in the process, inadvertently endangers the lives of his family and friends.

The reader is once again treated to a multiplicity of clues that provide them with the opportunity to try to best Faison as he races to free Neith, by finding Narcissus' Reflection. ➡ ➡ ➡

One By One
~ Fourth In The Series ~

A series of supposedly natural and accidental deaths causes the thirteenth Duke of Exeter to become a recluse and fear that he will be next to die. Each time he experiences chest pains, his doctor accuses him of imagining them or becoming a hypochondriac and his children are certain he is overreacting or, even worse, entering senility.

The arrival of his dear friends the world-famous Faison Quay, VI, and Dr. Stark Redfearne affords His Grace the opportunity to confide his fears to his guests and enlist their help in proving him correct.

Faison calls upon his wits and wealth to unravel the seemingly unrelated deaths and solve, before it is too late, why The Duke of Exeter's friends are dying One By One.

The First Stone
~ Fifth In The Series ~

Although The First Stone is based on the files of the world famous Faison Quay's exploits solving crimes, which directly or indirectly involve friends, it is unlike any of the other Faison Quay murder mystery series because of its' uniquely 'dark' edge.

Faison Quay's friend, Detective Sergeant Gregor Ferguson, of the Toronto Police Service, is initially assigned to investigate the discovery of a man's body, which had been found in a City of Toronto garbage bin outside the Abbey of Perpetual Blessings. In spite of discovering the man had been missing for twenty-seven years, Gregor is ordered to stop the investigation when the Coroner announces the cause of death to be Cancer.

Not satisfied that he must abandon the case, but unable to officially continue investigating, Gregor asks Faison Quay if he will continue. Faison agrees and immediately involves the full force of one of his many companies, Key Security International, to assist.

Faison Quay quickly discovers a web of nefarious situations that only he can bring to bay, before The First Stone.

Harcourt's Legacy
~ Sixth In The Series ~

Following the inaugural party of the supposedly impenetrable estate of Faison Quay scion, Faison Quay VII, fondly known as Veetwo, and his wife, Felicia, eight friends and family are abducted as they leave the estate. With no clues, and, seemingly, no reason behind the kidnappings, Faison mobilises his massive financial resources and staff.

When a number of employees of eponymous Key Construction are discovered murdered, Faison desperately attempts to determine if the deaths are connected to the abductions.

Eventually, Veetwo and Felicia, plus their entire staff, are forced to abandon their estate, which leads to the impossible occurring; in spite of totally being sealed to the outside world, the security of their home is compromised.

Faison races against all odds to unravel who is behind the crimes and what is motivating them, before the hostages are killed and the wrong person gains Harcourt's Legacy.

Perfection
~ Seventh In The Series ~

Several months after Pawel Piotrowicz, photographer extraordinaire and owner of the Picture Perfect Model Agency, was beaten and abandoned in a parking lot, by off-duty police, for having interrupted a Friday night drug-filled orgy, at Dr. Marshall Bendorff's Old Post Road mansion, and threatening to kill him for having performed cosmetic surgery on the perfect face of his client and world's top model, Vă; Piotrowicz was arrested and charged with the murder of Dr. Marshall Bendorff, owner of the world renown Yorkville area cosmetic surgery clinic known as Perfection.

When his lawyer, Barsla Panderric, is prevented from accessing the Coroner's and Police Reports, Pawel's discovery and friend, model and former Miss Black Canada, Ziam Ngout, implores her very close friend, Faison Quay VI, into proving Piotrowicz' innocence.

Utilising his resourceful and talented staff, at Key Security International, Faison unravels the seamy side of the doctor's life in an attempt to discover not only who killed him, but, how; as he uses his uncanny sleuthing abilities and phenomenal wealth to free Pawel Piotrowicz and prove Dr. Marshall Bendorff's murder was not Perfection.

➡ ➡ ➡

Final Curtain Call

~ Eighth In The Series ~

Two days after the opening, to rave reviews in a London revival, of Noel Coward's 'Private Lives', Dame Jocelyn Mahone disappears the same day her co-star and husband of thirty-one years, Sir Alistair Vickers, surprises her and the world, by announcing he is retiring.

Following a fortnight of inaction on the part of Scotland Yard, which feels it is a publicity stunt to boost ticket sales, Estelle Vickers, Dame Jocelyn and Sir Alistair's daughter calls the dear friend, Faison Quay, in Toronto, Canada, and asks for his assistance in locating her Mother.

Rather than merely having his famous Key Security International's London Agent take on the case, Faison, immediately flies to London on his private plane, along with his husband, Stark Redfearne, son, Faison Quay VII, affectionately known as Veetwo, Règinè Ouellette, Chief Operations Officer of Key Security International and former Commissioner of the Royal Canadian Mounted Police, and Faison's Personal Assistant, David Granpré.

Taking up residence in the Owner's Suite, of the six-star Key Hotel London, the world famous Faison Quay sets out to solve the mystery of Dame Jocelyn's disappearance, as well as two subsequent murders, before the Final Curtain Call.

Clod

To

Suave

The
Etiquette, Manners, Grooming & Dressing 'Make-Over' Handbook

For

 &

Michael James Stewart
Image & Etiquette Consultant

Available In Soft Cover & eBook From
www.Amazon.com & Other Retailers

Website: www.MichaelJamesStewart.com

Email: Author@MichaelJamesStewart.com ➡➡➡

Will & Estate Planning Inventory Kit

How Much Is Your Estate Worth?

For that matter, how much does anyone really know about you and your personal affairs? That doesn't mean you are expected to confide that kind of information to just anyone – but surely your husband, your wife, a child or your lawyer, solicitor, or attorney should be made aware of the whereabouts of your insurance, home and personal papers.

Okay, so they know you've made a will, signed a Power of Attorney – even prepaid your funeral. Good for you! Excellent!

BUT have you told anyone:

- Where you bank?
- Where your investments are?
- How about your insurance policies?
- And don't forget about your sources of income, as well as your debts and other liabilities pertaining to your estate.

Are Your Estate's Affairs Really in Order?

"Be Prepared" – the motto of the Boy Scouts, Girl Scouts and Girl Guides – has stood the test of time, been followed by millions of people, and should be a guiding light for everyone. Unfortunately, most of us continue to put off attending to anything that is even remotely associated with the possibility of becoming incapacitated (physically or mentally) and are no longer able or capable of taking care of our personal affairs and ourselves. Even more sobering – what will happen to those dependent upon us, or those we leave behind, when we die?

Obviously, no one likes to talk about death – even to think about it. Nevertheless, it doesn't do anyone any good to just bury their head in the sand, pretending it won't happen – because it will! And when it happens, will loved ones, significant others, relatives or friends know what to do?

Introducing an Estate Planning Tool

An excellent and helpful article in the Canadian senior citizens magazine, Good Times (Sept. 2001) dealt with this topic in a very general way when it advised its readers to "Share Financial Information; Introduce Professional Advisors; Assess Domestic Affairs; Prepare Contingency Plans and Take Advantage of Helping Hands." It is in that same spirit of helpfulness and "Be(ing) Prepared" that the comprehensive and detailed **Will and Estate Planning Inventory Kit** was prepared and is now available and useable to the general public, wherever they live throughout the world, with the hope that people will not procrastinate any longer, thereby taking the chance of leaving everything up to a spouse, lawyer, family member or friend to fret, worry and hunt for the many and sundry items, documents, information and property records that will be required by the various levels of government, care givers, etc.

Playing 'hide and seek' might be fun for kids – but it isn't fun for the person or persons left to finalize an estate and distribute various items – items that may or may not have been named in a formal will – items intended for 'specific' individuals. It is at that point where 'hide and seek' is no longer a game but instead, becomes a very real, serious and expensive business – expensive both in time and money. That's when the world's first, specially designed, comprehensive and inexpensive estate planning tool comes to the rescue!

Available In Soft Cover From www.Amazon.com & Other Retailers

CPSIA information can be obtained at www.ICGtesting.com
Printed in the USA
LVOW11s0114140614

389985LV00001B/70/P